Repetition in Dickens's *A Tale of Two Cities*

An Exploration into His Linguistic Artistry

Notes on the author

Keisuke Koguchi is Associate Professor of English Linguistics and Stylistics at Yasuda Women's University in Japan. His main research area is the language and style of Charles Dickens. He co-translated M. A. K. Halliday and R. Hasan's *Cohesion in English* into Japanese.

Repetition in Dickens's
A Tale of Two Cities
An Exploration into His Linguistic Artistry

Keisuke Koguchi

KEISUISHA

Hiroshima, Japan

2009

First published on March 21, 2009

Copyright ©2009 Keisuke Koguchi

All right reservrd. No part of this publication may be reproduced, stored in a retrieval system, or transmitted, in any form, or by any means electronic, mechanical, photocopying, recording or otherwise, without the prior permission in writing of Keisuisha Publishing Company.

Published in Japan by
Keisuisha Co., Ltd., 1-4 Komachi, Naka-ku, Hiroshima 730-0041

For my wife, Tomoko Koguchi

Contents

List of Tables	x
List of Figures	xii
Acknowledgements	xiii
Introduction	3
Chapter I Repetition of Participant Items	17
1.0 Introduction	17
1.1 Proper names	21
1.1.1 Madame Defarge's case	21
1.1.2 Sydney Carton's case	29
1.1.3 Lucie's case	40
1.2 Personal pronouns	44
1.2.1 Darnay's case	45
1.2.2 Doctor Manette's case	54
1.2.3 Repetition of personal pronouns in the dialogue	66
1.3 Other lexical expressions	71
Chapter II Repetition of Words for Character Description	81
2.0 Introduction	81
2.1 Repetition of "head" and "hair"	85
2.1.1 Repetition of Lucie's "head" and "hair"	91
2.1.2 Repetition of Dr. Manette's "head" and "hair"	93
2.1.3 Repetition of other characters' "head" and "hair"	99

2.2	Repetition of "eye" and "eyebrows"		102
	2.2.1	Repetition of Lucie's "eye" and "eyebrows"	108
	2.2.2	Repetition of Mr. Lorry's "eye" and "eyebrows"	110
	2.2.3	Repetition of Dr. Manette's "eye" and "eyebrows"	111
	2.2.4	Repetition of Madame Defarge's "eye" and "eyebrows"	114
	2.2.5	Repetition of a seamstress's "eye" and "eyebrows"	115
2.3	Repetition of "hand" and "finger"		116
	2.3.1	Repetition of Lucie's "hand" and "finger"	123
	2.3.2	Repetition of Carton's "hand" and "finger"	124
	2.3.3	Repetition of Jacques Three's "hand" and "finger"	126
	2.3.4	Repetition of a seamstress's "hand" and "finger"	128
	2.3.5	Repetition of Jerry Cruncher's "hand" and "finger"	129
2.4	Key words in *A Tale of Two Cities*		130
2.5	Repetition of "business" and "knit"		133
	2.5.1	Repetition of "business"	134
	2.5.2	Repetition of "knit"	137

Chapter III Distinctive Use of Repetition   145

3.0	Introduction	145
3.1	Repetition of "wine," "red," and "blood"	148
	3.1.1 Use of "wine" in the French scenes	151
	3.1.2 Use of "wine" in the English scenes	158
3.2	Repetition of "footstep," "foot," "tread," and "echo"	161
3.3	Repetition of words indicative of "light" and "dark"	167
3.4	Distinctive use of repetition among characters or scenes	173
3.5	Repetition of "plane-tree" and "fountain"	177

Final Remarks   185

Select Bibliography 193

Index of Names and Subjects 201

Index of Words 207

List of Tables

Table 1-1	Madame Defarge's participant items	22
Table 1-2	Statistical data of Table 1-1	23
Table 1-3	Transition of Madame Defarge's participant items in III, 3	27
Table 1-4	Carton's participant items	30
Table 1-5	Comparison of Carton's with Solomn's participant items including pronouns in III, 8	33
Table 1-6	Statistical data of Table 1-5	37
Table 1-7	Lucie's participant items	41
Table 1-8	(A) Carton's and Darnay's participant items in II, 4	46
Table 1-9	(B) Carton's and Darnay's participant items in II, 20	46
Table 1-10	(C) Carton's and Darnay's participant items in III, 13	47
Table 1-11	Carton's and Darnay's participant items in scene (C)	48
Table 1-12	Dr. Manette's participant items in I, 5 and I, 6	54
Table 1-13	Statistical data of Table 1-12	56
Table 1-14	Dr. Manette's participant items in II, 18 and II, 19	58
Table 1-15	Dr. Manette's participant items in III, 11, III, 12, and III, 13	60
Table 1-16	In Book III, Chapter 11	61
Table 1-17	In Book III, Chapter 12	61
Table 1-18	In Book III, Chapter 13	61
Table 1-19	Participant items of Lucie in Carton's speech	67
Table 1-20	Alternatives of Madame Defarge	72
Table 1-21	Alternatives of Carton	76
Table 2-1	The 50 highest-frequency content words in *A Tale of Two Cities* and the Dickens Corpus	83
Table 2-2	Comparative distribution of "hand," "head," and "eye"	85
Table 2-4	Frequencies of "head" and "hair" for each character	87

Table 2-5	Collocations of "head" and "hair" by character	89
Table 2-6	Use of "head" and "hair" in Bk. I, Ch. 6	95
Table 2-8	Frequencies of "eye" and "eyebrows" for each character	104
Table 2-9	Collocations of "eye" and "eyebrows" by character	105
Table 2-10	Instances of "eye" and "eyebrows" in Bk. I, Ch. 6	112
Table 2-12	Frequencies of "hand" and "finger" for each character	120
Table 2-13	Collocations of "hand" and "finger" by character	121
Table 2-14	Distribution of Carton's "hand" and "finger"	125
Table 2-15	Key words in *A Tale of Two Cities* as compared to the Dickens Corpus	131
Table 3-1	Structure of the opening sentences	146
Table 3-2	Frequencies of "wine," "red," and "blood"	148
Table 3-4	Words including "wine" and words related to the spilled wine	153
Table 3-5	Words denoting "wine," "red," "blood," and the mob's cruelty	156
Table 3-8	Frequency of "confidence" in the dialogue	174
Table 3-9	Descriptions of the English and the French courts	176

xi

List of Figures

Figure 2-3	Frequencies of "head" and "hair"	86
Figure 2-7	Frequencies of "eye" and "eyebrows"	103
Figure 2-11	Frequencies of "hand" and "finger"	117
Figure 2-16	Frequency of "knit"	139
Figure 3-3	Frequencies of "wine," "red," and "blood"	150
Figure 3-6	Frequencies of "footstep," "foot," "tread," and "echo"	162
Figure 3-7	Frequencies of words indicative of "light" and "dark"	169
Figure 3-10	Frequecies of "plane-tree," "pleasant," "fate," and "fountain"	179
Figure 3-11	Verbal chart of "fountain"	184

Acknowledgements

I am deeply and particularly grateful to Dr. Hiroyuki Ito, Professor Emeritus of English Philology and Stylistics, at Kumamoto University in Japan, who has guided me in the philological and stylistic study of the English language for more than twenty years, and taught me the importance, and at the same time the pleasure, of reading the literary text closely through words. Under his guidance I have studied the language and style of Charles Dickens since I wrote my first research paper on *A Christmas Carol*.

I also wish to express my deep obligations to Professor Sadahiro Kumamoto, my Ph.D. supervisor, of the Graduate School of Social and Cultural Sciences at Kumamoto University for his exhaustive guidance, considerable encouragement and invaluable discussion that make enormous contribution to my study. As to the present work, which is developed and improved through a Ph.D. thesis submitted to Kumamoto University, Dr. Ito and Dr. Kumamoto have generously read the manuscript in its various stages and offered helpful suggestions and comments for improvements beyond my power to discover for myself. Without their encouraging words, sound advice, and continuous guidance, this book would not have come into existence.

Moreover, my special gratitude and appreciation goes to my colleagues, Professors Ken Nakagawa, P. Timothy Ervin, Richard R. P. Gabbrielli, and John McLean. Dr. Nakagawa has kindly read an earlier draft of this book and given me invaluable advice and comments, which has improved the final version of this work. Professor Ervin, Dr.

Gabbrielli, and Assistant Professor McLean also have read the manuscript and pointed out various errors. Their comments and suggestions made an enormous contribution to my work. Of course, responsibility for the book with any surviving errors rests upon me.

In addition, I would like to express my gratitude to many others who indirectly supported me, especially, all the members of the Kumamoto English Stylistics and Philology Circle.

I am very grateful to Yasuda Women's University and Yasuda Institute of Education for the grant to write this book.

Finally, I would like to extend my indebtedness to my family for their endless love, understanding, support, encouragement and sacrifice throughout my study.

Hiroshima, Japan
March 2008

Keisuke Koguchi

Repetition in Dickens's *A Tale of Two Cities*

An Exploration into His Linguistic Artistry

Introduction

A careful and sensitive reading of Charles Dickens's novels makes us aware of peculiar qualities of the language by means of which characters and events are uniquely described, literary effects are skillfully produced, and themes are most aptly expressed. That is to say, the author uses various rhetorical and stylistic devices such as word-formation, variation, deviation, and repetition to instill upon his readers the depth of his works. Among these features, the repetition of words and phrases attracts special attention.

As Brook (1970: 143) states, repetition is one of the linguistic devices "of which Charles Dickens is very fond," and the novelist "makes things easy for his readers by his constant repetitions, and his habitual phrases are remembered by readers who are not used to reading with close attention." According to Monod (1968: 461), Dickens's "stylistic use of repetition reaches its climax in [*A Tale of Two Cities* (1859)]." It is therefore fruitful to deal with the language of Dickens, especially that of *A Tale of Two Cities*, from the point of view of repetition in order to explore his linguistic artistry with which the novelist, inheriting the language of the 18th century, improved upon the style of English prose.

Over the past several decades a considerable number of studies have been made on the language of Dickens's works. To mention just some of the major books, Yamamoto (2003) shows the growth and structure of Dickens's language, and explains colloquial idioms in it and the method of studying them. Brook (1970) points out many different varieties of, and possible ways of approaching, Dickens's English. Sørensen (1985) exemplifies many innovative aspects of the language of Dickens's prose as linguistically ahead of his time. Moreover, Hori (2004) provides profound insights into Dickens's language and style through a corpus-based study of collocation, and especially makes a close analysis of the two narratives in *Bleak House*. However, despite the numerous works on Dickens's language it seems that observations from a viewpoint of repetition have not fully been made on the language and style of the greatest of all Victorian novelists.

Repetition is a device "for constructing a meaning that is independent of the specific meanings of each of the repeated units" (Hasan 1989: 5), and often conveys the meaning of intensity; moreover, it contributes to the individualization of characters, the creation of symbolic meaning, foreshadowing, and an indication of dominant themes in literary works. As Leech (1969: 79) points out, "Although repetition sometimes indicates poverty of linguistic resource, it can ... have its own kind of eloquence."

Quirk (1974: 7) appreciates Dickens's use of language under four headings: use for individualization, use for typification, structural use, and experimental use. Dickens's use of repetition constitutes a very important factor in representation of these four aspects of the novelist's language, especially in the structural use of it, the use for individualizing the characters, and the use for reinforcing the major themes of *A Tale of Two Cities*.

From a literary angle, as Glancy (1991: 10) points out, "*A Tale of Two Cities* may lack the breadth of character and humor of the more typically Dickensian novels, but its neatly interlocking plot, every incident and character essential to the working out of the design is Dickens the storyteller at his best." For example, the chapter headings are intricately linked by repetition and provide "a strong sense of continuity and association within the story" (Glancy 1991: 61): "The Night Shadows" (Bk. I, Ch. 3) are identified and embodied in "The Substance of the Shadow" (Bk. III, Ch. 10); "The Fellow of Delicacy" (Bk. II, Ch. 12) and "The Fellow of No Delicacy" (Bk. II, Ch. 13) individualize two contrastive characters, Stryver and Carton; "A Hand at Cards" (Bk. III, Ch. 8) and "The Game Made" (Bk. III, Ch. 9) usher in "a form of metaphorical expression which will be adopted in the character's conversations" (Monod 1968: 467).[1] In these chapter titles, the same or related words are reiterated, suggesting strong connections between the two chapters in a lexical or contextual light.

My chief concern in this work is to demonstrate how repetition appears as a verbal medium for individualizing characters, exposing them through their speech, and representing the subject matter of *A Tale of Two Cities*. The present treatise is divided into three chapters. In Chapter I my attention is directed to repetition of participant items, in Chapter II my discussion is devoted to repetition of words for character description, and in Chapter III my concern is with the distinctive use of repetition. These three chapters are linguistically viewed from the following three features inherent to Dickens's repetition.

---

[1] Gross and Pearson (1962: 196) critically points out "a tendency towards heavy repetitions and parallelisms, brought out by the chapter-headings."

(1) Repetition of an expression

Leech and Short (1981: 244) describe formal repetition as "repeated use of an expression (morpheme, lexical item, proper name, phrase, etc.) which has already occurred in the context." In fact, Dickens exploits various types of repetition, that is, repetition of sounds, morphemes, words, phrases, and sentences for various stylistic purposes, say, association, implication, irony, characterization, or verbal iconicity. However, following their definition, I focus my attention on the repetitive use of words or phases, which include participant items as personal reference items. The reason for this is that the repetition of words or phrases seems to be most closely related to characterization and an indication of the themes of the novel.

Let me cite two examples of repetition of words or phrases from Dickens's novels to illustrate his technique of repetition. As the first instance, I examine a case where onomatopoetic words are reiterated. See the passage below, in which David, the hero of *David Copperfield*, visits Mr. Omer's shop to order a mourning dress after his mother's death:

> (a) The three young women, who appeared to be very industrious and comfortable, raised their heads to look at me, and then went on with their work. *Stitch, stitch, stitch.* At the same time there came from a workshop across a little yard outside the window, a regular sound of hammering that kept a kind of tune: *RAT—tat-tat, RAT—tat-tat, RAT—tat-tat*, without any variation. (*DC* 9)[2]

---

[2] The italics and the underlines are all mine unless otherwise indicated.

In the passage above, the word "stitch" indicates the sound of sewing a mourning dress, and the onomatopoeia "RAT—tat-tat" imitates the sound of the hammering of his mother's coffin. The word "RAT—tat-tat," especially, occurs as many as nine times in the same chapter. These are seemingly simple examples of repetition of onomatopoeic words, but being very frequently repeated and being brought to the foreground, they serve to imply death symbolically.

As the second instance, I scrutinize the repetitive use of participant items in the passage below from *Hard Times*:

> (b) (Sissy has been adjudged hopeless as to her progress according to Gradgrind's educational theory.)
>   'I fear, *Jupe*,' said Mr. Gradgrind, 'that your continuance at the school any longer would be useless.'
>   'I am afraid it would, Sir,' *Sissy* answered with a curtsey.
>   'I cannot disguise from you, *Jupe*,' said Mr. Gradgrind, knitting his brow...
>   'I am sorry, Sir,' she returned; 'but... Yet I have tried hard, Sir.'
>   'Yes,' said Mr. Gradgrind, 'yes, I believe you have tried hard; ...'
>   'Thank you, Sir. I have thought sometimes;' *Sissy* very timid here;...
>   'No, *Jupe*, no,' said Mr. Gradgrind, shaking his head...
>   'I wish I could have made a better acknowledgement...'
>   'Don't shed tears,' said Mr. Gradgrind...
>   'Thank you, Sir, very much,' said *Sissy*, with a grateful curtsey. (*HT* I, 14)

In this passage, Gradgrind's forms of addressing Sissy are all "Jupe" except the pronoun "you." His use of this uniform mode of address is well in keeping with his philosophy of facts. He "is obsessed with the doctrine of facts and neglects the normal human feelings."[3] On the other hand, we observe the item "Sissy" and the pronoun "she" as participant items in the reporting clauses. Dickens could have adopted "Jupe," or some other expression instead of "Sissy." Dickens intends to manifest a discrepancy in the view between Gradgrind and Sissy through the difference of items attributed to Sissy, who is not affected by Gradgrind's rigid theories. Furthermore, the consistent and repetitive use of different participant items for Sissy in Gradgrind's speeches and in her reporting clauses reveals Dickens's satirical attitude toward Gradgrind who is obsessed with facts.

(2) Collocation of repeated words

I examine cases in which the combination or collocation of repeated words with words co-occurring with them contributes to the characterization in Dickens's novels. As a typical case, I discuss the reiterated word "pride" in describing the main characters of *Great Expectations*. The word is repetitively used in the depictions of Drummle, Estella, and Joe in different contexts:

> (c) (Description of Drummle)
>   I had heard of her as leading a most unhappy life, and as being separated from her husband, who had used her with great cruelty, and who had become quite renowned as a compound of *pride*, avarice, brutality, and meanness. (*GE* 59)
>
> (d) (Description of Estella)
>   Why should I loiter on my road, to compare the state of mind in which I had tried to rid myself of the stain of the

---

[3] Greaves (1972), 74.

prison before meeting her at the coach-office, with the state of mind in which I now reflected on the abyss between Estella in her *pride* and beauty, and the returned transport whom I harboured? (*GE* 43)

(e) (Description of Joe)
Evidently Biddy had taught Joe to write. As I lay in bed looking at him, it made me, in my weak state, cry again with pleasure to see the *pride* with which he set about his letter.
(*GE* 57)

In each quotation, we see the collocation of the word "pride" with other words which represent the personalities of Drummle, Estella, and Joe. They are described respectively as characters who have their own pride. The examination of the relation between the recurrent word "pride" and words co-occurring with it helps us realize the different personalities of the three characters. In quotation (c), the word "pride" co-occurs with the words "avarice," "brutality," and "meanness." Drummle's pride is indicative of his evil personality. In quotation (d), the juxtaposition of "pride" and "beauty" represents Estella's personality, or her internal and external aspects. In the last quotation (e), the word "pride" co-occurs with the word "pleasure" which suggests Pip's feeling toward Joe. The word "pride," together with the help of the co-occurring words, imparts various flavors to the depictions of the three characters according to their personalities. We see how Pip considers them, or how the author intends to represent them, through the repetition of the word "pride" and the words co-occurring with it.[4]

---

[4] Moreover, the word "pride" in the quotations can be defined in two ways: "a high or overweening opinion of one's own qualities, attainments, or estate, which gives rise to a feeling and attitude of superiority over and contempt for others" (*OED 2*, s.v. Pride I. 1. a), and "a feeling of elation, pleasure, or high satisfaction derived from some action or possession" (*OED 2* s.v. Pride I. 4).

A similar technique is also employed in the descriptions of the two heroines in *David Copperfield*. That is to say, Dora, David's first wife, has the combination of the words "love and beauty," whereas Agnes, his life-long friend and second wife, has "love and truth" as seen in the passages below:

> (f) (Description of Dora, David's first wife)
> I was sensible of a mist of *love and beauty* about Dora, but of nothing else. (*DC* 33)
>
> (g) (Description of Agnes, David's second wife)
> When Agnes laid her bonnet on the table, and sat down beside her, I could not but think, looking on her mild eyes and her radiant forehead, how natural it seemed to have her there; how trustfully, although she was so young and inexperienced, my aunt confided in her; how strong she was, indeed, in simple *love and truth*. (*DC* 35)

The difference of these collocations in the framework of the repetitive use of "love" not only serves to individualize the two heroines but also suggests the distinction between David's feelings for Dora and for Agnes.

I will later show that the collocation or combination of repeated words with other particular words is a matter of vital importance in *A Tale of Two Cities* as well.

(3) Repetition of words with different connotations

Put simply, "pride" has both a good and a bad connotation. The repetitive use of "pride," therefore, can also be seen as a problem of repetition of words with different connotations.

I will also consider "the pregnant repetition of an item in different senses" (Leech 1969: 77-78), where the same word conveys two or more meanings. For example, the adjective "dark" is defined as "characterized by (absolute or relative) absence of light," and figuratively means "characterized by absence of moral or spiritual light."[5] Moreover, I deal with a case where repeated instances of the same word carry the same conceptual meaning and different connotative meanings, as seen in the passage below from *David Copperfield*:

> (h) (Miss Trotwood and Mr. Dick suddenly visit David.)
> 'My dear aunt!' cried I. 'Why, what an unexpected pleasure!'
> We *cordially* embraced; and Mr. Dick and I *cordially* shook hands; and Mrs. Crupp, who was busy making tea, and could not be too attentive, *cordially* said she had knowed well as Mr. Copperfull would have his heart in his mouth, when he see his dear relations. (*DC* 34)

In the context of this passage, David warmly welcomes Miss Trotwood and Mr. Dick, who have suddenly visited him, with spontaneous affection. The three instances of "cordially" bear the conceptual meaning of "with hearty friendliness or good-will."[6] However, the connotative meanings of the third instance of "cordially," which is employed for depicting Mrs. Crupp, is slightly different from the first two. That is to say, the first and second instances represent the affectionate and endearing actions between David, Miss Trotwood, and Mr. Dick with the help of the verb phrases "embraced" and "shook

---

[5] *OED* 2 s.v. Dark 1. a and 4.
[6] *OED* 2 s.v. Cordially 3.

hands." On the other hand, the third instance of "cordially" describes Mrs. Crupp's intentional and outward hospitality by word of mouth along with the verb "said." In this way, the iterative use of "cordially" with its different connotations creates a stylistic effect of irony.[7] The same or similar technique is often used on a larger and more dramatic scale in *A Tale of Two Cities*, being closely connected with its themes.

Furthermore, as an important factor which is closely linked with all the above-mentioned aspects of repetition, I will examine the "context" in which instances of repetition occur, to pursue the meanings or stylistic effects Dickens creates by means of repetition.

The clearest instance of repetition occurs when the same expression is found in two or more adjacent clauses or sentences in the same sense (i.e. in an immediate context). Moreover, repetition can also have a close cohesiveness in two or more clauses (sentences) which, although at intervals, namely in different contexts, are in close semantic relationship with each other (the so-called echo or resounding, which is a device to strengthen meaning and structure). Therefore, the use of repetition will be best discussed from the following two main angles: (i) cases in which words or phrases are repetitively employed in an immediate context; (ii) cases in which words or phrases are recurrently found at intervals, or in different contexts, or throughout the text.

By way of example, I look at one instance of repetition in an immediate context and another in different contexts. In the passage below, the apparent state of Vholes, a sinister solicitor in *Bleak House*,

---

[7] Noticeably enough, Mrs. Crupp's speech, "she had knowed well as Mr. Copperfull would have his heart in his mouth, when he see his dear relations" takes the Free Indirect Speech mode. The use of the speech presentation also serves to create irony in this scene.

is described through the repetitive use of "respectable" and "respectability" in an immediate context:

> (i) Mr. Vholes is a very *respectable* man. He has not a large business, but he is a very *respectable* man. He is allowed by the greater attorneys who have made good fortunes, or are making them, to be a most *respectable* man. He never misses a chance in his practice; which is a mark of *respectability*. He never takes any pleasure; which is another mark of *respectability*. He is reserved and serious; which is another mark of *respectability*. (*BH* 39)

Vholes behaves as morally upright, and his conduct is outwardly justified by the repetitive use of the words "respectable" (3 times) with the intensive adverbs "very" and "most," and "respectability" (3 times) in the passage above.[8] In fact, however, he entangles Richard in the Jandyce case, poisons his mind, and leads him to his ruin. It is clear that his essence, or "reality," is incompatible with the connotative meaning of the iterated words "respectable" and "respectability." The repetitive use of these words in the immediate context leads the reader to cast doubt on their positive flavor of meanings, and to notice Dickens's ironical attitude toward Vohles by the "blame by praise" technique.[9]

Next, consider the passages in which a word and its derivatives are repeated in different contexts to characterize John Wemmick, one of Dickens's finest creations in *Great Expectations*:

> (j) Casting my eyes on Mr. Wemmick as we went along, to

---

[8] Moreover, counting the frequencies of the two words in Chapter 39 of *Bleak House*, I come across the word "respectable" 6 times and "respectability" 7 times.

[9] Vholes intends to justify his deed and evade his responsibility by repeatedly using the word "openly" in his speech.

see what he was like in the light of day, I found him to be a *dry* man, rather short in stature, with a square wooden face, whose expression seemed to have been imperfectly chipped out with a dull-edged chisel. (*GE* 21)

(k) 'Did your client commit the robbery?' I asked.
'Bless your soul and body, no,' answered Wemmick, very *drily*. (*GE* 31)

(l) 'With money down?' said Wemmick, in a tone *drier* than any sawdust. (*GE* 36)

When I look at the descriptions of Wemmick at work, I easily notice that the word "dry" and its derivatives "drily" and "drier" are recurrently used. The iterated use of the words semantically suggests that he is "feeling or showing no emotions" or "wanting in sympathy or cordiality."[10] Moreover, Dickens often manages to individualize his characters through the repetitive use of a particular word and the expressions which convert the meaning of the particular word into tangible terms in different contexts. This technique can be seen in the description of Wemmick. That is to say, Wemmick is first described as "a dry man" in quotation (j), and then in quotation (k) Dickens employs "drily" to portray his manner of reply, and furthermore, in (l) the tone of his voice is depicted by the word "drier." The state of Wemmick being "dry" is concretely represented in diverse ways in the accumulated contexts. Through this technique he is delineated to the state of being inanimate.

Moreover, as Brook (1970: 36) points out, "this impression of lack of

---

[10] *OED 2* s.v. Dry II. 13.

animation is confirmed by Dickens's habit of describing his mouth as a post office." The metaphorical expression in which his mouth is compared to the post office is iteratively employed in the depiction of Wemmick throughout the novel. See one such example in the passage which follows:

> (m) 'I have an impending engagement,' said I, glancing at Wemmick, who was putting fish into *the post-office*, 'that renders me rather uncertain of my time...' (*GE* 43)

A reader who first looks at the clause "[Wemmick] was putting fish into the post-office" in isolation would hardly be able to realize that "the post-office" refers to Wemmick's mouth (cf. Sørensen 1985: 83-84). The repetitive and cumulative use of "the post-office" in different contexts helps us identify its referent, and contributes to the purpose of inviting the reader more closely into the text. Thus, Dickens exploits a number of repetitions to describe and individualize his characters.

In the following three chapters, with such contextual considerations in mind, I will explore the language and style of *A Tale of Two Cities* from the viewpoint of repetition, and investigate the essence of Dickens's stylistic and linguistic artistry that persists throughout his whole works. This study represents the linguistic idiosyncrasies of the work as one phase in the development of Dickens's English.

All quotations of Dickens's novels are taken from *The Oxford Illustrated Dickens* (OUP, 1947-58, 21 volumes). I also refer to electronic texts of Dickens's novels (*Like the Dickens* 1994, Bureau of Electronic Publishing, and those from *Project Gutenberg*[11]). I have

---

[11] The Gutenberg Corpus can be found at http://promo.net/pg/index.html.

checked the electronic texts with the printed ones, but I have not found any crucial differences between the two editions. For the statistical analysis of repetition, I adopt a computer-assisted approach to a self-made Dickens Corpus of his 22 novels.[12]

---

[12] The self-made Dickens Corpus includes the following novels: *Sketches by Boz* (1833-36), *The Pickwick Papers* (1836-37), *Oliver Twist* (1837-39), *Nicholas Nickleby* (1838-39), *The Old Curiosity Shop* (1840-41), *Barnaby Rudge* (1841), *A Christmas Carol* (1843), *Martin Chuzzlewit* (1843-44), *The Chimes* (1844), *The Cricket on the Hearth* (1845), *Battle of Life* (1846), *Dombey and Son* (1846-48), *The Haunted Man* (1848), *David Copperfield* (1849-50), *Reprinted Pieces* (1850-56), *Bleak House* (1852-53), *Hard Times* (1854), *Little Dorrit* (1855-57), T*he Uncommercial Traveller* (1860), *Great Expectations* (1860-61), *Our Mutual Friend* (1864-65), *Edwin Drood* (1869-70).

I also use such concordance software as "WordSmith Tools V. 3.0" and "CONC 1.76." WordSmith Tools is lexical analysis software for the PC, published by Oxford University Press (1998), and CONC 1.76 is a text retrieval tool for the Macintosh.

Chapter I

Repetition of Participant Items

1.0 Introduction

My chief concern in this chapter is the relationship between repetitive use of participant items and individualization of characters in *A Tale of Two Cities*. Such main characters as Sydney Carton, Charles Darnay, Lucie Manette, Dr. Manette, and Madame Defarge are carefully created and individualized through the appropriate choice and repetitive use of participant items. Participant items refer back to the same referent mentioned in different parts of the text. They are basically divided into three major types: characters' proper names, personal pronouns, and other lexical expressions (mostly, examples of elegant variation). Before my concrete investigation into the participant items, I will briefly introduce the three types of reference devices.

First, as Brook (1970: 208-9) points out, "the proper names of Dickens were not arrived at by accident" but "Dickens devoted a lot of care to the choice of suitable names for his characters." Their proper names often symbolize their traits. For example, the names for Sir Leicester Dedlock in *Bleak House* and Mr. Thomas Gradgrind in *Hard Times* suggest each character's nature, role, and fate in the stories. Sir Dedlock holds the strong opinion that "the world might get on without hills, but would be done up without Dedlocks" (*BH* 2). His wife, Lady Dedlock, however, has brought disgrace upon his honorable name. He is put in a situation in which it is impossible to proceed or act: he is in a "deadlock." Likewise, Mr. Gradgrind is obsessed with the doctrine of facts and brings up his two children by a strict adherence to facts without any imaginativeness or youthful tendencies. Dickens has obviously put bitter irony and satire into these names.

Some of the author's character's names have become very well known "to represent human traits or things and have remained part of our vocabulary: Gamp (an umbrella) [in *Martin Chuzzlewit*], Micawberism (jaunty improvidence) [in *David Copperfield*], Podsnappery (British Philistinism) [in *Our Mutual Friend*] and Scrooge (a miser) [in *A Christmas Carol*]" (Hawes 1998: 1).

In *A Tale of Two Cities*, Lucie, the heroine, whose name means "light," (Glancy 1991: 95) has a compassionate nature and the power to inspire great love and peace of mind in other characters by figuratively casting light on them. Needless to say, it is unquestionably fruitful to examine the proper names given to characters, but here, I am more interested in how and why the proper names are repeated in a particular context or throughout the text.

Secondly, as Leech and Short (1981: 246-47) state, "the most common form of reduction [to avoid the repeated expression of repeated ideas] is by means of third-person pronouns." Accordingly, a pronoun is often regarded as an unmarked cohesive item referring back to the same referent. A careful examination of the contrastive and repetitive use of personal pronouns between the characters or between the contexts reveals some of the stylistic devices that we are liable to overlook in our text. The seemingly intentional repetition of personal pronouns in the novel contributes to the individualization of the characters and indication of their states of mind.

Furthermore, Leech and Short (1981: 247) also point out that "there is a principle of variety: too much repetition, either of lexical items or of reduced forms, can be tedious, and hence ELEGANT VARIATION becomes an allowable, and indeed welcome, device of cross-reference." Therefore, we are led to think that a variety of expressions or items will be applied to characters according to the plot development or the context. In case proper names or personal pronouns are excessively repeated at the expense of variation, we should consider that such repetition is rhetorically necessary.

Elegant variation is recognized as an alternative item or "use of an alternative expression (not a pronoun or a substitute) as a replacement for an expression in the context" (Leech and Short 1981: 244). It is not merely a long-winded substitute for a name but serves to build up a multi-sided picture of characters. It is regarded as opposite to repetition and as a means of avoiding repetition and monotony. I do not intend to examine each instance of elegant variation at full length, but I shall make a general view of such participant items as proper names, personal pronouns, and other lexical items (for example, "the woman" and "the gentlemen").[1] It is true that the items given to Madame Defarge, the most formidable woman of this novel, like "the dreadful woman of whose unrelenting character" and "a tigress," offer a significant clue to her nature and role by themselves. However, I am more concerned with

---

[1] As means of cross-reference, substitution (use of pro-forms such as "one" and "ones") and ellipsis (omission or deletion of referent items) should be mentioned, but I have focused my attention on proper names, personal pronouns, or other lexical items including instances of elegant variation.

cases where a character's proper name is repetitively employed in an immediate context, and where a personal pronoun or a particular lexical item (for instance, the repetitive use of "the spy" for Solomon in Section 1.1.2) is constantly assigned to the character's interlocutor for a rhetorical or stylistic purpose, say, contrast or irony. In such cases, repetition seems to reveal the author's intentional and elaborate scheme for individualizing the characters.

Needless to say, each instance of the participant items must be seen in relation to other instances in the contextual light. The scrutiny of repetition of the participant items must certainly contribute to a fuller understanding and appreciation of Dickens's stylistic and linguistic techniques in describing his characters. It could also be a means to discover a medium for the establishment of unity and coherence in the novel: how the structural unity of *A Tale of Two Cities* is created through the appropriate choice and repeated use of the participant items.

In the following sections, the instances of participant items will be classified into three cases: repetitive use of proper names, personal pronouns, and other lexical expressions. I will first make a general survey of the type of participant items applied to a character, and then I will deal with repetitive use of such participant items indicative of characters' individualization, their roles, and their relation with the subject matter of this novel.

The participant items investigated in this chapter are mainly observed in the descriptive and narrative parts. The items in the two parts allow us to directly observe Dickens's general attitude toward his characters.[2]

---

[2]   cf. Koguchi (1993). In *Hard Times*, an investigation of items referring to Sissy in Gradgrind's speeches and in the description and narrative shows a significant difference in kind and quality, which may reveal Dickens's satirical attitude toward Gradgrind, who is obsessed with facts.

1.1 Proper names

This section is concerned with repeated use of characters' proper names. The proper names of the novel's characters imply Dickens's intentions and devices for creating and individualizing colorful and lifelike characters. I can see cases where the proper names of such characters as Madame Defarge, Sydney Carton, and Lucie Manette are deliberately repeated in a particular context. In such cases, repetition conveys an additional meaning that is independent of the special meanings of each proper name; for instance, an indication of the role change a character plays according to the plot development. Additionally, examining the frequencies of name occurrences and their distribution in a particular context or throughout the whole text throws light on the cohesive net in which the author repeats the proper names appropriate to the characters' roles and the subject matter.

In the following subsections, I will focus my attention on repetitive use of proper names, but I will also examine the use of personal pronouns and other expressions for comparison, or for highlighting the effects of the repetition of proper names.

1.1.1 Madame Defarge's case

First, I consider the recurrent use of the proper name "Madame Defarge." From her first appearance in this book, Madame Defarge is depicted as a mysterious and uncanny figure: her cruel and inhuman character is not descriptively revealed, especially before the Revolution. This is partly because of Dickens's intention that the characters should be expressed through narration rather than through description and dialogue, and partly because of the role she plays in the novel. The choice and arrangement of her participant items is closely associated with her personality and role in the novel. The following table shows her participant items, excluding pronouns, in the descriptive and narrative parts throughout the text.[3]

Table 1-1 Madame Defarge's participant items

Participant items	Book I	Book II	Book III
Madame Defarge	12	34	58
The Defarges, husband and wife		2	
the Defarges, man and woman			1
The Defarges		2	2
these Defarges			1
madame		38	8
his wife	2	4	3
madame his wife		2	
a stout woman	1		
(the husband and) wife			1
one quite steady figure			1
the figure			1
the figure of a dark stout woman		1	
the woman who stood knitting		1	
the one woman who stood conscious, knitting			1
that lady		1	
the admirable woman		1	

---

[3] Madame Defarge's participant items in Book I are found in two chapters, that is, Chapters 5 and 6; and the items in Book II in five chapters, Chapters 7, 15, 16, 21, and 22; and those in Book III in eight chapters, Chapters 3, 5, 6, 8, 9, 10, 12, and 14. In Table 1-1, "two women" refer back to Madame Defarge and The Vengeance, and "two figures" to Defarge and Madame Defarge. I regard these two as Madame Defarge's items.

a woman's	1
two women (Madame Defarge & the Vengeance)	1
the two (Madame Defarge & the Vengeance)	1
her questioner	1
the woman	1
all the three	1
two figures (Defarge & Madame Defarge)	1
that terrible woman	1
the dreadful woman of whose unrelenting character	1
his feasting wife	1
a tigress	1
this ruthless woman	1
a figure	1
the family's malevolent enemy	1
the furious woman	1
the body	1
Total	15 86 93

A glance at the table clearly reveals the change of her proper name and the item "madame" in frequency between the Books.

Table 1-2 below summarizes the use of her participant items in Table 1-1 and shows the frequencies of her proper name, "Madame Defarge," her title "madame," and other items.

Table 1-2 Statistical data of Table 1-1

Items	Book I	Book II	Book III
"Madame Defarge"	12 (80%)	34 (39.5%)	58 (62.4%)
"madame"	0 (0%)	38 (44.2%)	8 (8.6%)
Others	3 (20%)	14 (16.3%)	27 (29.0%)
Total	15 (100%)	86 (100%)	93 (100%)

The total number of her participant items in Book I, 15, is so small that it is not useful for comparison with the results of the other two Books.[4] I will focus my attention, therefore, on the frequencies of her items in Book II and Book III.

What is worthy of examination between Books II and III is the decreased use of "madame" [38 (44.2%) to 8 (8.6%)] and the higher frequency of occurrences of her proper name, "Madame Defarge [34 (39.5%) to 58 (62.4%)]." This drastic shift of her participant items in frequency between the two Books is closely related to the role she plays in the novel, especially the revelation of her real personality in Book III.

Before the outbreak of the Revolution, Madame Defarge remains in the background, quietly and secretly waiting for the Revolution to break out, when she can inflict vengeance on her enemies and the upper class. Such an image of Madame Defarge is partly formed through the frequent use of "madame."

"Madame" in "Madame Defarge" is the title prefixed to the surname of a French married woman, corresponding to "Mrs." in English. The item "madame" is non-vocatively employed as the substituted form for the name of Madame Defarge in the description and narrative.[5] In this novel, though several French women appear, the item "madame" is not applied to them but only to Madame Defarge. Therefore, it should be

---

[4] "The Defarges, husband and wife," "the Defarges, man and woman," "The Defarges," and "these Defarges" include her proper name, but I do not classify them into the "Madame Defarge" group because these items also represent her husband, Defarge. Moreover, "madame his wife" has two items, "madame" and "his wife," in apposition, but I classify the item into the "madame" group.

[5] In the characters' speeches, "madame" is also used vocatively to address Madame Defarge (18 times). The item is not vocatively applied to any other character.

regarded as a kind of proper name, or an indicator of Madame Defarge herself.[6] It seems that the item indicates her presence more explicitly than personal pronouns, and more implicitly than her proper name. See an example illustrating the nature of the use of "madame":

(1) (A road-mender stays at the Defarges' and demonstrates a level of terror with Madame Defarge.)
Worse quarters than Defarge's wine-shop, could easily have been found in Paris for a provincial slave of that degree. Saving for a mysterious dread of *madame* by which he was constantly haunted, his life was very new and agreeable. But, *madame* sat all day at *her* counter, so expressly unconscious of him, and so particularly determined not to perceive that his being there had any connexion with anything below the surface, that he shook in his wooden shoes whenever his eye lighted on *her*. For, he contended with himself that it was impossible to foresee what *that lady* might pretend next; and he felt assured that if *she* should take it into *her* brightly ornamented head to pretend that *she* had seen him do a murder and afterwards flay the victim, *she* would infallibly go through with it until the play was played out.
Therefore, when Sunday came, the mender of roads was not enchanted (though he said he was) to find that *madame* was to accompany monsieur and himself to Versailles. It was additionally disconcerting to have *madame* knitting all the way there, in a public conveyance; it was additionally disconcerting yet, to have *madame* in the crowd in the

---

[6] See the passage below. The item "madam" is applied to Mrs. Stryver. The passage is in a kind of FIS of Mr. Stryver:

He was also in the habit of declaiming to Mrs. Stryver, over his full-bodied wine, on the arts Mrs. Darnay had once put in practice to 'catch' him, and on the diamond-cut-diamond arts in himself, *madam*, which had rendered him 'not to be caught.' (Bk. II, Ch. 21)

afternoon, still with *her* knitting in *her* hands as the crowd waited to see the carriage of the King and Queen.

(Bk. II, Ch. 15)

In the passage above, the cohesive items referring back to Madame Defarge are "madame," "that lady," and personal pronouns ("she" and "her"). The participant line of the items indicative of her is as follows:

> (In the first paragraph)
> madame – madame – (her counter) – her – that lady – she – (her brightly ornamented head) – she – she
>
> (In the second paragraph)
> madame – madame – madame – (her knitting) – (her hands)

In most cases, "madame" could be substituted for the proper name, personal pronouns, or other lexical expressions. The repetitive use of "madame" at the beginning of each paragraph serves to enhance her existence implicitly as the driving force behind the Revolution.[7] Together with her husband, in the context of the passage above, she takes the road-mender to see the King and Queen. The couple's purpose is to initiate him into the revolutionary movement and make him a bloodthirsty revolutionist.[8] The recurrent use of the item "madame" discloses her inner self less obtrusively than that of her proper name before the outbreak of the Revolution.

---

[7] The item "monsieur" in the passage refers to her husband, Monsieur Defarge. This is the only instance where the item is non-vocatively employed to refer to him in the narrative. "Monsieur Defarge" (30 times) and "Monsieur Defarge's" (2 times) are frequently used in this work.

[8] In this scene the road-mender, who becomes a member of the revolutionaries, cheers the King, Queeen, and other nobles, caught up in the splendor of Versailles. His change of heart represents the folly of the mob.

On the other hand, during the Revolution, or in Book III, as mentioned above, her proper name occurs more frequently than in Book II.[9] This finding is strongly associated with the fact that she steps out of the shadow and into the limelight.

The meaning constructed through the repetitive use of her proper name in Book III will be more clearly confirmed by investigating the device of repetition in an immediate context. Table 1-3 below shows the participant items of Madame Defarge in Chapter 3 of Book III, where she visits Lucie with her husband and The Vengeance so as to identify her and her daughter. She schemes secretly for Lucie's and her child's death on the guillotine because of her all-engrossing lust for vengeance on the Evrémonde.

Table 1-3 Transition of Madame Defarge's participant items in III, 3

1 two women; one, knitting	8 Madame Defarge	**17 Madame Defarge**
	9 Madame Defarge	**18 Madame Defarge**
2 her	10 all the three (Defarge, Madame Defarge and The Vengeance)	19 Madame Defarge
3 she		20 her
4 the women (Madame Defarge and The Vengeance)		**21 Madame Defarge**
	11 his wife	22 her questioner
	12 Madame Defarge	**23 Madame Defarge**
5 They (Mr. Lorry, Defarge, Madame Defarge and The Vengeance)	13 the two (Madame Defarge and The Vengeance)	24 Madame Defarge
		25 Madame Defarge
		26 She
	14 Madame Defarge	27 these Defarges
6 they	15 Madame Defarge	
7 his wife	16 Madame Defarge	

(The horizontal lines in the table represent paragraph boundaries. The boldfaced items serve as subjects of their reporting clauses.)

---

[9] The proper name "Defarge" may come from the French word "défaire," which means "to demolish," "to destroy," etc. (Mansion (1972) s.v. Défaire 1.)

The above table demonstrates that the item "Madame Defarge" is applied to Madame Defarge at a very high ratio, 13 of 27 items (48.1%). From items 7 to 26, where Lucie speaks to Madame Defarge, the proper name of the latter is exploited in 11 of 16 paragraphs. Dickens could have given her the item "madame," or other expressions, instead of the proper name. The repeated use of her proper name here brings her presence into the foreground, and more strongly serves to represent the menacing presence of Madame Defarge.

In the following passage, where items 15 and 16 in Table 1-3 are present, repetition of "Madame Defarge" describes the ominous aspect of Madame Defarge with the repetition of the words "shadow" and "threatening and dark":

> (2) The shadow attendant on *Madame Defarge* and her party seemed to fall so threatening and dark on the child, that her mother instinctively kneeled on the ground beside her, and held her to her breast. The shadow attendant on *Madame Defarge* and her party seemed then to fall, threatening and dark, on both the mother and the child. (Bk. III, Ch. 3)

Madame Defarge is a typical woman of the Revolution. She functions as the center of the revolutionaries in the Paris suburb of St. Antoine, and in a sense, becomes the revolutionary impulse incarnate. She knits the names of her intended victims into her own register and exemplifies the driving force behind the Revolution. As a character, she plays a symbolic role in that she sums up the intensity and blood thirst behind the Revolution. The change of her participant items between the Books, especially the repeated use of her proper names in Book III leads to the revelation of her real nature, or her personality affected by the

Revolution.[10] The different frequencies of the item "madame" and her proper name reflect the change of her traits between the Books or the revelation of her true personality during the Revolution, and expose the author's elaborate scheme in the novel's structure. The repetitive use of the alternatives given to Madame Defarge will be further discussed in Section 1.3.

1.1.2 Sydney Carton's case

Next, I will observe the repetitive use of Sydney Carton's proper name. Glancy (1991: 16) talks about the two heroes of our text, "biographers of Dickens have found much of interest in *A Tale of Two Cities*. They have pounced upon the name Charles Darnay and its closeness to Charles Dickens, and of course Dickens identifies himself with Sydney Carton in his preface to the novel, through his acting the part of Carton's literary predecessor Richard Wardour in the play *The Frozen Deep*, written by Wilkie Collins but heavily influenced and amended by Dickens." The individual role the author assigns to Carton in this novel is reflected through the arrangement of his proper name between the Books.

---

[10] As Dickens frequently suggests in this novel, the French Revolution was inevitable because the aristocracy exploited and plundered the poor until they were driven to revolt. First, the objects of the people's vengeance under oppression are the aristocrats who form a privileged class and by birth or fortune occupy a position distinctly above the rest of the community. As the Revolution progresses, however, many innocent people, including good citizens and even a poor seamstress, are jailed and killed on the guillotine by the mobs. It seems that Dickens delineates Madame Defarge as a representative of the mob, who are particularly bloodthirsty.

The following table shows his participant items, excluding pronouns, in the description and narrative throughout the text.[11]

Table 1-4 Carton's participant items

Participant items	Book II	Book III
Sydney Carton	12	18
Sydney	9	11
Carton	26	49
Mr. Carton	7	
Mr. Carton (FIS)	1	
this Mr. Carton	1	
the old Sydney Carton	1	
another wigged gentleman	1	
the one wigged gentleman	1	
the wigged gentleman	1	
my learned friend (FIS)	2	
this one man	1	
the first	1	
Another person	1	
the barrister	1	
this Double of coarse deportment	1	
this disagreeable companion	1	
this strange being	1	
Stryver's great ally	1	
the two (Carton & Stryver)	1	
an amazingly good jackal	1	
the jackal	9	
his jackal	1	
the same moody and morose lounger	1	
this man	1	

---

[11] In the table, FIS indicates that the item is seen in a situation where it is difficult to decide whether the sentence which includes the item is in the narrative or in a character's Free Indirect Speech.

Chapter I Repetition of Participant Items

the man	1	2
his friend	1	
the first person	1	
the first stranger		1
the owner of the rising coat		1
another voice		1
The speaker		1
the two gentleman (Carton & Lorry)		1
the former		1
the listener		1
The English customer		2
a stranger		1
an apparition of his own imagining		1
one man		1
Evrémonde		2
The supposed Evrémonde		1
The two (Carton & a seamstress)		1
these two children of the Universal Mother (Carton & a seamstress)		1
Total	87	97

Before investigating the repetitive use of the proper name applied to Carton, I will provide a broad overview of his participant items. What attracts my attention first is the difference, in number and in quality, of the items excluding the proper name between Book II and Book III of this novel.[12] The frequency of occurrences of the items (the alter-

---

[12] Sydney Carton first appears in Book II, so the distribution of his participant items is shown as follows: his items in Book II are found in nine chapters, that is, Chapters 2, 3, 4, 5, 6, 11, 13, 20, and 21, and the items in Book III in seven chapters, Chapters 5, 8, 9, 11, 12, 13, and 15. In Table 1-4, some items refer back to both Carton and other characters: "the two" in Book II refers to Carton and Stryver, and "the two gentlemen" in Book III, to Carton and Mr. Lorry. These are listed as items applied to Carton.

natives) in Book II is 30 of 21 kinds, and in Book III, 18 of 16 kinds. Expressions vary more widely in Book II than in Book III. In addition, the items given to him in Book III, with the exception of "the man," are quite different from those in Book II. He is delineated to becoming a different person. (A more detailed discussion about these items is resumed in Section 1.3.)

Further attention is attracted to the use of his proper names — Carton, Sydney, and Sydney Carton. The proper names for him appear more frequently in Book III (78 instances, 80.4%) than in Book II (57 instances, 65.5%). In other words, the use of his proper names is in reverse proportion to that of the other items (the alternatives) between the two Books. This shift of the participant items for him is directly connected to the change of his personality and role, and serves to bring his existence and unselfish act into the foreground, which is in marked contrast to the French Revolution, the inhuman and terrible reality recurrently depicted in Book III.

The effect of this repetition of Carton's proper names in Book III can be more clearly demonstrated by comparing his items with the items for Solomon Pross (Barsad) in a particular context. Solomon Pross is described as a thoroughly bad character. He was an informer for the government in England and drifted over to Paris, where he becomes a spy on the prisoners. Table 1-5 denotes Carton's and Solomon's participant items in the description and narrative in Book III, Chapter 8. The comparison shows that the two persons are contrastively individualized through the repetitive use of the proper name and the item "spy."

In Tables 1-1 and 1-4, I have excluded pronouns among the items given to Madame Defarge and Sydney Carton. In Table 1-5, however, I list Carton's and Solomon's items including pronouns. The methods of examining participant items depend on the roles the characters play in the novel.[13]

Table 1-5 Comparison of Carton's with Solomn's participant items including pronouns in III, 8

Par.	Carton's items	Solomon's items	In Carton's speeches
(1)		1 a man 2 he 3 he	
(2)		4 a man 5 the man	
(3)		**6 the man**	
(4)		**7 the man**	
(5)		**8 Solomon**	
(6)		9 her by no means affectionate brother	
(7)		**10 Solomon**	
(8)		**11 Solomon**	
(9)		**12 Solomon**	
(10)		**13 Solomon**	
(11)		**14 her brother Solomon**	
(12)		**15 her brother**	
(13)		16 this precious brother	
(14)		17 He 18 he 19 him	
(15)		20 The official	
(16)	**1 another voice**		Barsad
(17)	2 The speaker 3 Sydney Carton 4 He 5 him 6 he 7 he		

---

[13] The cohesive element "his" of "his sister" and the item "Barsad" are co-referential, but I do not regard "his" as one of Solomon's participant items because the item "his sister" refers back to Miss Pross. Incidentally, the possessive form "his" of the third person pronoun "he" is not included in this table.

(18)			your Brother Mr. Barsad Mr. Barsad
(19)	8 him 9 he	21 The spy	
(20)	**10 Sydney**		Mr. Barsad
(21)			Mr. Barsad
(22)		**22 the spy**	
(23)			Mr. Barsad
(24)		**23 the spy**	
(25)			Mr. Barsad
(26)	11 he 12 he		
(27)		**24 the spy**	
(28)	**13 Sydney**		Mr. Barsad
(29)			Mr. Barsad
(30)	14 him 15 the man	25 Solomon 26 the brother	
(31)	16 They (Carton, Cruncher, Barsad) 17 Carton	27 They (Carton, Cruncher, Barsad) 28 John Barsad, or Solomon Pross	
(32)	18 they (Carton, Cruncher, Barsad)	29 they (Carton, Cruncher, Barsad) 30 a stranger	
(33)	**19 Sydney**		Miss Pross's brother Mr. Barsad
(34)	**20 Carton**		Mr. Barsad
(35)	21 he 22 himself 23 he	31 his new visitor	
(36)	**24 Sydney**		Mr. Barsad the affectionate brother
(37)			Mr. Barsad
(38)	**25 Sydney**		Mr. Barsad
(39)	**26 Sydney**		Mr. Barsad
(40)	27 Carton		
(41)	**28 Sydney**		Mr. Barsad
(42)		**32 the spy**	

Chapter I Repetition of Participant Items   35

(43)	29 him 30 he		
(44)	**31 he**		Mr. Barsad Sheep of the prisons emissary of Republican committees turnkey prisoner spy and secret informer Mr. Barsad Mr. Barsad Mr. Barsad
(45)		**33 the spy**	
(46)			Mr. Barsad Mr. Barsad
(47)	32 He 33 He 34 himself 35 he	34 the spy 35 him	
(48)			Mr. Barsad
(49)	36 Sydney Carton	36 he 37 Mr. Barsad 38 he 39 he 40 he 41 He 42 he 43 him 44 He 45 he 46 him 47 He 48 He 49 he 50 he 51 he 52 him 53 he 54 he 55 him 56 he	
(50)	**37 Sydney**		
(51)		**57 the spy** 58 he	

(52)	**38 Carton**		Mr. Barsad
(53)		**59 the spy**	
(54)	**39 Sydney Carton**		her brother
(55)	40 Carton **41 Carton**	60 the spy 61 he 62 him 63 he	
(56)		**64 the spy**	
(57)	**42 Carton** 43 he	65 him	
(58)		**66 the spy**	
(59)	**44 Carton**		
(60)		**67 the spy**	
(61)	**45 Sydney Carton**		
(62)		**68 the spy**	
(63)	**46 Carton**		
(64)		**69 Barsad**	
(65)		**70 the spy** 71 he	
(66)		72 the spy 73 him	
(67)		74 Barsad	
(68)	47 the two gentlemen (Carton and Lorry) 48 they (Carton and Lorry)	75 The spy	
(69)	49 Sydney Carton		
(70)	**50 Carton**		Mr. Barsad
(71)		**76 the spy**	
(72)	51 Sydney Carton	**77 The Sheep of the prisons**	
(73)			a turnkey
(74)		**78 the spy**	
(75)			a turnkey
(76)	52 Sydney Carton **53 he**		

("Par." represents a paragraph and the numbers in the "Par." column the paragraph numbers of this scene. The dotted lines represent paragraph boundaries. The "In Carton's Speeches" column shows how Carton calls Solomon in his speeches, excluding the personal pronoun "you." The boldfaced items serve as subjects of their reporting clauses.)

The following table summarizes the use of Carton's and Solomon's participant items in Table 1-5.

Table 1-6   Statistical data of Table 1-5

Carton's Case		Solomon's Case	
Proper names	25 (47%)	Proper names	10 (13%)
Pronouns	24 (45%)	Pronouns	35 (45%)
		"the spy"	19 (24%)
Other items	4 (8%)	Other items	14 (18%)
Total	53 (100%)	**Total**	78 (100%)

The ratio of the proper names applied to Carton is 47% (25 of 53 items). Items excluding proper names and personal pronouns only reach 8% (4 in number) of 53 items, and most of them include general words like "man" and "speaker." Moreover, 17 (85%) of 20 boldfaced items, which serve as the subjects of reporting clauses, are Carton's proper names.

On the other hand, in Barsad's case, his proper name is only used at a ratio of 13% (10 of 78), and the item "the spy" is most frequently used as his participant item. Although he is a mere minor character, Solomon plays a contrastive role to dramatize Carton's nobility and heroic self-sacrifice, which is based on his love for Lucie. The proper name of "Solomon" itself, which implies "a profoundly wise man," indicates Dickens's ironical attitude toward the owner.

Furthermore, a careful scrutiny of Solomon's participant items according to the progress of the plot suggests that his items are deliberately applied to him in contrast to Carton's. Concretely, the major changes of his participant items can be seen after the item "Solomon" in Paragraph 5 and the item "The spy" in Paragraph 19 of Table 1-5. The two items are respectively observed in the passages below:

(3) '<u>Brother, brother!</u>' cried Miss Pross, bursting into tears. 'Have I ever been so hard with you that you ask me such a cruel question?'
'Then hold your meddlesome tongue,' said *Solomon*, 'and come out, if you want to speak to me. Pay for your wine, and come out. Who's this man?' (Bk. III, Ch. 8)

(4) 'Yes. T'other one's was one syllable. I know you. You was a spy-witness at the Bailey. What, in the name of the Father of Lies, own father to yourself, was you called at that time?'
'<u>Barsad</u>,' said another voice, striking in.
'That's the name for a thousand pound!' cried Jerry.
The speaker who struck in, was Sydney Carton...
'Don't be alarmed, my dear Miss Pross. ... I wish for your sake Mr. Barsad was not a Sheep of the Prisons.'
Sheep was a cant word of the time for a spy, under the gaolers. *The spy*, who was pale, turned paler, and asked him how he dared — (Bk. III, Ch. 8)

In the context of passage (3), Miss Pross and Jerry Cruncher enter a wine-shop, where both are startled by the sight of a man who is about to leave. Miss Pross recognizes him as her brother, Solomon Pross. The sudden encounter with her brother frightens her to speechless excitement. From the item "a man" in Paragraph 1 to the item "the man" in Paragraph 4, the general word "man" and the third person pronoun "he" repeatedly occur in the narrative to reflect Miss Pross's agitated state of mind even though she calls him "Solomon" in her speech between Paragraphs 3 and 4. The item "Solomon" and his items that include the common noun "brother" appear in the narrative just after she addresses him as "Brother, brother!" as seen in passage (3). From then forward, from Paragraphs 5 to 15, his proper name "Solomon" and the word "brother" are recurrently used.

Cruncher also remembers him from Darnay's trial in England, but he cannot remember his assumed name. He only knows that it was not Solomon. At the time, as seen in passage (4), or in Paragraph 16 of Table 1-5, Sydney Carton suddenly joins the three and tells them the name was "Barsad." Carton also discloses to them that Barsad is a prison informer. From then onward, that is, from Paragraph 19 to the end, the item "the spy" frequently recurs in marked contrast to the repetitive use of Carton's proper names. Concretely speaking, "the spy" is repeatedly applied to Solomon at the ratio of 68% (19 of 28 items excluding pronouns), in spite of the fact that his proper name, Solomon Pross, is already revealed. The very frequent use of "the spy" makes us realize his morally depraved and shameful character with the associative meaning of the word "spy."[14]

In addition, when I focus my attention on the boldfaced items themselves, the author's intention of allocating such items to Barsad is made even clearer. That is to say, from Paragraph 19 to the end, the

---

[14] Item 35 "Mr. Barsad," the combination of a title for a man, "Mr.," and his false name, is a marked instance among his participant items. The use of the item, viewed in the contextual light, may be inseparably connected with and foreshadow the plot of this chapter. That is to say, as seen in the passage below, Solomon still covers up a secret which is to be exposed later:

It was a poorer hand than he suspected. *Mr. Barsad* saw losing cards in it that Sydney Carton knew nothing of. (Bk. III, Ch. 8)

item "the spy" accounts for the high frequency of items (13 of 15) excluding the item "Barsad" in Paragraph 64 and the item "The Sheep of the prisons" in Paragraph 71. Through such a consistent use of the item as the subjects of his reporting clauses, Dickens endeavors to express not only Solomon's corrupt personality with which he tries to protect his own interests but also the deceitful and empty words he utters.

Carton tries to force Barsad to co-operate in his plan to rescue Darnay from the Conciergerie for the sake of Lucie, while Barsad carries out acts of self-protection and his own interests. The contrastive use of their participant items enhances the difference of their character traits and roles in the novel.[15]

What is more, while blackmailing Solomon in Bk. III, Ch. 8, Carton recurrently addresses him as "Mr. Barsad" (24 times), even though he already knows that "Barsad" is an assumed name. Consciously using his false name, Carton forces him to gain Darnay's release. The repeated use of "spy" as Solomon's participant item in the descriptive and narrative contrasts sharply with that of "Mr. Barsad" as his proper name in Carton's speeches.

1.1.3 Lucie's case

As a final example of the repeated use of proper names, I will deal with

---

[15] As to the repetition of words seen in Chapter 8 of Book III, I see the frequent use of the words "card," "hand," and "face," which attracts attention. Notice that Carton won't "show his cards" or "tip his hands," but deliberately tries to deal with the situation in the right way so that he is successful in making Solomon help with Darnay's freedom. The repeated use of "face" foreshadows that Carton will rescue Darnay by the striking resemblance between the two men.

the use of Lucie's proper names. Her Christian name "Lucie" allegorically means "light," and therefore its recurrent use symbolizes the role she plays in the novel. Table 1-7 shows her participant items, excluding pronouns, in the description and narrative:[16]

Table 1-7 Lucie's participant items

Participant items	Book I	Book II	Book III
Miss Manette	6	1	
Lucie Manette		5	36
Lucie		30	
Mrs. Darnay (FIS)		1	
Lucie Darnay		1	
The Manettes (Lucie and Manette)			1
a young lady	2		
the young lady	4	2	
the poor young lady	1		
a young lady of little more than twenty		1	
his fair young lady		1	
the daughter	2		
his daughter	2	7	3
(the father and) daughter	1	3	
the Doctor's daughter		2	1
His lonely daughter			1
a perfectly happy young wife		1	
the wife of an emigrant prisoner			1
his wife			10
The wretched wife of the innocent man			1
his beloved wife			1
the wife of an aristocrat			1
a short, slight pretty figure	1		
the figure	1		

---

[16] Lucie's participant items in Book I are found in three chapters, that is, Chapters 4, 5, and 6; the items in Book II in 14 chapters, that is, Chapters 2, 3, 4, 5, 6, 10, 12, 13, 17, 18, 19, 20, 21, and 24; and those in Book III in 12 chapters, that is, Chapters 2, 3, 4, 5, 6, 7, 9, 10, 11, 12, 13, and 14.

the two figures (Lucie and Manette)		1	1
a child		1	
the child of his old master	1		
the patient	1		
the two strangers (Lucie and Lorry)	1		
the young mother		1	
her mother			1
the mother			1
her unconscious mother			1
the beautiful bride		1	
the bride		1	
the newly-married pair (Lucie & Darnay)		1	
the golden thread		1	
the afflicted heart			1
Her Darling		1	
his darling			1
her Ladybird		1	
two persons (Lucie and Manette)		1	
her natural enemies (Lucie & Little Lucie)			1
her prey (Lucie & Little Lucie)			1
Total	**23**	**65**	**64**

A close investigation of the use of her proper name arouses at least the following questions:[17]

(i) In Book I, the item "Miss Manette" occurs 6 times, but why is her Christian name "Lucie" not used? Meanwhile, the item "Lucie Manette" first appears in Chapter 4 of Book II.

(ii) On the contrary, in Book II and III, even after her marriage

---

[17] A careful scrutiny of Table 1-7 suggests that a variety of alternatives are applied to Lucie as the plot progresses. For example, the common noun, "lady," is most frequently employed in the items in Book I, the word "daughter" in Book II, and the word "wife" in Book III respectively. They show Lucie's various aspects at each stage of her life.

with Charles Darnay, her first name "Lucie" is recurrently used. The items "Mrs. Darnay" and "Lucie Darnay" occur only once each.[18] Why do these items not occur more often? (Incidentally, in Madame Defarge's case, as we have already observed, the item "Madame Defarge" as a married woman, is most frequently applied to her, especially in Book III.)

One possible answer to these questions is that Lucie's role in the book is "to provide the moral center from which the people surrounding her draw their strength" (Glancy 1991: 97), as her Christian name indicates. In reality, she is the sole support of her mentally deranged father, her imprisoned husband, and the self-destructive Sydney Carton. Thinking of the role she plays, we clearly understand why Dickens intentionally uses "Lucie" so often. The frequent use of her first name is regarded as the antithesis to Madame Defarge's family name, who represents the mad turbulence of the Revolution. To put it another way, Dickens, throughout the novel, clearly intends to show Lucie and Madame Defarge as opposites.[19]

---

[18] See the following passages:

> Now, Heaven defeat the fancy of *Lucie Darnay*, and keep these feet far out of her life! For, they are headlong, mad, and dangerous; and in the years so long after the breaking of the cask at Defarge's wine-shop door, they are not easily purified when once stained red. (Bk. II, Ch. 21)

> He was also in the habit of declaiming to Mrs. Stryver, over his full-bodied wine, on the arts *Mrs Darnay* had once put in practice to 'catch' him, and on the diamond-cut-diamond arts in himself, madam, which had rendered him 'not to be caught.' (Bk. II, Ch. 21)

[19] In addition, the item applied to Lucie in Book II, "the golden thread," which is also the title of Book II, has religious connotations. As Glancy (1991: 97) states, "it is traditionally a metaphor for the inviolable heart of things, the sac-

As we have observed so far, Madame Defarge and Sydney Carton are "round" characters,[20] not stereotyped ones. They present several traits and a sort of development and change according to the plot and the subject matter. The repetition of their proper names as a verbal medium serves to individualize their personalities who have those names.

On the other hand, Lucie can be seen as a "flat" character. She remains unchanged and underdeveloped throughout the text. Her predominant trait, the sacred core of truth and love, is symbolized through the repetitive and constant use of her proper name "Lucie."

1.2 Personal pronouns

In this section I will turn to the repetitive use of personal pronouns. Personal pronouns are unmarked reference items and have anaphoric, cataphoric, or situational reference. As is well known, the commonest textual reference is an anaphoric reference. We usually expect to find an antecedent, especially a character's proper name, to identify the referent of the personal pronouns in context. In the novel, however, we observe cases where the repeated and consistent use of personal pronouns without their antecedents is felt to be anaphorically ambiguous and intentional with some stylistic effect: individualization of characters or an indication of their states of mind.

---

red core of truth and honesty that binds together the more vulnerable pieces of the fabric... Lucie's golden thread is contrasted throughout the novel with the wool that Madame Defarge silently and purposely knits into her register, condemning those named in her pattern to the guillotine."

[20] See Forster (1927), 106.

1.2.1 Darnay's case

I consider first the repetitive use of personal pronouns in the participant items of Charles Darnay in comparison with Sydney Carton's items. Carton and Darnay are depicted as characters who bear a strong resemblance in appearance, but play markedly contrastive roles in the work. They both express love for Lucie Manette and try to win her favor. In the end, it is Darnay who finally wins her love. Carton realizes his own aspired courtship as hopeless because of his idle life and, therefore, does not seek to disturb the love between her and his rival in any way. From a certain angle, Carton acts as a foil. Their roles, however, have been reversed when Carton contrives to exchange places with Darnay in the condemned cell and willingly sacrifices himself on the guillotine because of his devotion to Lucie. The change of their roles is reflected through their participant items, especially the frequent use of personal pronouns among Darnay's items, which will be discussed below.

Now, I will compare their participant items in the three scenes where both Carton and Darnay appear and talk with each other: (A) when they are in a restaurant after the trial at the Old Baily in Bk. II, Ch. 4; (B) when Carton asks Darnay's permission to be allowed to visit the family a few times a year after the Darnays' return from their honeymoon in Bk. II, Ch. 20; and, (C) when Carton enters the cell to take Darnay's place in Bk. III, Ch. 13. In each scene their participant items are examined and listed below. The total numbers for their items are different in each scene, so the frequency percentages of the items are added.

Table 1-8

(A) Carton's and Darnay's participant items in II, 4

Carton		Darnay	
Proper Name	8 (42%)	Proper Name	9 (56%)
Pronoun	9 (47%)	Pronoun	5 (31%)
Others	2 (11%)	Others	2 (13%)
Total	19 (100%)	**Total**	16 (100%)

(In Carton's case, "Proper Name" group includes "Carton" (8 times); "Others," "the Double of coarse deportment" and "this disagreeable companion." In Darnay's case, "Proper Name" group includes "Darnay" (5 times) and "Charles Darnay" (4 times); "Others," "his companion" and "the other.")

No great difference is seen in the use of their participant items. More proper names, if any, are applied to Darnay, but the number is insignificant.

Table 1-9

(B) Carton's and Darnay's participant items in II, 20

Carton		Darnay	
Proper Name	6 (38%)	Proper Name	5 (56%)
Pronoun	9 (56%)	Pronoun	3 (33%)
Others	1 (6%)	Others	1 (11%)
Total	16 (100%)	**Total**	9 (100%)

(In Carton's case, "Proper Name" group includes "Carton" (4 times) and "Sydney Carton" (once); "Others," "the first person." In Darnay's case, "Proper Name" includes "Darnay" (3 times) and "Charles Darnay" (twice); "Others," "the newly married pair.")

Here, the total number of participant items is quite different. This is partially because some of Darnay's speeches are in Free Direct Speech without their reporting clauses. In percentage terms, more proper names are given to Darnay and more pronouns to Carton.

Table 1-10
(C) Carton's and Darnay's participant items in III, 13

Carton		Darnay		
Proper Names	12 (50%)	Proper Names	1 (3%)	
Pronouns	10 (42%)	Pronouns	18 (55%)	
		"the prisoner"	12 (36%)	14 (42%)
Others	2 (8%)	Others	2 (6%)	
Total	24 (100%)	**Total**	33 (100%)	

In scene (C), a greater difference of participant items can be seen in comparison with scenes (A) and (B). In scenes (A) and (B), Darnay's proper name occurs at the ratio of more than 50%. In scene (C), however, his proper name is applied to him only once. Instead, the third person pronouns (55%) and the item "the prisoner" (36%) are frequently used. On the contrary, the use of Carton's participant items does not indicate any remarkable differences between the three scenes. Because of the marked increase of pronouns and decrease of proper names, Darnay is put into the shade, while Carton is brought out into the light. The contrastive use of their participant items in scene (C) may reflect the role change they play in this scene, and thus foreshadow the dramatic climax to this novel: Carton's heroic self-sacrifice.

Furthermore, I will turn my attention to the cohesive ties of the items referring to the two men within one paragraph in scene (C). The items are all shown in Table 1-11 below. [21]

Table 1-11 Carton's and Darney's participant items in scene (C)

Par.	Carton's items	Darnay's items	Modes of address
(1)	(his lip) Sydney Carton	him him	
(2)	(his look) him an apparition of his own imagining he (his voice) he (his real grasp)	the prisoner (the prisoner's hand)	
(3)	he		
(4)			dear Darnay
(5)		The prisoner	
(6)		The prisoner	
(7)	Carton	the prisoner him him	
(8)			Carton
(9)	he	him The prisoner	
(10)			Carton Dear Carton
(11)			my dear Darnay
(12)			friend

---

[21] The cohesive element "his" of "his lip" in Paragraph 1 of the table and the item "Sydney Carton" are co-referential, or have a cohesive tie, but I do not regard "his" as one of his participant items. So, "his lip" is put in brackets; the other brackets represent the same situation.

Chapter I Repetition of Participant Items

(13)	Carton (his right hand) (his breast)	(his hand) (his bewildered head) Darnay him
(14)	Carton	
(15)	Carton (his hand) (his breast)	The prisoner him
(16)	**Carton**	
(17)	He (his hand) (his breast)	the prisoner (his hurried wonder) he
(18)	**Carton**	
(19)	he (his eyes) (his hand)	He the writer (the writer's face)
(20)		(Darnay's fingers) he him
(21)		**he**
(22)	Carton Carton (his hand) (his breast)	(his memory) (his faculties) the prisoner (his attention) he him
(23)		The prisoner
(24)	(Carton's hand) Carton	(the prisoner's face)
(25)	(Carton's hand) (his breast) (Carton's hand) (Carton's left arm) the man	The prisoner (his nostrils) him he him he
(26)	(his heart) Carton himself (his hair) he	the prisoner the prisoner
(27)	**Carton** he	the insensible figure

("Par." represents a paragraph and the numbers in the "Par." column the paragraph numbers of this scene. The dotted lines represent paragraph boundaries: in the first paragraph the item "Sydney Carton" is applied to Carton and "him" to Darnay twice.[22] The boldfaced items serve as the subjects of their reporting clauses.)

Examining the cohesive chains of the items referring to Darnay in each paragraph, I notice that most of the chains begin with "the prisoner" or a personal pronoun as in (7) "the prisoner – him – him" or (19) "He – the writer – (the writer's face)." In Carton's case, on the other hand, most of the chains contain the structure "Carton – personal pronouns" as in (13) "Carton – (his hand) – (his breast)."[23] It is said that we can more easily clarify the identity of the pronouns within a paragraph in Carton's case than in Darnay's, as Halliday and Hasan (1976: 296-7) note, "in principle, we shall expect to find a greater degree of cohesion within a paragraph than between paragraphs." The choice and arrangement of the cohesive items referring to Carton indicates the denser cohesive ties within each paragraph more so than Darnay's items. As a result, Carton's active and prominent presence or his heroic action in this scene is very much in the foreground, and Darnay's passive and unobtrusive presence in the background.

The boldfaced items serve as the subjects of the reporting clauses leading their speeches. In Darnay's case, "he" in Paragraph 21 is the

---

[22] In scene (C), before Carton comes to see Darnay in the cell, Darnay was writing letters to Lucie, Dr. Manette, and Mr. Lorry. This is a type of monologue, in which the item "Charles Darnay" first appears, and then the third person singular pronouns are recurrently used to refer to him. Therefore, in this table, Darnay's items start with the personal pronoun "him."

[23] In Paragraph 9, the cohesive chain of Carton's items begins with the personal pronoun "he." This is partly because Darnay addresses him as "Carton" in the foregoing paragraph.

only instance. Most of his speeches are in the Free Direct Speech mode. In Carton's case, (3) "he," (16) "Carton," (18) "Carton," and (27) "Carton" work as the subjects of his reporting clauses. This also contributes to making Carton's presence more conspicuous.

The frequent use of personal pronouns as Darnay's participant items are present not only in scene (C) but also in several scenes after he returns to France and is imprisoned as an emigrant aristocrat in Book III. This suggests Darnay's role and fate in the Book. As a typical example, I will discuss the following passage. The passage, long as it is, must be quoted to observe all his items in context:

(5) (Darnay is acquitted and rescued from the mob execution and the threat of the guillotine by Dr. Manette's testimony on his behalf.)
 Then, began one of those extraordinary scenes with which the populace sometimes gratified their fickleness, or their better impulses towards generosity and mercy, or which they regarded as some set-off against their swollen account of cruel rage... No sooner was the acquittal pronounced, than tears were shed as freely as blood at another time, and such fraternal embraces were bestowed upon *the prisoner* by as many of both sexes as could rush at *him*, that after *his* long and unwholesome confinement *he* was in danger of fainting from exhaustion; none the less because *he* knew very well, that the very same people, carried by another current, would have rushed at *him* with the very same intensity, to rend *him* to pieces and strew *him* over the streets.
 His removal, to make way for other accused persons who were to be tried, rescued *him* from these caresses for the moment. Five were to be tried together, next, as enemies of the Republic, forasmuch as they had not assisted it by word or deed. So quick was the Tribunal to compensate itself and the nation for a chance lost, that these five came down to *him*

before *he* left the place, condemned to die within twenty-four hours. The first of them told *him* so, with the customary prison sign of Death — a raised finger — and they all added in words, "Long live the Republic!"

The five had had, it is true, no audience to lengthen their proceedings, for when *he* and <u>Doctor Manette</u> emerged from the gate, there was a great crowd about it, in which there seemed to be every face *he* had seen in Court — except two, for which *he* looked in vain. On his coming out, the concourse made at *him* anew, weeping, embracing, and shouting, all by turns and all together, until the very tide of the river on the bank of which the mad scene was acted, seemed to run mad, like the people on the shore.

(Bk. III, Ch. 6)

This passage appears just after Darnay is found innocent and released in the Revolutionary Tribunal. The reader's attention should be directed to him and to Dr. Manette who saved him. We should also expect to find descriptions of Darnay, who is much delighted with his discharge, through the use of his proper names. His participant items in the above passage, however, are the item "the prisoner" (once), and the pronouns "he" (6 times) and "him" (8 times). His proper names are not employed as the item referring to him in any of the three paragraphs at all, while Dr. Manette is given the item "Doctor Manette" as his participant item.

After the passage above, Darnay, who is rather apprehensive of his own safety, is carried home by the mob, and Lucie celebrates her husband's release from prison. Once again, his proper names are found neither in the narrative nor in the dialogue.

In fact, in the scenes following the passage above, Darnay is captured and tried again, and then sentenced to death because of an incriminating document penned by Dr. Manette. The consistent use of personal pronouns applied to Darnay is closely related to, and serves to make the reader forebode, his inevitable and cruel fate.

In such a case, repetitive use of personal pronouns not only serves to individualize the characters but also is utilized to produce ambiguity about identification of the referents. See the next passage, in which the personal pronouns refer back to Darnay and/or Carton:

> (6) (Mr. Lorry, Doctor Manette, and his family escape from France.)
> The night comes on dark. (i) *He* moves more; (ii) *he* is beginning to revive, and to speak intelligibly; (iii) *he* thinks (iv) *they* are still together; (v) *he* asks (vi) *him*, by his name, what (vii) *he* has in his hand. O pity us, kind Heaven, and help us! Look out, look out, and see if we are pursued.
> (Bk. III, Ch. 13)

Each of the personal pronouns in the passage refers back to Darnay and/or Carton as follows:

(i) He: Darnay   (ii) he: Darnay   (iii) he: Darnay
(iv) they: Darnay and Carton   (v) he: Darnay
(vi) him: Carton   (vii) he: Carton

Within the passage and in its vicinity, I cannot find any element to identify the reference items, or the antecedent of the personal pronouns — the proper name of Darnay or Carton. Darnay, who is drugged by Carton, still loses consciousness. Lucie and Mr. Lorry identify Darnay as Carton by mistake. The repetition of the personal pronouns reflects the ambiguity with identifying the two heroes.

1.2.2 Doctor Manette's case

In Doctor Manette's case, the repetition of personal pronouns reflects his deflective state of mind, his dehumanization. The Doctor was imprisoned in the Bastille for 18 years because of his knowledge of the evil doings of the French aristocratic St. Evrémonde twins. While incarcerated, he lost his memory and worked as a shoemaker. Even after his liberation, he continues to cobble shoes in Defarge's garret. The following table shows Dr. Manette's participant items in the description and narrative at the end of Book I, Chapter 5 and in the Book I, Chapter 6, where he first appears in the scene.

Table 1-12   Dr. Manette's participant items in I, 5 and I, 6

(Bk. I, Ch. 5)	16 him	33 he
1 a faint voice	17 himself	34 he
2 him	18 he	35 him
3 a white haired man	19 he	36 he
(Bk. I, Ch. 6)	20 him	37 him
4 a very faint voice	21 he	38 He
5 the voice	22 the shoemaker	39 he
6 the shoemaker	23 He	40 he
7 The shoemaker	24 he	41 him
8 him	25 he	42 he
9 him	26 The shoemaker	43 the captive of many years
10 the workman	27 the shoemaker	44 him
11 He	28 He	45 him
12 He	29 he	46 him
13 He	30 he	47 him
14 he	31 him	48 him
15 He	32 he	49 him

50 him	80 He	109 him
51 him	81 he	110 he
52 He	82 he	111 him
53 him	83 him	112 He
54 he	84 he	113 him
55 he	85 he	114 he
56 him	86 he	115 he
57 he	87 him	116 him
58 him	88 he	117 him
59 he	89 he	118 He
60 he	90 him	119 They (Defarge, Lorry, Dr. Manette, & Lucie)
61 him	91 him	
62 He	92 him	120 They (Defarge, Lorry, Dr. Manette, & Lucie)
63 He	93 him	
64 He	94 He	121 he
65 he	95 the father	122 he
66 him	96 He	123 he
67 him	97 him	124 him
68 He	98 him	125 he
69 him	99 him	126 him
70 he	100 him	127 him
71 he	101 they (Dr. Manette & Lucie)	128 he
72 he		129 he
73 he	102 the captive	130 he
74 he	103 him	131 The prisoner
75 He	104 he	132 him
76 he	105 he	133 monsieur with the white head
77 He	106 him	
78 he	107 he	134 the buried man
79 He	108 he	135 him

(The horizontal lines in the table represent paragraph boundaries.)

Table 1-13 below summarizes the results of Table 1-12, showing the frequencies of use of Dr. Manette's participant items.

Table 1-13 Statistical data of Table 1-12

Items	Frequency	
He (he)	69	
him	46	119 (88%)
himself	1	
They (they)	3	
The (the) shoemaker	5	
the captive	2	
a faint voice	1	
a white haired man	1	
a very faint voice	1	
the voice	1	16 (12%)
the workman	1	
the father	1	
the prisoner	1	
monsieur with the white head	1	
the buried man	1	
Total	135	135 (100%)

A careful observation of the two tables above shows the following:

(i) In the description and narrative, his participant items, including his proper name or a title such as "Doctor Manette" and "the Doctor," which are frequently seen in later chapters, are not applied to him in this scene. On the other hand, in the dialogue, the two characters address him as "Monsieur Manette" (4 times), Mr. Lorry (3 times), and Defarge (once).[24] It is often observed that the addressing

---

[24] Tables 1-12 and 1-13 do not cover participant items in the dialogue because I think that the items in the dialogue indicate a character's viewpoints and emotions to other characters, and that those in the description and narrative directly denote the author's attitude toward the characters.

forms of a character in the dialogue are repeated in the description and narrative, but no items containing his proper name are found in the description and narrative.

(ii) The ratio of personal pronouns as his participant item reaches 88%. The complete disuse of his proper name and the extensive use of pronouns is closely related to his state of mind in this scene. At his first appearance in the novel, Dr. Manette is a man completely stripped of his identity by the ordeal of his imprisonment; he works quietly at his shoemaking at Defarge's garret and passively submits to others. The particularly frequent use of pronouns as his participant item reflects his complete loss of himself.

(iii) A variety of expressions are used to suggest his various aspects, and serve to build up a many-sided picture of Dr. Manette in this scene. The figurative expression "the buried man" shows a strong link with the contents of the foregoing chapter: in Book I, Chapter 3, Mr. Lorry repeats the question "Buried how long?" to Dr. Manette in his dream. This is one of the devices Dickens often exploits to conjure up a phrase which is already represented.

Throughout the novel, Dr. Manette can never really escape his prison experience, and in moments of great stress he reverts to the insanity which prison inflicted on him: 1) when he learns Darnay's true identity, and 2) when he ultimately feels responsible for Darnay's condemnation by the Revolutionary Tribunal. In each case, the repeated and structural use of pronouns as his participant item suggests his mental collapse. These two cases will be investigated in detail.

First, the following table shows Dr. Manette's participant items in Book II, Chapter 18 and Book II, Chapter 19. In the former chapter, Doctor Manette has temporarily reverted to shoemaking because of the shock of Charles Darnay's revelation, on the morning of his wedding to Lucie, of his identity as a member of the St Evrémonde family. In the latter chapter, after a nine-day absorption in cobbling, Dr. Manette fully recovers and is unaware of what has happened in the interim. Mr. Lorry tactfully questions him and learns the cause of the recurrence of his old illness. The boldfaced items in Table 1-14 serve as the subjects of his reporting clauses.

Table 1-14 Dr. Manette's participant items in II, 18 and II, 19

Items	Bk. II, Ch. 18		Bk. II, Ch. 19	
he (He)	37		12	
he (He)	2	62 (79.5%)	1	19 (42.2%)
him	20		6	
himself	3		0	
they	4	6 (7.7%)	1	1 (2.2%)
them	2		0	
the Doctor	5		12	
the Doctor	0	6 (7.7%)	8	24 (53.4%)
Doctor Manette	1		1	
Doctor Manette	0		3	
the shoemaker	2		0	
her father	2	4 (5.1%)	0	1 (2.2%)
his friend	0		1	
Total	78	78 (100%)	45	45 (100%)

The table shows a great difference in the use of his participant items between the two chapters. In Book II, Chapter 18, such third person pronouns as "he," "him," and "himself" are employed at the ratio of nearly 80%. The use of the items "the Doctor" and "Doctor Manette" comprises only 6 (7.7%) of 78 instances. In Book II, Chapter 19, on the other hand, the items with "Doctor" or "Manette" reach a 53.4% majority of the 45 instances and the pronouns ratio falls to 42.2%. Especially noteworthy, the two items "the Doctor" and "Doctor Manette" which function as the subjects do not occur in Book II, Chapter 18, but appear as many as 11 times in the following chapter.

The difference of his participant items in frequency between the two chapters is closely connected with Dr. Manette's mental state. The high frequency of the personal pronouns in Book II, Ch. 18 reminds us of the relationship between the use of the pronouns and his mental collapse in the scene where Dr. Manette first appears in the novel. To put it another way, the repeated use of the personal pronouns are made to describe Dr. Manette as a colorless figure losing his personality in both scenes. The increase of items including "Doctor" and "Manette" in Book II, Ch. 19 throws his recovery into light in contrast with the extensive use of pronouns in the foregoing chapter.

Next, I will examine the relationship between Dr. Manette's mental state and the use of his participant items in the scene where Charles Darnay is finally sentenced to death by the Revolutionary Tribunal. The seemingly deliberate and intentional use of personal pronouns denotative of Dr. Manette's state of mind can be found again with some modification.

Doctor Manette is instrumental at first in gaining Darnay's release from prison when he is arrested as a member of the notorious St. Evrémondes. But Darnay is re-arrested and condemned to death on the evidence of Doctor Manette's written testimony of the wrongs committed by the St Evrémonde twins, which Defarge had found in the

Bastille. Because of the consciousness of regret the Doctor reverts to his old insanity again.

The following table represents his participant items in Chapters 11, 12, and 13 of Book III.

Table 1-15 Dr. Manette's participant items in III, 11, III, 12, and III, 13

(Bk. III, Ch. 11)	18 him	39 itself	59 himself
1 Her father	19 he	40 the Doctor	60 her father
2 him	20 him	41 the rocking figure	61 her father
3 him	21 he	42 it	62 himself
4 her father	22 he	43 it	63 her father
5 Her father	23 he	44 it	64 him
6 they (Lucie,	24 he	45 it	65 him
Carton, Lorry,	25 him	46 it	66 he
and Dr. Manette)	26 he	(Bk. III, Ch. 13)	67 them (Dr. Manette,
7 her father	27 he	47 her father	Lucie, and little
8 the latter	28 he	48 he	Lucie)
9 He	29 he	49 her father	68 he
10 Doctor Manette	30 he	50 him	69 this helpless,
(Bk. III, Ch. 12)	31 he	51 he	inarticulately
11 Her father	32 him	52 he	murmuring,
12 he	33 him	53 he	wandering old
13 He	34 him	54 her father	man
14 he	35 he	55 him	70 him
15 Doctor Manette	36 He	56 he	
16 the Doctor	37 him	57 he	
17 Doctor Manette	38 The figure	58 himself	

The tables below show items of Dr. Manette's participant items and their frequencies in each chapter.

Table 1-16　In Book III, Chapter 11

Items		Frequency
Doctor Manette	1	1 (10%)
her father	4	5 (50%)
the latter	1	
he (him)	3	4 (40%)
they	1	
Total	10	10 (100%)

Table 1-17　In Book III, Chapter 12

Items		Frequency
Doctor Manette	2	4 (11%)
the Doctor	2	
her father	1	3 (8%)
the (rocking) figure	2	
he (him)	23	29 (81%)
it (itself)	6	
Total	36	36 (100%)

Table1-18　In Book III, Chapter 13

Items		Frequency
her father	6	7 (29%)
this … man	1	
he (him, himself)	16	17 (71%)
them	1	
Total	24	24 (100%)

What can be observed in common among the three chapters is that the frequency of the items including his proper name and his title, "Doctor," is very low, especially in Book III, Chapter 13, where the items are not present at all. The low frequency of items reflects his distressed mental state, his insanity, as we have already observed in the foregoing two scenes.

Furthermore, the use of his participant items in each chapter has its own characteristics, depending on the change of his state of mind. These need to be examined in detail.

In Book III, Chapter 11, Dr. Manette does not revert to his mental illness, but he is in a state of great anguish because he thinks Darnay was condemned to death on account of his own written testimony. Observing his participant items in this chapter, I notice that the frequency of personal pronouns is not as high as that of the other two chapters. The item "her father" recurs most frequently among his participant items. Through the use of this item, Dr. Manette is seen and depicted in relation to his daughter, Lucie. This shows that his mental illness is not serious yet, but that his self-confidence is shaky and crushed.

In Chapter 11 of Book III, the item "Doctor Manette" occurs only once in the context where his mental state of recovering his self-confidence is suggested:

> (6) 'You had great influence but yesterday, Doctor Manette; let it at least be tried. These judges, and all the men in power, are very friendly to you, and very recognisant of your services; are they not?'
> 'Nothing connected with Charles was concealed from me. I had the strongest assurances that I should save him; and I did.' *He* returned the answer in great trouble, and very slowly.
> 'Try them again. The hours between this and to-morrow afternoon are few and short, but try.'

'I intend to try. I will not rest a moment.'

'That's well. I have known such energy as yours do great things before now — though never,' he added, with a smile and a sigh together, 'such great things as this. But try! Of little worth as life is when we misuse it, it is worth that effort. It would cost nothing to lay down if it were not.'

'I will go,' said *Doctor Manette*, 'to the Prosecutor and the President straight, and I will go to others whom it is better not to name. I will write too, and — But stay! There is a celebration in the streets, and no one will be accessible until dark.' (Bk. III, Ch. 11)

Although knowing the case to be hopeless, Carton urges Dr. Manette to see if he can use his personal influence again as a last resort in order to rescue Darnay. The item "Doctor Manette," which appears as the subject of his reporting clause, suggests his recovered confidence and inflexible determination to do anything to save Darnay.

In Book III, Chapter 12, Dr. Manette returns from his fruitless mission in a demented state. After he relapses into his former insane state, personal pronouns are applied to him at a higher frequency, as Table 1-17 above shows.

The item "her father" is used only once before he returns, and after his return it never occurs in the chapter.

The items "Doctor Manette" and "the Doctor" occur four times. All of those items depict a Dr. Manette who is not in a mental collapse. Let us look at the two passages below in which the items can be seen:

(7)　(i) Mr. Lorry waited until ten; but, *Doctor Manette* not returning, and he being unwilling to leave Lucie any longer, it was arranged that he should go back to her, and come to the banking-house again at midnight. In the meanwhile,

Carton would wait alone by the fire for *the Doctor*.

(ii) He waited and waited, and the clock struck twelve; but *Doctor Manette* did not come back. Mr. Lorry returned, and found no tidings of *him*, and brought none. Where could *he* be?

(iii) They were discussing this question, and were almost building up some weak structure of hope on his prolonged absence, when they heard *him* on the stairs. The instant *he* entered the room, it was plain that all was lost.

(iv) Whether *he* had really been to any one, or whether *he* had been all that time traversing the streets, was never known. As *he* stood staring at them, they asked *him* no question, for his face told them everything.

(v) 'I cannot find it,' said *he*, 'and I must have it. Where is it?'

(vi) His head and throat were bare, and, as *he* spoke with a helpless look straying all around, *he* took his coat off, and let it drop on the floor.

(vii) 'Where is my bench? I have been looking everywhere for my bench, and I can't find it. What have they done with my work? Time presses: I must finish those shoes.'

(viii) They looked at one another, and their hearts died within them.

(ix) 'Come, come!' said *he*, in a whimpering miserable way; 'let me get to work. Give me my work.'

(x) Receiving no answer, *he* tore his hair, and beat his feet upon the ground, like a distracted child.

(xi) 'Don't torture a poor forlorn wretch,' *he* implored them, with a dreadful cry; 'but give me my work! What is to become of us, if those shoes are not done to-night?'

(Bk. III, Ch. 12)

Carton and Mr. Lorry have expectantly waited for Dr. Manette's good result. The repeated use of "Doctor Manette" and "the Doctor" in paragraphs (i) and (ii) reflects their anxious waiting for a Dr. Manette who is not insane. Dr. Manette, however, returns in a mentally demented state against their expectation. The items attributed to Dr. Manette in paragraph (iii) are all personal pronouns. From then on, from paragraph (iii) to (xi), the personal pronouns occur again and again in referring to Dr. Manette.

The shift from the items "Doctor Manette" and "the Doctor" to the pronouns reminds us of the use of his participant items between Book II, Chapters 18 and 19, whose shift is quite reverse. Such an appropriate and structural use of his participant items reflects the character's mental state, and at the same time create a strong link between the scenes.

Next, note another use of "the Doctor" in Book III, Chapter 12 in the passage below:

> (8) (i) Carton stooped to pick up the coat, which lay almost entangling his feet. As he did so, a small case in which *the Doctor* was accustomed to carry the list of his day's duties, fell lightly on the floor. Carton took it up, and there was a folded paper in it. "We should look at this!" he said. Mr. Lorry nodded his consent. He opened it, and exclaimed, "Thank GOD!" ...
> (ii) Though he said it with a grave smile of earnestness, and though he even put the old man's hand to his lips, he did not part from him then. He helped him so far to arouse *the rocking figure* before the dying embers, as to get a cloak and hat put upon *it*, and to tempt *it* forth to find where the bench and work were hidden that *it* still moaningly besought to have. (Bk. III, Ch. 12)

The item "the Doctor" in paragraph (i) refers to Dr. Manette not in a defective mental state but in a good state of mind. The items which in fact refer to Dr. Manette in a state of mental illness in paragraph (ii) are "the rocking figure," which seems "to produce an impression of specified character on the beholder,"[25] and the pronoun "it," which is the neuter pronoun of the third person singular.

The anaphoric reference of "it" to "the rocking figure" is commonly seen, but the usage of these reference items gives us an impression that he is described as a being who does not possess characteristics associated with a mere member of the human race.

In Book III, Chapter 13, as I have already stated, no items with "Manette" and "Doctor" are found in the description and narrative. Dr. Manette is on the way back to England with Mr. Lorry, Lucie, her daughter, and Darnay. Among Dr. Manette's participant items in Table 1-18, the item "her father" occurs 6 times, and the personal pronouns recur at a high frequency (71%). The repeated use of the personal pronouns and the item "her father" indicate Dr. Manette's suffering from a serious mental illness and his being taken care of by his daughter.

1.2.3 Repetition of personal pronouns in the dialogue

So far I have made an investigation of participant items in the description and narrative. In this section, I will deal with the repetitive use of personal pronouns reflective of Carton's secret love for Lucie in the dialogue. The following table shows Lucie's participant items in Carton's speeches when he refers to her in front of others.

---

[25] *OED2* s.v. Figure 7. a.

Table1-19 Participant items of Lucie in Carton's speech

(Bk. II, Ch. 3)	19. Her	41. her
1. that young lady	20. She	42. his daughter
2. haer	21. She	43. They (Lucie, her
3. she	22. her	child, her father)
4. the young lady	23. her	44. They (Lucie, her
5. the witness,	24. her	child, her father)
Miss Manette	25. her	45. Her
6. She	26. She	46. her
(Bk. II, Ch. 4)	27. She	47. She
7. Miss Manette	28. she	48. they (Lucie, her
8. a fair young lady	29. She	child, her father)
9. a fair young lady	30. She	49. her
10. She	**(Bk. III, Ch. 11)**	50. she
11. her	31. her	51. her
12. she	32. her	52. her
13. she	33. she	53. her
(Bk. II, Ch. 5)	34. her	54. she
14. She	35. she	55. her
15. She	36. her	**(Bk. III, Ch. 13)**
16. A golden-hair doll	37. her	56. her — your wife
(Bk. II, Ch. 6)	38. her	57. her
17. Miss Manette	39. she	58. his wife
(Bk. III, Ch. 9)	40. her	
18. She	**(Bk. III, Ch. 12)**	

The table above shows that Carton tends to use personal pronouns in referring to Lucie, especially after she and Darnay get married, that is, from item 18 in Table 1-19 onward. Before their marriage he calls her "Miss Manette" three times (items 5, 7 and 17), but after the marriage he does not mention her by name even once. As is shown from item 18 in the table to the last, he repeatedly and constantly uses the third person pronouns except for items 42 "his daughter," 56 "her — your wife," and 58 "his wife" to refer to her. [26]

Observing the cohesive ties of the items in his speech, I cannot find one element to identify the reference items, or the antecedent of the personal pronouns. There are a few instances where his interlocutor mentions Lucie by her proper name and then Carton uses personal pronouns. Moreover, the personal pronouns are sometimes used situationally, to refer to some person whose identity can only be inferred from the extralinguistic context. This is supported grammatically, of course, as indicated by Quirk's definition, "much more frequently, however, the identity of the referents of 3rd person pronouns is supplied by the linguistic context" (Quirk, et al. 1985: 6.15). It is unnatural that personal pronouns are frequently used when Lucie is first referred to in the contexts as the normal procedure stipulates that a pronoun is employed as back-reference when a noun or a name has previously been introduced. Sørensen (1985: 71) talks about Dickens's use of pronouns as follows: "The normal procedure when a noun or a name has been introduced is to employ a pronoun for back-reference. Dickens has, however, a very strong tendency to avoid using pronouns for this purpose. He contrives to avoid pronominalization in two ways: either by repeating the nominal or by introducing a variant, and both procedures involve a greater or lesser degree of deviation from normal style." Seen in this light, I should think that Carton intentionally avoids using Lucie's proper name as if naming her would profane his love for her. His consistent use of the personal pronouns reflects his mental

---

[26] Item 58 "his wife" is uttered to a little seamstress, who recognizes Carton's imposture and asks him to hold her hand on the way to the guillotine.

attitudes toward Lucie.[27]

As a good example, see item 56 "her — your wife" in the above table. This item is spoken to Darnay in the cell when Carton intends to sacrifice himself for Lucie and her husband. The personal pronoun "her" is first utilized situationally to refer to Lucie, and then "your wife" cataphorically. Such a use of pronouns may reflect Carton's avoidance of directly mentioning her name, or his innermost love for her.

Another good instance in the passage below furthermore supports what is just mentioned:

(9) (Darnay, who was once released, is imprisoned again with the accusation of the Defarges.)
'To return to poor Darnay,' said Carton. 'Don't tell *Her* of this interview, or this arrangement. It would not enable *Her* to go to see him. *She* might think it was contrived, in case of the worse, to convey to him the means of anticipating the sentence.'
Mr. Lorry had not thought of that, and he looked quickly at Carton to see if it were in his mind. It seemed to be; he returned the look, and evidently understood it.
'*She* might think a thousand things,' Carton said, 'and any of them would only add to *her* trouble. Don't speak of me to *her*. As I said to you when I first came, I had better not see *her*. I can put my hand out, to do any little helpful work for *her* that my hand can find to do, without that. You are going to *her*, I hope? *She* must be very desolate to-night.'
(Bk. III, Ch. 9)

---

[27] This deliberate use of personal pronouns is very common in Dickens's novels. For example, the appearance of a mysterious character in *Oliver Twist*, Monks, is described through the repetitive use of personal pronouns, keeping the reader in suspense. See Hori (1981), 54-55.

Needless to say, the italicized pronouns "Her (her)" and "She" in the passage refer back to Lucie.[28] But the identity of the referent of the third person pronouns is supplied neither in Carton's speech nor in the narrative. In the first paragraph Carton mentions Darnay by use of his proper name, and he could have referred to Lucie by the cohesive items such as "Mrs. Darnay," "Lucie" or "his wife," but in fact he repeatedly employs the personal pronouns. The identity of the person involved has to be inferred from the contents of the sentence or the mention of her husband "Darnay." The use of the personal pronouns in this context seems to suggest that Carton, who is strongly anxious for Darnay's and Lucie's safety, shuns mentioning her name because of his secret love for her.

In addition, the repeated use of personal pronouns indicative of Carton's inner emotions toward Lucie can also be reflected and seen in the narrative. In other words, his point of view is mirrored in the use of personal pronouns in the narrative. Consider the passage below:

(10) (Carton attends Darnay's new trial in the Revolutionary Tribunal in great anxiety about Darnay and Lucie.)
The court was all astir and a-buzz, when the black sheep — whom many fell away from in dread — pressed him into an obscure corner among the crowd. Mr. Lorry was there, and Doctor Manette was there. *She* was there, sitting beside *her* father.
When *her* husband was brought in, *she* turned a look upon him, so sustaining, so encouraging, so full of admiring love and pitying tenderness, yet so courageous for his sake, that it called the healthy blood into his face, brightened his glance,

---

[28] One minor point that must undoubtedly be deliberate is the use of an initial capital in "Her." I must suppose that the author uses the capital here to express Carton's feelings for Lucie. Some visual effect of the initial capital could be achieved for the reader as well.

Chapter I Repetition of Participant Items 71

and animated his heart. If there had been any eyes to notice the influence of *her* look, on Sydney Carton, it would have been seen to be the same influence exactly. (Bk. III, Ch. 9)

The italicized items "She (she)" and "her" all refer back to Lucie. As seen in Carton's speech, however, the element to clarify the identity of the person the pronouns refer back to cannot be found in the passage.

Mr. Lorry and Dr. Manette, being with her in the court, are given the items "Mr. Lorry" and "Doctor Manette." Dickens could have supplied her with the items such as "Lucie," "his daughter," or "the accused's wife." From the first mention of her in the context, however, the author gives her the pronouns without using the antecedent or another lexical equivalent. We have to recover the appropriate antecedent of the pronouns from the context in which each of the pronouns appears.

From these facts I can say that the personal pronouns in the narrative stand out against the other characters' participant items and reflect Carton's mental attitude toward Lucie, his hidden love for her, as suggested in his speech.

Personal pronouns are unmarked referent items, but Dickens deliberately repeats the items and exploits them to compare the characters, to make the identity of the referents obscure, and to indicate the characters' states of mind.

1.3 Other lexical expressions

In the foregoing sections, I have concentrated my attention on the repetitive use of proper name and personal pronouns applied to the characters. I have not discussed other lexical expressions (the alternatives) in detail in order to focus the discussion on the two kinds of participant items. I have only dealt with the alternatives for comparison with the proper names and personal pronouns. In this section, however, I will examine repeated use of the alternatives (for example, "a steady figure" for Madame Defarge) in the descriptions of Madame Defarge and Sydney Carton.

First, look at Table 1-20 below, in which Madame Defarge's participant items (the alternatives) excluding her proper names, personal pronouns, and the item "madame" from Table 1-1, are rearranged into four groups: 1) items including "wife," 2) items including "woman," 3) items including "figure," and 4) Others.

Table 1-20 Alternatives of Madame Defarge

	Items	Book I	Book II	Book III	Total
wife	his wife	2	4	3	9
	madame his wife		2		2
	(the husband and) wife			1	1
	his feasting wife			1	1
	Subtotal	**2**	**6**	**5**	**13**
woman	a stout woman	1			1
	the woman who stood knitting		1		1
	the admirable woman		1		1
	the one woman who stood conscious, knitting			1	1
	a woman's			1	1
	two women (Madame Defarge & the Vengeance)			1	1
	the woman			1	1
	the dreadful woman of whose unrelenting character			1	1
	this ruthless woman			1	1
	the furious woman			1	1
	that terrible woman			1	1
	Subtotal	**1**	**2**	**8**	**11**

figure	the figure of a dark stout woman	1		1
	one quite steady figure		1	1
	the figure			1
	two figures (Defarge & Madame Defarge)		1	1
	a figure		1	1
	Subtotal	**1**	**4**	**5**
Others	that lady	1		1
	the two (Madame Defarge & the Vengeance)		1	1
	her questioner		1	1
	all the three		1	1
	a tigress		1	1
	the family's malevolent enemy		1	1
	the body		1	1
	Subtotal	**1**	**6**	**7**
	Totals	**3**	**10**	**23**	**36**

The table makes us realize the fact that the items including the common nouns "wife," "woman," and "figure," are very frequently used to refer back to Madame Defarge. Moreover, a close inspection of the adjectives seen in the items with these common nouns suggests that they are quite different in quality between the three Books. The adjectives in the items used in Book I and II such as "stout," "dark" in "the figure of a dark stout woman," and "steady" in "one quite steady figure" are denotative of her inner self from her outer appearance, except for "admirable" in "the admirable woman." The word "admirable" is employed to praise Madame Defarge's patience and urge to retaliate in the context where she encourages her husband, Defarge, to be patient toward the French Revolution. The adjective might apparently indicate a good quality of her nature, but, in fact, it reveals her fierce dedication to the cause of the Revolution.

In Book III, on the other hand, observing her alternatives including the repeated common nouns, "wife," "woman," and "figure," I immediately notice that the adjectives, "terrible," "dreadful," "ruthless," "furious," and "unrelenting," which all contain the seme <– FAVORABLE >,[29] or the affective meaning of minus qualities, are used.[30] They are all denotative of her inner qualities, say, cruelty, atrocity, and inhumanity. Though the adjective "feasting" in the item "his feasting wife" contains the seme <+ FAVORABLE > or the associative meaning of religion, it leads itself to irony. The word is employed to describe Madame Defarge as a person who is quite delighted to see Dr. Manette, Lucie and Darnay in great agony in the court.

In the framework of the recurrent use of the common words, "wife," "woman," and "figure," in the alternatives assigned to Madame Defarge, the change of the adjectives modifying them is correspondent to that of her personality traits expressed in the Books portraying the situations before and during the French Revolution. The use of adjectives of minus quality in her alternatives after the outbreak of the Revolution serves to unveil her real nature, or her personality affected by the Revolution.

Moreover, Madame Defarge's inner self after the Revolution is sometimes indicated, through the cohesive structure of her alternatives and the related words co-occurring with them in the same context. See the next passage which contains typical examples:

(11) (Madame Defarge hews off the head of the governor of the

---

[29] See Fowler (1977), 33-38.
[30] Considering the types of meaning for words, I follow the "Seven Types of Meaning" in Leech (1981: 9-23).

Bastille.)

(i) In the howling universe of passion and contention that seemed to encompass this grim old officer conspicuous in his grey coat and red decoration, there was but *one quite steady figure*, and that was *a woman's*. (ii) "See, there is my husband!" *she* cried, pointing him out. (iii) "See Defarge!" (iv) *She* stood <u>immovable</u> close to the grim old officer, and <u>remained immovable</u> close to him; <u>remained immovable</u> close to him through the streets, as Defarge and the rest bore him along; <u>remained immovable</u> close to him when he was got near his destination, and began to be struck at from behind; <u>remained immovable</u> close to him when the long-gathering rain of stabs and blows fell heavy; was so close to him when he dropped dead under it, that, <u>suddenly animated</u>, *she* put her foot upon his neck, and with her cruel knife — long ready — hewed off his head.

(v) The hour was come, when Saint Antoine was to execute his horrible idea of hoisting up men for lamps to show what he could be and do. (vi) Saint Antoine's blood was up, and the blood of tyranny and domination by the iron hand was down — down on the steps of the Hôtel de Ville where the governor's body lay — down on the sole of the shoe of *Madame Defarge* where *she* had trodden on the body to <u>steady</u> it for <u>mutilation</u>. (Bk. II, Ch. 21)

In sentence (i) of the passage above, the items, "one quite steady figure" and "a woman's" are used as her participant items. The omniscient author initially withholds the information that the figure is Madame Defarge until her proper name occurs in sentence (vi). Accordingly, the reader is kept in suspense and has to understand cataphorically who "one quite steady figure" refers to, only to be revealed at the end of this passage.

The adjective "steady" in the item "one quite steady figure" shows her being "firm in standing or movement,"[31] but it does not explicitly

---
[31] *OED2* s.v. Steady 2.a.

expose her real character. Her inhuman character is revealed through the cohesive arrangement of the words associated with the adjective. That is to say, the adjective "immovable," which is a near-synonym of "steady," and is seen in the recurrent phrase "remained immovable," is repeated as many as five times to show and emphasize her being motionless or physically fixed in sentence (iv). At the end of sentence (iv), the repetition dramatizes her sudden movement and her cruel action of beheading, which will culminate in the clauses "suddenly animated" and "she put her foot upon his neck, and . . . hewed his head."

In addition, in sentence (vi), the word "steady" is again used as a verb. The verb is closely related to her cruel action of "mutilation." Madame Defarge's inhuman character is exposed through the repetitive use of the words which co-occur with her alternatives.

Next, I will examine the use of the alternatives attributed to Carton. Take a look at Table 1-21 below, in which Carton's alternatives from Table 1-4 are reshuffled into the seven groups according to the common words included in the alternatives, "gentleman," "jackal," friend," "person," "man," "stranger," and Others.

Table 1-21 Alternatives of Carton

	Items	Book II	Book III	Total
gentle-man	another wigged gentleman	1		1
	the one wigged gentleman	1		1
	the wigged gentleman	1		1
	Subtotal	**3**		**3**
jackal	an amazingly good jackal	1		1
	the jackal	9		9
	his jackal	1		1
	Subtotal	**11**		**11**

friend	my learned friend (FIS)	2		2
	his friend	1		1
	Subtotal	**3**		**3**
person	Another person	1		1
	the first person	1		1
	Subtotal	**2**		**2**
man	this one man	1		1
	this man	1		1
	the man	1	2	3
	one man		1	1
	Subtotal	**3**	**3**	**6**
stranger	the first stranger		1	1
	a stranger		1	1
	Subtotal		**2**	**2**
Others	the barrister	1		1
	this Double of coarse deportment	1		1
	this disagreeable companion	1		1
	this strange being	1		1
	Stryver's great ally	1		1
	the two (Carton & Stryver)	1		1
	the first	1		1
	the same moody and morose lounger	1		1
	the owner of the rising coat		1	1
	another voice		1	1
	The speaker		1	1
	the former		1	1
	the listener		1	1
	the two gentleman (Carton & Lorry)		1	1
	The English customer		2	2
	an apparition of his own imagining		1	1
	Evrémonde		2	2
	The supposed Evrémonde		1	1
	The two (Carton & a seamstress)		1	1

these two children of the Universal Mother (Carton & a seamstress)		1	1
Subtotal	8	14	22
Totals	30	19	49

In Madame Defarge's case, the three words "wife," "woman," and "figure" are used in her alternatives at a very high frequency of 80.1% (in 29 of 36 items). In Carton's case, on the other hand, I cannot see such a repeated use of the common words throughout the text. The general words "gentleman," "friend," and "person" are mainly used in the items attributed to him in Book II. What interests me most among the items seen in the Book is the iterated use of the word "jackal" in figurative expressions like "an amazingly good jackal" and "the (his) jackal." It is said that a jackal "hunts up the lion's prey for him."[32] The recurrent use of the items including "jackal" (11 times) evokes the derogative association of the word "jackal" in the reader's mind, and it is, so to speak, in harmony with his characterization and role in Book II. In the Book, Carton is introduced as a heavy drinker and a dissolute person through lack of willpower and self-discipline for all his outstanding natural gifts as a young barrister. These items serve to describe him as an unfavorable person in a superficial sense. At the same time, the repetition foretells that Carton is given a role to stay in the background, and to save Darnay in secret later.

Another thing to be stated is that at his first appearance, the word "wigged" is repeatedly used as Carton's alternatives, "another wigged gentleman" (once), "the one wigged gentleman" (once), and "the wigged gentleman" (twice). The repetitive use of the word not only

---

[32] de Vries (1976) s.v. Jackal 1.

suggests his professionalism as a barrister in the court of law but also a hidden reality behind his untidy and undignified appearance.[33]

On the other hand, the items applied to him in Book III (mainly seen in the "Others" column of Table 1-21) are quite different from those in Book II. He is delineated as if he has become a different person. The expressions denotative of his negative qualities, like "the jackal" and "this disagreeable companion," cannot be found in Book III at all.

In Book III, in reality, Sydney Carton dies for Charles Darnay on the scaffold, with a strong physical resemblance between the two. He performs this ultimate act of self-sacrifice for the sake of Darnay's wife, Lucie, whom he loves. The change of his alternatives symbolically suggests that of the role he plays between the two Books. At the same time, this change implies one of the dominant themes of this book — Resurrection.[34]

As remarked above, repetition of participant items — proper names, personal pronouns, and the other lexical expressions — reflects Dickens's deliberate and conscious intention for character creation, development of plot, and description of scenes.

---

[33] The linguistic and stylistic meanings of the repetitive use of the word "wigged" are discussed later in Chapter III.

[34] This dominant theme of "Resurrection" is often alluded to in various forms throughout the book. For example, the expression "recalled to life" applied to Dr. Manette at the beginning of the novel is closely related to this theme. Moreover, Sydney Carton himself repeatedly mentions the following Biblical passage: "I am the resurrection and the life, saith the Lord: he that believeth in me, though he were dead, yet shall he live: and whosoever liveth and believeth in me, shall never die."

Chapter II
Repetition of Words for Character Description

2.0 Introduction

Dickens has a strong predilection for particular words in describing his characters; moreover, he also varies words co-occurring with them according to the characters. In this chapter, I will turn my attention to the repetitive use of words which are frequently present in the descriptions of the characters, and at the same time, to habitual co-occurrence of the repeated words with words co-occurring with them. I will investigate cases in which the collocation of repeated words with co-occurring words contributes to characterization. I take into account two collocational patterns. In the first case, some repeated words regularly collocate with particular words in juxtaposition: in a [(determiner +) modifier + noun] construction. In the second case, some repeated words co-occur with words that appear in proximity — in the same sentence or in adjacent sentences — demonstrating the tendency to share the same lexical environment.[1]

Concretely, in the following sections, special concern is first directed to repeated use of common nouns of a character's body parts like

---

[1] cf. Halliday & Hasan (1976), 284-86.

"head," "eye," "hand," and words modifying them. Attention will then turn to repetitive use of the words "business," "knit," and words co-occurring with them.

Before focusing on the repetitive use of the three body words, it is important to see how these words are used in a corpus of Dickens's works.

Table 2-1 on the next page illustrates the 50 highest-frequency content words in *A Tale of Two Cities* and in the Dickens Corpus. The total number of words in the corpus is approximately 4.38 million, while *A Tale of Two Cities* has approximately 137,000 words. In constructing Table 2-1, I have followed the procedure by which Hori (2004: 117-20) created a corpus of content words for 23 of Dickens's works. According to the procedure, "the following types of words have been removed from the wordlist: function words (pronouns, articles, prepositions, conjunctions, auxiliaries, and relatives) and proper nouns. In addition to these removals, words having different parts of speech, such as *have*, *had* (auxiliary and verb), *so* (conjunction, adverb, pronoun) and *do* (verb and auxiliary) are also omitted as they are highly frequent in numerous texts and registers and thus, similar to function words, show no distinctive features among particular texts or registers." I have followed Professor Hori's procedure, but the results of the two corpora (Hori's Dickens Corpus and mine) differ to some degree. He shows much greater interest in collocation, "a relationship of habitual co-occurrence between words," and in his corpus, "word forms that differ in number, tense or aspect are treated as different words" (Hori 2004: 23). In my own Dickens Corpus, I consider word lemmatization: that is to say, the word "say" in Table 2-1 contains the word-forms "say," "said," and "saying"; the word "young" includes "young," "younger," and "young-

Chapter II Repetition of Words for Character Description 83

est"; when I mention the frequency of the word "head," this includes the frequency of its plural form "heads." This is mandated by my interest with the repetition of words of the same form. Table 2-1 may not provide sufficient and adequate statistical data on the word frequencies of Dickens's novels, but at least it does indicate Dickens's preference for particular words. See the table below.

Table 2-1 The 50 highest-frequency content words in *A Tale of Two Cities* and the Dickens Corpus

Rank	*A Tale of Two Cities* (Approx. 137,000 words)			Dickens Corpus (Approx. 4,380,000 words)		
	Word	Freq.	%	Word	Freq.	%
1	say	874	0.64	say	40,053	0.91
2	no	542	0.40	no	16,001	0.37
3	look	482	0.35	go	14,248	0.33
4	see	426	0.31	know	13,453	0.31
5	go	420	0.31	look	13,137	0.30
6	know	409	0.30	come	12,931	0.30
7	man	375	0.27	very	12,929	0.30
8	hand	370	0.27	see	11,432	0.26
9	come	363	0.26	little	11,199	0.26
10	take	318	0.23	man	11,122	0.25
11	make	303	0.22	make	11,022	0.25
12	little	266	0.19	take	10,635	0.24
13	more	264	0.19	time	9,788	0.22
14	now	262	0.19	think	9,769	0.22
15	then	257	0.19	old	9,221	0.21
16	day	246	0.18	more	9,013	0.21
17	face	241	0.18	hand	8,912	0.20
18	some	229	0.17	now	8,756	0.20
19	again	228	0.17	some	8,180	0.19
20	night	228	0.17	then	7,454	0.17
21	doctor	226	0.16	any	7,447	0.17
22	any	224	0.16	like	7,159	0.16
23	two	224	0.16	good	7,040	0.16
24	good	222	0.16	never	6,869	0.16
25	head	219	0.16	again	6,754	0.15
26	very	217	0.16	great	6,747	0.15
27	like	216	0.16	other	6,670	0.15

28	other	212	0.15	here	6,667	0.15
29	long	208	0.15	much	6,658	0.15
30	way	204	0.15	such	6,649	0.15
31	eye	200	0.15	well	6,302	0.14
32	think	200	0.15	dear	6,195	0.14
33	old	196	0.14	head	6,144	0.14
34	never	194	0.14	get	5,991	0.14
35	great	186	0.14	young	5,886	0.13
36	here	186	0.14	eye	5,884	0.13
37	much	185	0.13	day	5,859	0.13
38	turn	181	0.13	gentleman	5,809	0.13
39	such	178	0.13	way	5,653	0.13
40	life	176	0.13	face	5,247	0.12
41	lie	174	0.13	house	5,237	0.12
42	prisoner	169	0.12	give	5,218	0.12
43	father	163	0.12	tell	5,213	0.12
44	get	163	0.12	return	5,146	0.12
45	door	162	0.12	two	5,112	0.12
46	own	161	0.12	night	4,912	0.11
47	ask	158	0.12	own	4,880	0.11
48	even	158	0.12	lady	4,879	0.11
49	leave	153	0.11	door	4,870	0.11
50	nothing	151	0.11	back	4,797	0.11

As this table shows, the three body words, "head," "eye," and "hand," are employed at high frequencies both in *A Tale of Two Cities* and the Dickens Corpus. As percentage figures show, these words are more frequently exploited in *A Tale of Two Cities*: for example, "hand" is used at the frequency of 0.27%, at Rank 8 in *A Tale of Two Cities*, and at the frequency of 0.20%, at Rank 17 in Dickens's other novels.

Furthermore, in order to demonstrate Dickens's preference for the three words, compare the frequencies in Dickens's works with those in Jane Austen's works, which were written a little earlier in the nineteenth century.[2]

---

[2] The following eight novels are examined: *Love And Freindship* (1790), *Sense and Sensibility* (1811), *Pride And Prejudice* (1813), *Mansfield Park* (1814), *Emma* (1815), *Northanger Abbey* (1817), *Persuasion* (1818), *Lady Susan* (1871).

Chapter II Repetition of Words for Character Description

Table-2-2 Comparative distribution of "hand," "head," and "eye"

Word	A Tale of Two Cities (Approx. 137,000 words)		Dickens Corpus (Approx. 4,380,000 words)		Austen's works (Approx. 781,000 words)	
	Freq.	%	Freq.	%	Freq.	%
hand	370	0.27	8,912	0.20	380	0.05
head	219	0.16	6,144	0.14	253	0.03
eye	200	0.15	5,884	0.13	477	0.06

The tokens for the words are quite different between the two authors' works, so the frequency of each word is expressed as a percentage. As Table 2-2 indicates, the three words occur more frequently in Dickens than in Austen. For example, Dickens uses the word "hand" in *A Tale of Two Cities* alone at almost the same frequency of occurrence as Austen does in all eight of her works (370 to 380), and in percentage figures the word is employed in *A Tale of Two Cities* approximately five times as frequently as in Austen's eight novels. This fact also statistically shows Dickens's strong preference for the words in the descriptions of the characters.

2.1 Repetition of "head" and "hair"

First, let us examine the repetitive use of and collocational patterns of the words "head" and "hair" in the outward depictions of characters, and how the words and their related words are distributed throughout *A Tale of Two Cities*. The word "head" (219 instances) is realized in the word-forms "head" (176), "heads" (38), "heading" (1), "headed" (4). As I have confined my attention to the word "head" indicative of "the top part of our body," the words "heading" (1) and "headed" (4) are excluded. Sixteen of the 176 instances of "head" do not refer to "the top part of our body," so these are also excluded. In addition, the plural form "heads" (38) is also excluded because most of them represent the public's or the crowds' body parts. As a result, we are left with 160 instances of "head."

The word "hair" and its related word "-haired" occur 74 times, and 73 of them refer to "the mass of things like fine threads that grows on our head." The frequencies of "head" and "hair" by chapter are shown in Figure 2-3 below.

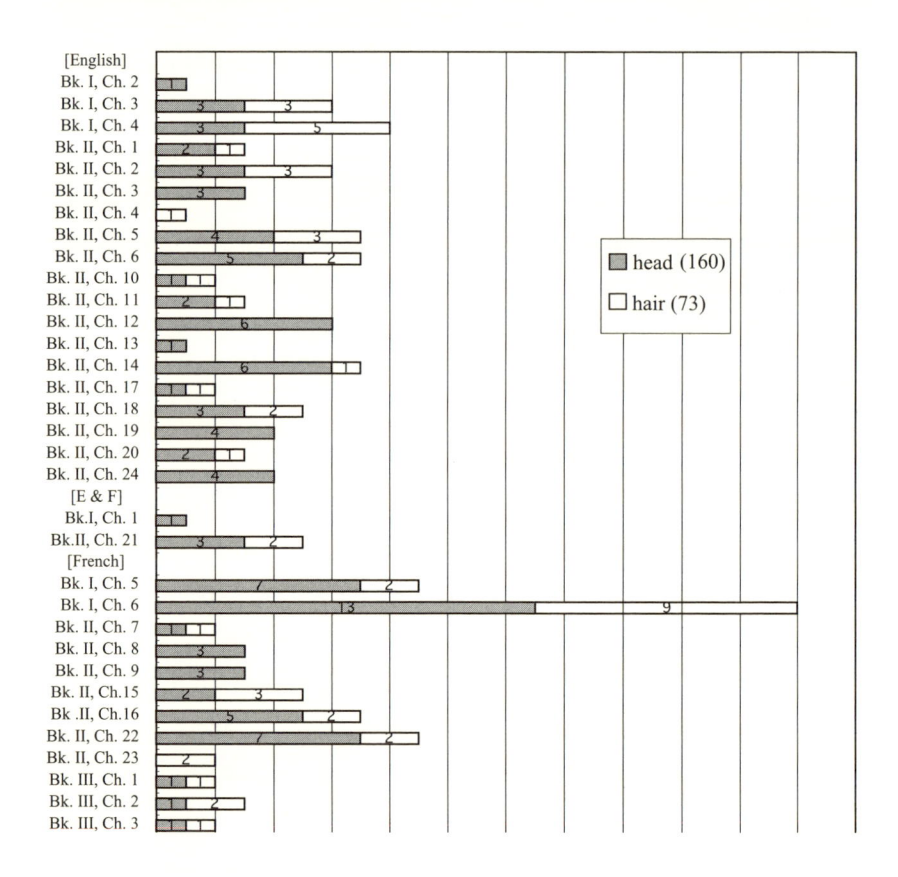

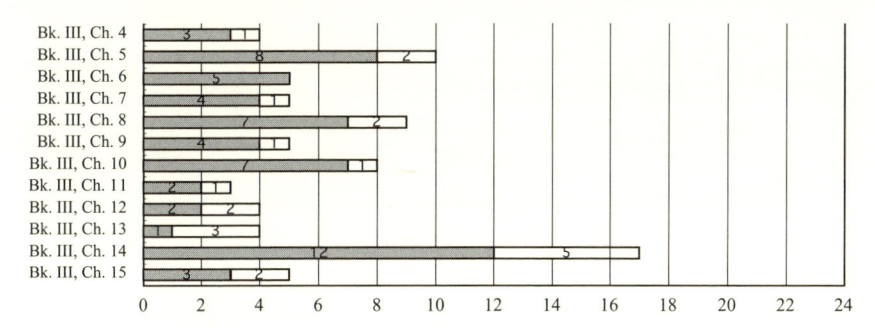

```
Bk. III, Ch. 4
Bk. III, Ch. 5
Bk. III, Ch. 6
Bk. III, Ch. 7
Bk. III, Ch. 8
Bk. III, Ch. 9
Bk. III, Ch. 10
Bk. III, Ch. 11
Bk. III, Ch. 12
Bk. III, Ch. 13
Bk. III, Ch. 14
Bk. III, Ch. 15
```

Figure 2-3 Frequencies of "head" and "hair"

From even a cursory examination of Figure 2-3, the following facts emerge: (i) the words "head" and "hair" occur in all chapters of the novel; (ii) they happen most frequently in Chapter 6 of Book I and Chapter 14 of Book III; (iii) though it is natural, the two words co-occur in most chapters. On this last fact, it must be noted that the words "head" and "hair" are often contextually synonymous. The two words literally refer to different things, but the "head" often includes the "hair" in reference.

Secondly, I will demonstrate how the words "head" and "hair" are allocated to each character.

Table 2-4 Frequencies of "head" and "hair" for each character

Characters	"head"	"hair"	Total
Dr. Manette	26	13	39
Lucie	13	19	32
Jerry	16	5	21
Darnay	11	4	15
Mr. Lorry	12	2	14
Miss Pross	10	3	13
Carton	7	5	12
Madame Defarge	8	2	10

Defarge	7	2	9
Barsad	3	2	5
Jacques Three	1	2	3
Young Jerry	1	1	2
Others	45	13	58
Total	**160**	**73**	**233**

As Table 2-4 shows, the words are assigned to most of the characters in the novel at various frequencies, but they occur at much higher frequencies in the descriptions of Dr. Manette and Lucie. This indicates that the words are more closely related to the two characters' individualization.

Thirdly, investigating particular collocational patterns of those words, I find Dickens's elaborate scheme of representing his characters through the repetition of the words and their collocates. The collocations I deal with are in either of two kinds of construction: [(determiner +) modifiers + "hair" / "head"] and [(determiner +) color adjective + "-haired" + noun]. In the following table, these word collocations for each character are divided into two columns: E and F. The instances in E indicate that they occur in the English scenes and those in F, the French scenes.[3] In addition, note that the examples in quotation marks are seen in a character's speech.[4]

---

[3] As discussed in the following pages, the instances of such collocations in the French scenes carry subtle but significant differences of implication before and during the French Revolution.

[4] Not listed in Table 2-5, the instance of "the poor shoemaker's white locks" (Bk. II, Ch. 18) is also found in the description of Dr. Manette.

Table 2-5 Collocations of "head" and "hair" by character

Dr. Manette	E	his white hair (II, 10) / his white hair (II, 17)
	F	a white-haired man (I, 5) / his confused white hair (I, 6) / his white hair (I, 6) / the white head (2 times) (I, 6) / "the white head" (I, 6) / his ruined head (I, 6) / His cold white head (I, 6) / white-haired man (3 times) (II, 15) / His streaming white hair (III, 2) / a steady head (2 times) (III, 4) / the white head, a steady head (III, 5) / his poor head (III, 6) / his white hair (III, 11)
Lucie	E	a quantity of golden hair (I, 4) / flowing golden hair (I, 4) / her golden hair (I, 4) / "golden-haired doll" (3 times) (II, 5) / her rich hair (II, 6) / "the golden-haired doll" (II, 11) / the bright golden hair (II, 18) / the golden hair (II, 18) / the golden hair (II, 20) / the golden head (II, 20)
	F	her drooping head (I, 5) / Her golden hair (I, 6) / her radiant hair (I, 6) / her beautiful head (III, 6) / "her darling's golden hair" (III, 7) / "your pretty head" (III, 7) / her own fair head (III, 12) / "a fine head" (III, 14) / "golden hair" (III, 14)
Jerry	E	stiff, black hair (I, 3) / his spiky hair (II, 1) / his spiky head (II, 14)
	F	his spiky head (III, 7) / the risen and stiff hair (III, 8)
Darnay	E	his own head (II, 24)
	F	his bewildered head (III, 13)
Carton	F	his long brown hair (III, 9) / his wild hair (III, 12)
Miss Pross	E	red hair (I, 4) / her own hair (II, 6)
	F	her loving and rejected head (III, 8)
Madame Defarge	F	her brightly ornamented head (II, 15) / her dark hair (III, 14) / "that dark hair" (III, 14)
Defarge	F	his own crisply-curling short dark hair (I, 5) / dark curling hair (III, 3)
Mr. Lorry	E	his erring head (II, 12)
Barsad	F	black hair (2 times) (II, 16)
Jacques Three	F	the shaggy black hair (II, 23), a shaggy-haired man (II, 23)

Out of 233 examples of "head" / "hair," 79 instances (34 %) contain the above-mentioned constructions. Scrutiny of Table 2-5 at least reveals the following:

(i) Different color words modifying "hair" and "head" are given to each of the characters: the words "golden" and "white" are respectively applied to Lucie and Dr. Manette; "black" for Jerry, Barsad, and Jacques Three; "red" for Miss Pross; "dark" for Madame Defarge and Defarge; and "brown" for Carton. In some characters' cases, moreover, the color adjectives are repeated in the same chapter. For example, the collocation "white head / hair" recurs as many as six times to represent Dr. Manette's outer appearance in Chapter 6 of Book I. In Madame Defarge's case, the words "dark hair" are repeated twice in Chapter 14 of Book III.

(ii) In addition to the color words, in some characters' cases, modifiers indicative of size or shape repetitively collocate with "head" and "hair": "spiky" and "stiff" co-occur with Jerry Cruncher's "head" and "hair"; "shaggy" with Jacques Three's.

(iii) Furthermore, modifiers denoting human tendencies like fear and confidence, so-called transferred epithets, frequently co-occur with the characters' "head" and "hair," especially in the description of Dr. Manette.

As already mentioned, repetition often serves to convey the meaning of intensity to each of the repeated units, and the units are brought to the foreground. This stylistic device also contributes to character individualization. It goes without saying that the repetitive use of the words "head" and "hair" and the distinctive use of their modifiers serve to individualize the characters themselves. The use of the words "head" and "hair" in the two kinds of constructions mentioned above most frequently occur in the description of Lucie (21 times) and Dr. Manette (20 times). I first examine how the repetition of the two words serves to individualize these two characters and then investigate two other characters, Jerry Cruncher and Madame Defarge, as contrasting examples.

2.1.1 Repetition of Lucie's "head" and "hair"

In Lucie's case, the modifiers expressive of the outward appearance of her "head" / "hair," that is to say, "golden," "bright," "beautiful," "fair" are repetitively found both in the English and the French scenes. Among the modifiers, the color adjective "golden" habitually modifies Lucie's "head" and "hair." In her very first appearance in the novel, in Chapter 4 of Book I, the collocation "golden hair" is reiterated three times, and is emphasized as a verbal means of individualizing the heroine. Lucie's "golden hair" itself indicates "sun-rays" and her good personalities of "purity" and "virtue."[5] Moreover, the expression recurs again in Chapter 6 of Book I, in the French scene, followed by the less familiar collocation "her radiant hair," which is uncommon in Dickens's

---

[5] cf. de Vries (1976) s.v. Hair 16.

works.[6] In the Dickens Corpus, "radiant" often collocates with "face," "smile," and "look." Only one other instance of "radiant hair" is found in the description of Miss Podsnap in *Our Mutual Friend*.[7] The unique collocation "radiant hair" serves to enhance the relation between Lucie's "head" / "hair" and words indicative of "light," in addition to the repetition of "golden hair."

The adjectival modifiers expressive of "light" directly modify Lucie's "head" / "hair" like "golden hair" and "radiant hair"; at the same time they are often scattered around in descriptions of the heroine, as seen in the two passages below:

(12) (Lucie comes to the garret of Defarge's wine shop in order to rescue her father, who is clearly mad because of his long imprisonment.)
His cold white head mingled with *her radiant hair*, which warmed and *lighted* it as though it were *the light of Freedom shining* on him. (Bk. I, Ch. 6)

(13) (The wedding of Lucie Manette and Charles Darnay takes place with the blessings of Dr. Manette, Mr. Lorry and Miss Pross.)
Besides *the glancing tears* that *shone* among the smiles of the little group when it was done, some diamonds, very *bright* and *sparkling*, glanced on the bride's hand, ... They returned home to breakfast, and all went well, and in due course *the golden hair* that had mingled with the poor

---

[6] *OED2* serves as a useful corpus of the literary texts, but the collocation "radiant hair" is not listed.

[7] See the following passage:

As he[Fledgeby] mounted, the call or song began to sound in his ears again, and, looking above, he saw the face of the little creature looking down out of a Glory of *her long bright radiant hair*, and musically repeating to him... (*MF* II, 5)

shoemaker's white locks in the Paris garret, were mingled with them again in *the morning sunlight*, on the threshold of the door at parting. (Bk. II, Ch. 18)

Such a co-occurrence of Lucie's "head" / "hair" with the words significant of "light" repeatedly occurs throughout the novel. The repetitive use of her "golden hair / head" and of adjectives indicative of light in the outward descriptions of Lucie contributes to individualizing her.

There is one other thing that must not be ignored. In both passages above, Lucie's "golden hair" and "radiant hair" contrast remarkably with Dr. Manette's "cold white head" and "white locks." The contrast represents the two characters' different roles in the novel. Lucie is the sole support of her mentally deranged father. Just as the recurrent use of her Christian name "Lucie" as her participant item symbolizes the role she plays in the novel (see Section 1.1.3), her personality traits and role are reflected by the recurrent use of words indicative of light in the collocations of her "head" / "hair." In other words, the frequent and consistent use of such words in those collocations and that of "Lucie" as her participant item are connected to make a strong cohesive tie, and thus serve to characterize her.[8]

2.1.2 Repetition of Dr. Manette's "head" and "hair"

Next, I will turn to the descriptions of Dr. Manette's "head"/ "hair." Most attractive in his case, as seen in Table 2-5, is the frequent

---

[8] The word "golden" is also used in one of Lucie's participant items as seen in the following sentence: "She was *the golden thread* that united him to a Past beyond his misery, and to a Present beyond his misery: and the sound of her voice, the light of her face, the touch of her hand, had a strong beneficial influence with him almost always." (Bk. II, Ch. 4).

collocation of the words "hair" and "head" with the color adjective "white" and such transferred epithets as "confused" and "steady." Moreover, most of the collocations in the two kinds of construction under consideration occur in the French scenes. That is to say, in the English scenes, the collocation "his white hair" is found only twice. On the other hand, in the French scenes, not only the collocations "white hair" and "white head" but also the combinations of his "hair" / "head" with transferred epithets, say, "his ruined head," "his steady head," are found 18 times.

The transferred epithets in the collocations of Dr. Manette's "hair" / "head" in Table 2-5 being closely examined, they can be divided into two types: those of negative quality like "confused," "ruined," "cold," and "poor," and the one of positive quality, "steady." Brook (1970: 21) acutely points out Dickens's use of adjectives as follows:

> One feature of Dickens's style ... is his readiness to use adjectives freely. As we have seen, the adjectives are often conventional, adding little to a description that a reader could not have imagined for himself, but they are sometimes very effective, giving a life-like picture in a very concise way.

The skillful exploitation of the transferred epithets suggestive of the contrastive qualities according to Dr. Manette's psychological states exposes his dual personality.

Dickens's genius for creative use of repetition is demonstrated more clearly in examining the repeated use of the collocations "white hair" and "white head" in Doctor Manette's case. First, consider the repetitive use of the words "head" and "hair" and their collocations in Chapter 6 of Book I, where Dr. Manette first appears in the scene. The table

Chapter II Repetition of Words for Character Description 95

below shows how each instance of the words "head" and "hair" is assigned to the characters in the chapter.

Table 2-6 Use of "head" and "hair" in Bk. I, Ch. 6

	Collocations	Characters
1	the white head	Dr. Manette
2	the head	Dr. Manette
3	his confused white hair	Dr. Manette
4	his ruined head	Dr. Manette
5	Her golden hair	Lucie
6	a very little quantity of hair	Lucie's mother
7	one or two long golden hairs	Lucie's mother
8	her hair	Lucie
9	her head	Lucie's mother
10	his white hair	Dr. Manette
11	his head	Dr. Manette
12	His cold white head	Dr. Manette
13	her radiant hair	Lucie
14	"my hair"	Lucie
15	a beloved head	Lucie's mother
16	his head	Dr. Manette
17	her hair	Dr. Manette
18	her head	Lucie
19	his head	Dr. Manette
20	his head	Dr. Manette
21	the white head	Dr. Manette
22	the white head	Dr. Manette

Of the 22 occurrences of "head" and "hair," thirteen of them are applied to Dr. Manette (59.1%); among these thirteen examples, the color adjective "white" collocates with his "head" and "hair" six times (46.3%). In addition to the recurrent use of the word "white," the transferred epithets, "confused," "ruined," and "cold," revealing his deranged state of mind, co-occur with his "hair" / "head" — "his confused white hair" and "His cold white head." With the help of those transferred epithets, the repetition of his "white hair" and "white head" serves to emphasize his mental illness as well as his old age at his first emergence.[9]

The most important addition to be made to this observation about the repetition of the collocations "white hair" and "white head" is that as the story goes on, the two kinds of collocation serve to reveal or foreshadow Dr. Manette's insanity in two different ways.

The "white hair" collocation recurrently occurs just before Dr. Manette actually reverts to his defective mental state. To put it another way, the symbolic and structural use of the collocation is a bad omen for his relapse into a demented state of mind. Let me cite the next three passages which contain this collocation:

(14)　He[Dr. Manette] turned towards him[Darnay] in his chair, but did not look at him, or raise his eyes. His chin dropped upon his hand, and *his white hair* overshadowed his face: ...
(Bk. II, Ch. 10)

(15)　So, the time came for him to bid Lucie good night, and they separated. But, in the stillness of the third hour of the morning, Lucie came down stairs again, and stole into his room; not free from unshaped fears, beforehand.
　　　　All things, however, were in their places; all was quiet; and he lay asleep, *his white hair* picturesque on the untroubled pillow, and his hands lying quiet on the coverlet.
(Bk. II, Ch. 17)

---

[9] At the same time, "white" implies "purity," "chastity," and "(eternal) life," and therefore is closely associated with Dr. Manette's innocence and one of the major themes of the book — resurrection. (cf. de Vries (1976) s.v. White 1 and 4)

(16)　Her father's only answer was to draw his hands through *his white hair*, and wring them with a shriek of anguish.
(Bk. III, Ch. 11)

Passage (14) appears in the context where Darnay asks Dr. Manette's permission to propose to Lucie. The Doctor has an overwhelming fear that he might lose his daughter, who has been his emotional mainstay since his release from prison. After his interview with Darnay, he is absorbed in cobbling again as he used to do in prison.[10] Passage (15) is found at the end of Chapter 17 of Book II, where Lucie's "unshaped fears" are just hinted at, and no sign of his reversion to the mental illness is shown. The collocation "his white hair," however, is an ill omen for Dr. Manette in spite of the use of the adjective "picturesque" postmodifying "his white hair." In fact, in Chapter 18 of Book II, Dr. Manette relapses into a mental collapse when he learns Darnay's true identity. Likewise, he goes mad just after passage (16), where he feels responsible for Darnay's condemnation because of his own incriminating document. In each case, or each chapter, the expression "his white hair" occurs independently without being connected with other collocations of his "hair" and "head," and symbolically presages Dr. Manette's coming relapse. It can be said that the collocation serves as a cohesive indicator of his defective mental state.

The collocation of "white head" foreshadows Dr. Manette's state of mental illness through its cohesive and cumulative use with other collocations of his "head." This is typically observed in Chapters 4, 5, and 6 of Book III. In those three chapters, we come across three kinds of collocation of the word "head": "a steady head" (3 times), "his white

---

[10] The word "overshadowed" in passage (14) also serves to hint at his mental collapse.

head" (once), and "his poor head" (once). The collocation "a steady head" represents Dr. Manette's unperturbed mind; on the contrary, "his white head" and "his poor head" imply his deranged mental state. However, the implication is subtly different from the case of the collocation "white hair." The four passages below, where these collocations occur, are quoted according to the progress of the plot:

> (17)   Among these terrors, and the brood belonging to them, the Doctor walked with *a steady head*: confident in his power, cautiously persistent in his end, never doubting that he would save Lucie's husband at last. ... Still, the Doctor walked among the terrors with *a steady head*. (Bk. III, Ch. 4)

> (18)   But, from the hour when she had taken *the white head* to her fresh young bosom in the garret of Saint Antoine, she had been true to her duties. (Bk. III, Ch. 5)

> (19)   These occupations brought her round to the December month, wherein her father walked among the terrors with *a steady head*. (Bk. III, Ch. 5)

> (20)   She laid her head upon her father's breast, as she had laid *his poor head* on her own breast, long, long ago. He was happy in the return he had made her, he was recompensed for his suffering, he was proud of his strength.
> (Bk. III, Ch. 6)

As seen in passages (17) and (19), the collocation "a steady head" repeatedly appears in the scene where Dr. Manette has a fixed determination to do anything to save Darnay. Through that expression, Dr. Manette's physical and mental situations in Chapters 4 and 5 of Book III are exposed: his head is "free of giddiness" and he is "not easily perturbed or discomposed."[11]

The collocations "the white head" in passage (18) and "his poor head" in passage (20) also occur in the context where Dr. Manette is still steady and confident, but they carry a negative implication of Dr. Manette's psychological state. That is to say, the two kinds of collocation serve to remind us that Dr. Manette used to be in a mental collapse, and that he can easily revert to his mental illness owing to his emotional stress.

The arrangement of these collocations in the three chapters: the repeated use of "a steady head" in Chapter 4 of Book III, the co-occurrence of "the white head" and "a steady head" in Chapter 5 of Book III, and the sole occurrence of "his poor head" in Chapter 6 of Book III, make a cohesive chain and produce an accumulative effect of foreshadowing Dr. Manette's fatal tragedy in the following chapters. In reality, after the occurrence of "his white hair" in Chapter 11 of Book III, as seen in passage (16), he reverts to his old demented state.

2.1.3 Repetition of other characters' "head" and "hair"

As stated in Section 2.1.1, different color adjectives modifying "hair" and "head" are allocated to each of the characters. The allocation is closely related to their characterization. For example, Jerry Cruncher's "black hair" is connected with his midnight work of exhuming bodies, and Barsad's with his task of spying. The collocation of the word "dark" with Defarge's and Madame Defarge's "hair" corresponds to their evil nature, and remarkably contrasts with Lucie's "golden hair" and Dr.

---

[11] *OED2* s.v. Steady 3.a.

Manette's "white hair."

Furthermore, modifiers denotative of size or shape such as "spiky" in Jerry Cruncher's "spiky hair" and "spiky head" contributes not only to individualizing characters but also suggesting their personal traits.

Here, as typical examples I investigate the descriptions of Jerry Cruncher's and Madame Defarge's "hair / head" in more detail.

In Jerry Cruncher's case, such particular collocations as "his spiky hair" and "his spiky head" are so striking for his individualization that we can easily identify him. Indeed, the adjective "spiky" occurs four times throughout our text, and it is always employed to depict his "hair" and "head" together with synonyms like "stiff" and "risen." It should also be added that the plural noun form of the adjective "spikes," which represents his "hair," occurs three times in the novel, two instances are for Jerry Cruncher and one for his son.[12] Let me cite one example of "his spiky head" in the passage below, which is present in the context where Jerry Cruncher joins the funeral of Roger Cly, one of the police spies, with the intention of digging up his corpse later. The use of the collocations conveys a flavor of humor in the painful and solemn funeral procession scene:

(21) Among the first of these volunteers was Jerry Cruncher himself, who modestly concealed *his spiky head* from the observation of Tellson's, in the further corner of the mourning coach. (Bk. II, Ch. 14)

---

[12] In the description of Jerry, we come across an unusual collocation, "all eyes, ears, and spikes," which conveys a sense of humor: "The way out of court lay in that direction, and Jerry followed him[Mr. Lorry], *all eyes, ears, and spikes.*" (Bk. II, Ch. 3)

The repetitive combination of "spiky" with "head" / "hair" adds some humor to the description of Jerry Cruncher. At the same time, the words "spiky head / hair" and "spikes" call up suggestions of his grave robbery because they recurrently remind us of the nails in a coffin. In the same chapter, in fact, Jerry and his companions dig up Cly's coffin, remove the nails, and pry it open. Thus, these repetitions serve to characterize him.

In Madame Defarge's case, attention is drawn to the collocation of the words "dark" and "hair." Words significant of "dark" are often found in the descriptions of Madame Defarge from her first appearance, for example, "her *darkly* defined eyebrows" (I, 5) and "a *dark* stout woman" (II, 7). In addition, these words repeatedly occur with unpleasant word associations, and make a contribution to indicating her personal traits. The collocation "dark hair," however, is not present at her first emergence in this story, in spite of the fact that her husband Defarge is depicted by the phrase "his own crisply-curling short dark hair" at his first appearance in Chapter 5 of Book I. Likewise, as I have already pointed out, in Lucie's and Dr. Manette's cases, "golden hair / head" and "white head / hair" are respectively applied to them repetitively at their first appearances. In Madame Defarge's case, it is not until Chapter 14 of Book III, where Madame Defarge's intention of inflicting revenge on Lucie's family is revealed, that "dark hair" first occurs as seen in the passage below, and then the expression is repeated twice in the chapter:

> (22) (After Darnay was given a sentence of beheading, Madame Defarge goes to Lucie's apartment to find her upset and to hear her impeach the justice of the Republic.)
> To appeal to her[Madame Defarge], was made hopeless by her having no sense of pity, even for herself...

Such a heart Madame Defarge carried under her rough robe. <u>Carelessly</u> worn, it was a becoming robe enough, in a certain <u>weird</u> way, and *her dark hair* looked rich under her <u>coarse</u> red cap. (Bk. III, Ch. 14)

In Section 1.1.1, I discussed the repeated use of the proper name "Madame Defarge" in Book III. I concluded that the repetition is closely related to the revelation of her true personality according to the progress of the story. The use of "dark hair" in Chapter 14 of Book III also serves to represent the menacing presence of Madame Defarge, together with the words of negative associations (note, for example, the underlined words in the passage above), in the context where her real nature, or her personality is unveiled.

2.2 Repetition of "eye" and "eyebrows"

In the previous subsections, I have focused my attention on the repetition of the words "head" / "hair" and their collocational patterns. Here, I turn to the repetition of the words "eye" / "eyebrows" and their collocates in the descriptions of the characters. Incidentally we must remember that the eye can be as eloquent as the mouth. It is quite natural the word "eye" frequently occurs in the novels which depict human relations. First, I exemplify the words distributed throughout *A Tale of Two Cities*. The word "eye" (200 instances) is realized in the word-forms "eye" (165), "eyes" (34), and "eyeing" (1), and 196 of them refer to "the organ of sight." I exclude one instance of "eyeing" and the three instances of "Bull's Eye," which is "a reference to the handsome antechamber to the State Apartments at Versailles."[13] The word

---

[13] Sanders (1988), 107-108.

Chapter II Repetition of Words for Character Description

"eyebrows" occurs 12 times, and all instances refer to "the fringe of hair along the upper orbit of the eye."[14] The frequencies of the two words "eye" (196) and "eyebrows" (12) are represented in serial order of chapters in Figure 2-7 below.

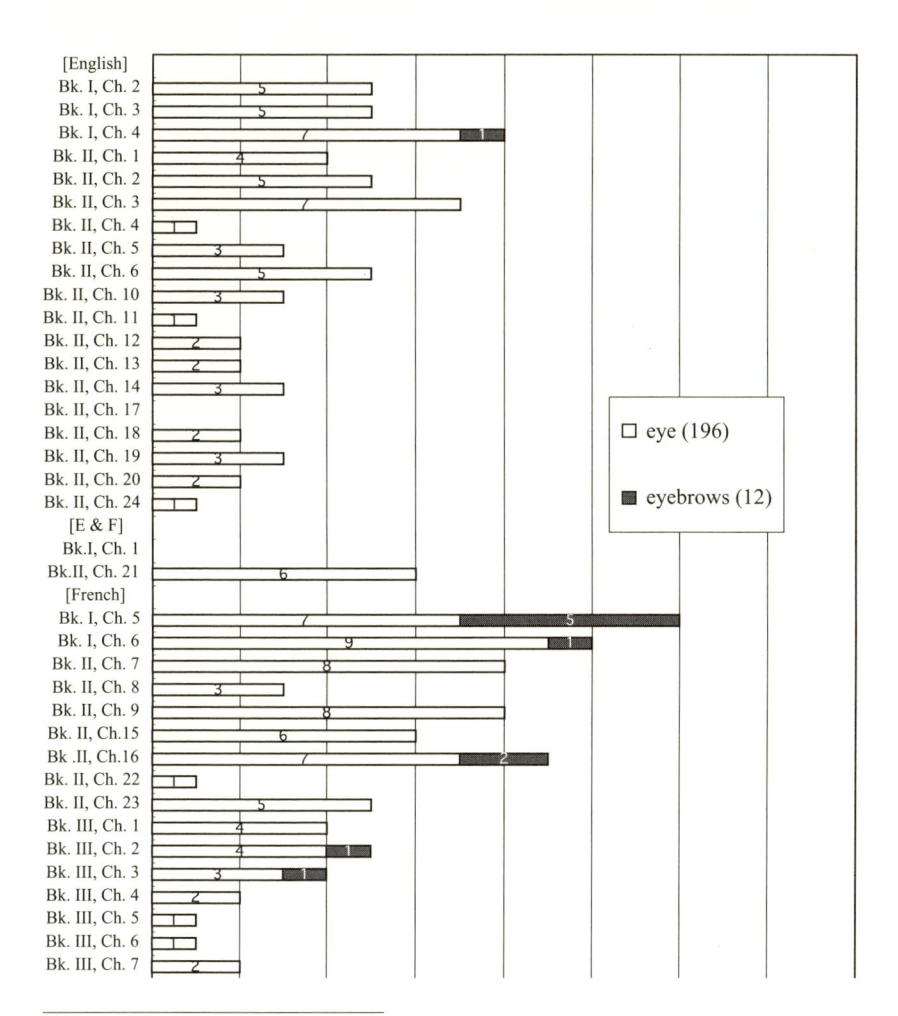

[English]	
Bk. I, Ch. 2	5
Bk. I, Ch. 3	5
Bk. I, Ch. 4	7 / 1
Bk. II, Ch. 1	4
Bk. II, Ch. 2	5
Bk. II, Ch. 3	7
Bk. II, Ch. 4	1
Bk. II, Ch. 5	3
Bk. II, Ch. 6	5
Bk. II, Ch. 10	3
Bk. II, Ch. 11	1
Bk. II, Ch. 12	2
Bk. II, Ch. 13	2
Bk. II, Ch. 14	3
Bk. II, Ch. 17	
Bk. II, Ch. 18	2
Bk. II, Ch. 19	3
Bk. II, Ch. 20	2
Bk. II, Ch. 24	1
[E & F]	
Bk.I, Ch. 1	
Bk.II, Ch. 21	6
[French]	
Bk. I, Ch. 5	7 / 5
Bk. I, Ch. 6	9 / 1
Bk. II, Ch. 7	8
Bk. II, Ch. 8	3
Bk. II, Ch. 9	8
Bk. II, Ch.15	6
Bk .II, Ch.16	7 / 2
Bk. II, Ch. 22	1
Bk. II, Ch. 23	5
Bk. III, Ch. 1	4
Bk. III, Ch. 2	4 / 1
Bk. III, Ch. 3	3 / 1
Bk. III, Ch. 4	2
Bk. III, Ch. 5	
Bk. III, Ch. 6	
Bk. III, Ch. 7	2

□ eye (196)
■ eyebrows (12)

---

[14] As the single form of "eyebrows" is not found in the novel, I use only the word "eyebrows."

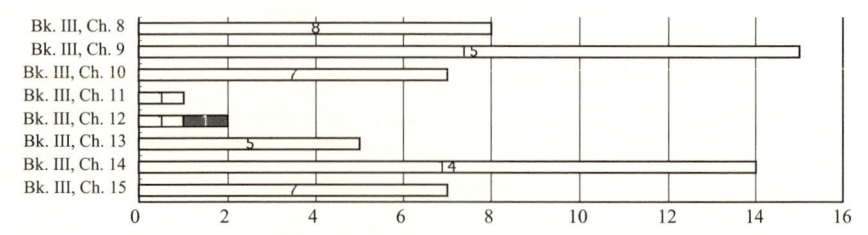

Chapter	Value
Bk. III, Ch. 8	8
Bk. III, Ch. 9	15
Bk. III, Ch. 10	
Bk. III, Ch. 11	
Bk. III, Ch. 12	1
Bk. III, Ch. 13	5
Bk. III, Ch. 14	14
Bk. III, Ch. 15	

Figure 2-7 Frequencies of "eye" and "eyebrows"

An examination of Figure 2-7 shows the following: (i) the word "eye" occurs in almost all the chapters of the novel; (ii) the words "eye" and "eyebrows" occur more frequently in the French scenes than in the English ones; (iii) most of the instances of "eyebrows" are present in the French scenes (the only instance of the word in the English scene is assigned to Lucie).

Next, I demonstrate how the words "eye" and "eyebrows" are allocated to each character in Table 2-8 below.

Table 2-8 Frequencies of "eye" and "eyebrows" for each character

Characters	"eye"	"eyebrows"	Total
Dr. Manette	19	1	20
Madame Defarge	12	8	20
Mr. Lorry	19		19
Lucie	13	2	15
Miss Pross	10		10
Carton	9		9
road-mender	8		8
Jerry	7		7
Defarge	7		7
Darnay	6		6
Marquis	6		6
Young Jerry	5		5
Barsad	4		4

seamstress	4	4
Stryver	3	3
Lucie's daughter	1	1
Others	63	1	64
Total	**196**	**12**	**208**

Table 2-8 shows that the word "eye" is used in the descriptions of most characters in the novel with varying frequencies, which exhibits Dickens's predilection for the word in character creation. The word "eyebrows," which is regarded as "the abode of pride after it has been generated in the heart,"[15] is mostly employed in the portrayals of Madame Defarge, Lucie, and Dr. Manette. Especially apparent are the eight out of the twelve instances (66.6%) in the description of Madame Defarge. This statistically indicates that the word "eyebrows" is most closely associated with Madame Defarge's characterization.

Moreover, I illustrate what words pre-modify the words of "eye" / "eyebrows" repeated in the descriptions of the characters. I deal with the collocations with the type of construction: [(determiner +) modifiers + "eye" / "eyebrows"]. In the table below, the collocations are shown separately for each character.

Table 2-9 Collocations of "eye" and "eyebrows" by character

Lucie	E	blue eyes (I,4) / "those blue eyes" (II,4) / clear eyes (II, 6) / the soft blue eyes (II, 20)
	F	the lifted eyebrows (III, 3) / her alarmed eyes (III, 3) / "blue eyes" (III, 14)
Dr. Manette	F	haggard eyes (3 times) (I, 6) / exceedingly bright eyes (I, 6) / the yet dark eyebrows (I, 6) / the kindled eyes (III, 4)

---

[15] de Vries (1976) s.v. Eyebrow.

Mr. Lorry	E	half-shut eyes (I, 3) / moist bright eyes (I, 4) / his bright eye (II, 6) / the business eye (II, 6) / his business eye (II, 6)
	F	Mr. Lorry's business eye (III, 8) / his troubled eyes (III, 8)
Madame Defarge	F	a watchful eye (I, 5) / her darkly defined eyebrows (I, 5) / steady eyebrows (I, 5) / quick eyes (II, 16) / flashing eyes (II, 16) / her dark eyebrows (III, 12) / dark eyes (2 times)
Defarge	F	good eyes (I, 5) / his bright eye (I, 5)
Carton	F	His practised eye (III, 8) / reverently shaded eyes (III, 9)
Darnay	E	a dark eye (II, 2)
	F	clouded eyes (III, 13)
Miss Pross	F	a wary eye (III, 8) / her tear-fraught eyes (III, 8)
Lucie's daughter	F	"blue eyes" (III, 14)
Stryver	E	sharp eyes (II, 1)
Marquis	F	his contemptuous eyes (II, 7)
seamstress	F	large widely opened patient eyes (III, 13) / the patient eyes (III, 13) / the uncomplaining eyes (III, 15)

An inquiry of Table 2-9 reveals the following:

1) The words that modify "eye" / "eyebrows" are roughly divided into three types:

   (i) Modifiers "blue," "clear," "bright," "shaded," "opened," etc. which refer to the physical appearances of "eye" / "eyebrows"
   (ii) Modifiers "haggard," "patient," "troubled," etc. which imply the characters' states of mind
   (iii) Modifiers "watchful," "sharp," etc. which suggest

Chapter II Repetition of Words for Character Description 107

functions of "eye" / "eyebrows" or their owner's properties.

2) As examined in Section 2.1.1, different color words for "head" and "hair" are allocated to each of the characters for individualization: "golden" to Lucie, "white" to Dr. Manette, and "dark" to Monsieur and Madame Defarge. As for the characters' "eye" / "eyebrows," the same method is employed in Lucie's "blue eyes" and Madame Defarge's "dark eyes." That is to say, the same combination of "eyes" / "eyebrows" with a particular modifier is repeated in an immediate context or in different contexts for individualization.

3) Such combinations as Mr. Lorry's "business eyes" and Madame Defarge's "steady eyebrows" are less common, at least in Dickens's works: no other examples of these collocations appear in the Dickens Corpus. These uncommon collocations are also used for individualization or typification of the characters.

4) On the other hand, the collocation "bright eye(s)" is commonly seen in the descriptions of Dr. Manette, Mr. Lorry, and Defarge. According to McMaster (1987: 37), "bright eyes belong ... to a number of other sympathetic characters, such as Pickwick, Mr. Dick, Mrs. Bagnet and Betty Higden." This kind of collocation is employed to

indicate common semantic features, say, thoughtfulness and intelligence, for the characters in *A Tale of Two Cities*.

5) Dr. Manette and Carton appear both in the English and French scenes, but the combinations of "eye" and "eyebrows" with modifiers occur only in the French scenes. We can say Dickens describes the characters' "eye" and "eyebrows" with modifiers when he manages to reveal their leading attributes. That is to say, in Carton's case, the collocation of "shaded eyes" with "reverently," which is connotative of religious coloring, occurs in the context where his determination of self-sacrifice is hinted at.

Now, in the following subsections, I discuss the peculiarities of the repetition of "eye" and "eyebrows" for five characters.

2.2.1 Repetition of Lucie's "eye" and "eyebrows"

Lucie's "blue eyes" occur from her first appearance in Chapter 4 of Book I, and then are repeated in the descriptions of the heroine and in other characters' speeches. The habitual use of Lucie's "eyes" with the adjective "blue" serves to make a visual representation of her personality much like her "golden hair."[16]

In Dickens's novels, "blue eyes" are often used in the descriptions of such "innocent, ingenuous, favoured" characters as Dora in *David*

---

[16] According to de Vries (1976), "blue eyes" are used in "the good fairies and heroines of fairy-tales." (s.v. Eye II. 1)

Copperfield and Joe in *Great Expectations*.[17] This kind of character creation may be thought of as a kind of "inter-textual repetition,"[18] an echo of semantic features among characters with "blue eyes." Through the inter-textual repetition of "blue eyes" in Dickens's works, Lucie's lovable personality traits are emphasized and impressed on the reader.

In addition, her "blue eyes" are recurrently juxtaposed with her "golden hair" from her first appearance. The repeated co-occurrence of "blue eyes" and "golden hair" serves to put more emphasis on her good nature as seen in the passage below:

(23) As his eyes rested on a short, slight, pretty figure, <u>a quantity of golden hair</u>, *a pair of blue eyes* that met his own with an inquiring look, and a forehead with a singular capacity...

(Bk. I, Ch. 4)

Next, I turn attention to the expression "the lifted eyebrows" from the passage below:

(24) There was something in its touch that gave Lucie a check. She stopped in the act of putting the note in her bosom, and, with her hands yet at her neck, looked terrified at Madame Defarge. Madame Defarge met *the lifted eyebrows* and forehead with a cold, impassive stare. (Bk. III, Ch. 3)

This passage appears when Defarge carries a note to Lucie from her

---

[17] Hori (2004: 21) says, "What seems peculiar to Dickens's typification is a tendency to create personality traits common to two or more characters for whom he uses the same collocation of the word *eye*."

[18] Imai (2004, 30) regards this term "inter-textual repetition" as "the borrowed use of motifs, as in *King Horn* and *Havelok the Dane*."

husband along with Madame Defarge and The Vengeance. Lucie thanks Madame Defarge and begs her to help Darnay. But Madame Defarge reacts coldly to Lucie's entreaties. Lucie feels frightened by Madame Defarge's reaction. The collocation "the lifted eyebrows" expresses Lucie's fright, and at the same time symbolically suggests an attitudinal difference between the two women. Unlike "blue eyes," it is not repeated as part of her individualization, but serves to appropriately describe the situation in which she is kept. Dickens often exploits this kind of technique of character and situational description.

2.2.2 Repetition of Mr. Lorry's "eye" and "eyebrows"

As another example of the repetition of "eye" / "eyebrows" with the same modifier, I will examine Mr. Lorry's case. One of the characteristics of the iterative use of Mr. Lorry's "eye" is displayed in the combination of "eye" with "business." This is one demonstrative instance of "a regional, social, occupational, or philosophical typification by language."[19] The less familiar collocation "business eye" occurs twice in Chapter 6 of Book II, and recurs in Chapter 8 of Book III again.[20] Incidentally, in Dickens's novels, I find no instance of "business eyes" except for the three examples given to Mr. Lorry. It cannot be said that the combination is frequently used, but it is closely related to the repetitive use of "business" in Mr. Lorry's speech and in the descriptions of Mr. Lorry. In fact, the word "business" occurs 134

---

[19] Quirk (1974), 8.
[20] I also consulted *Nineteenth-Century Fiction* (2000, Chadwyck-Healey), but I couldn't find any instances of "business eyes" except for the three examples in *A Tale of Two Cities*.

times throughout the novel. Eighty-nine of these instances are seen in the characters' speeches, and 50 of 89 instances (56%) in Mr. Lorry's speech. Moreover, 15 of the remaining 45 instances (33%) in the descriptive and narrative parts are found in such expressions related to him as "the man of business" and "his business eye." As a result, readers naturally draw a close association between Mr. Lorry and "business," or his businesslike manner.

The employment of "business eye" also shows that he has the ability to look at things objectively as seen in the following example:

(25) (Carton informs Mr. Lorry that Darnay, who was once released owing to Dr. Manette's testimony, has been arrested again.)
Mr. Lorry's business eye read in the speaker's[Carton's] face that it was loss of time to dwell upon the point. Confused, but sensible that something might depend on his presence of mind, he commanded himself, and was silently attentive.
(Bk. III, Ch. 8)

However, Mr. Lorry's ways of dealing with other characters are not always businesslike. He often displays great affection to Lucie and her father even though he repetitively uses "a man of business" in his speech. The collocation "business eyes" literally manifests his businesslike habits, and at the same time implies his human attributes.

2.2.3 Repetition of Dr. Manette's "eye" and "eyebrows"

In Dr. Manette's case, his "eye" and "eyebrows" co-occur with different and contrastive modifiers. In order to demonstrate this concretely, observe the instances of his "eye" and "eyebrows" in Chapter 6 of Book

I, where Dr. Manette, who is deranged after his long prison term, first appears. In the chapter, as shown in Figure 2-7, the words "eye" (9 times) and "eyebrows" (once) occur 10 times, and 9 of them are assigned to Dr. Manette (90%).

Table 2-10 Instances of "eye" and "eyebrows" in Bk. I, Ch. 6

	Instances of "eye" & "eyebrows"	Characters
1	a pair of haggard eyes	Dr. Manette
2	the haggard eyes	Dr. Manette
3	exceedingly bright eyes	Dr. Manette
4	his yet dark eyebrows	Dr. Manette
5	his eyes	Dr. Manette
6	His haggard eyes	Dr. Manette
7	His eyes	Dr. Manette
8	his eyes	Dr. Manette
9	his eyes	Dr. Manette
10	the eyes	an officer

As Table 2-10 indicates, five of nine instances (56%) of "eye" and "eyebrows" given to Dr. Manette are pre-modified with the adjectives expressive of their outward appearance: "haggard" (3 times), "dark" (once), and "bright" (once). The adjectives "haggard" and "dark" are antonymous with "bright" in the contextual light. Dr. Manette's "haggard eyes" and "dark eyebrows" represent his deranged state of mind, or his mental illness in this scene as his "white hair / head" does.[21] On the other hand, the "exceedingly bright eyes" suggest that he has other attributes, probably his natural or positive personality hidden

---

[21] In the description of Dr. Manette, I find the use of the adjective "haggard": "the old haggard, faded surface of face" (Bk. II, Ch. 18), in the context where he reverts to the mental collapse after the wedding between Lucie and Darnay.

beneath his "haggard eyes." This statement is supported by the fact that these collocations co-occur in adjacent sentences as seen in the next passage; therefore, the opposing meanings of "haggard" and "bright," which is pre-modified by the intensive adverb "extremely," are highlighted:

> (26) (Dr. Manette is in the garret of Defarge's wine-shop, absorbed in cobbling shoes.)
> Some minutes of silent work had passed: and *the haggard eyes* had looked up again: not with any interest or curiosity, but with a dull mechanical perception, beforehand, that the spot where the only visitor they were aware of had stood, was not yet empty...
> The opened half-door was opened a little further, and secured at that angle for the time... He had a white beard, raggedly cut, but not very long, a hollow face, and *exceedingly bright eyes*. (Bk. I, Ch. 6)

To understand Dickens's stylistic purpose in depicting Dr. Manette's "eye" as "exceedingly bright eyes," an examination of the expression "the kindled eyes" in the following passage will serve to clarify:

> (27) And when Jarvis Lorry saw *the kindled eyes*, the resolute face, the calm strong look and bearing of the man whose life always seemed to him to have been stopped, like a clock, for so many years, and then set going again with an energy which had lain dormant during the cessation of its usefulness, he believed. (Bk. III, Ch. 4)

In the above context, feeling strong in his power as a Bastille survivor, Dr. Manette is confident that he will be able to set Darnay free. The word "kindled" in Dr. Manette's "kindled eyes" figuratively represents his excited and elevated state of mind in this scene. The use of the near-synonyms "bright" and "kindled" to modify Dr. Manette's "eye" in two different scenes, although at intervals, are in close semantic relationship with each other as a resounding echo. Dickens assigns the expression "exceedingly bright eyes" to Dr. Manette in the former scene in order to foreshadow the role he will play later.

2.2.4 Repetition of Madame Defarge's "eye" and "eyebrows"

With regard to Madame Defarge, her "eye" and "eyebrows" are characterized by the use of a cluster of adjectives "watchful," "steady," and "quick" which express the diverse functions of her "eye" and "eyebrows," and by the repeated use of "dark" and "darkly."[22] In other words, her personality is first suggested by the depictions of the vigilant, alert, and firmly directed "eye" or "eyebrows" before the outbreak of the Revolution, and then after that, her evil nature is unveiled and symbolized by her "dark eyes" and "dark eyebrows" as is the case with the repetition of her "dark hair" (see Section 2.1.3). One such example of "her dark eyes" is cited in the passage below:

> (28) He[the wood-sawyer] was so very demonstrative herein, that he might have been suspected (perhaps was, by *the dark eyes* that looked contemptuously at him out of Madame Defarge's

---

[22] In the descriptions of Madame Defarge, I frequently notice unique collocations including the words "dark" and "darkly," as in the following:

> In that same juncture of time when the Fifty-Two awaited their fate, Madame Defarge held *darkly ominous council* with The Vengeance and Jacques Three of the Revolutionary Jury. (Bk. III, Ch. 14)

head) of having his small individual fears for his own personal safety, every hour in the day. (Bk. III, Ch. 14)

The context of the passage is the secret conference with Jacques Three and the Vengeance, where Madame Defarge declares her insane determination to wipe out the whole Evrémonde family including Lucie and her daughter. At the clandestine meeting she also casts suspicion upon one of her comrades, the wood-sawyer. In Chapter 14 of Book III, which contains passage (28), her "dark hair" is repeated twice. The repetitive use of the collocation in proximity serves to expose Madame Defarge's "absence of moral or spiritual light" with the help of the figurative meaning of the word "dark."[23]

2.2.5 Repetition of a seamstress's "eye" and "eyebrows"

As a final example, a seamstress's case is examined. The seamstress with whom Sydney Carton traveled in the tumbrel to the guillotine plays the role of a representative of the poor innocent victims of the Revolution.

She is given four instances of "eyes" (see Table 2-8). Three of the four include the construction [modifier + "eyes"]. That is to say, "patient eyes" is repeated twice in proximity in Chapter 13 of Book III as seen in the passage below. In Chapter 15 of Book III, her "eyes" are pre-modified by the word "uncomplaining," which is semantically related to "patient." The repetitive combination of her "eyes" with the modifiers effectively evokes great sympathy for her. Additionally, her

---

[23] *OED2* s.v. Dark a. 4.

"opened eyes" in "large widely opened patient eyes" suggests her depressed state of mind and her inevitable fate in the following passage:[24]

> (29) (A seamstress, who notices that Carton makes himself a vicarious sacrifice, asks him to hold her hand on the way to the guillotine.)
> A very few moments after that, a young woman, with a slight girlish form, a sweet spare face in which there was no vestige of colour, and *large widely opened patient eyes*, rose from the seat where he[Carton] had observed her sitting, and came to speak to him...
> 'If I may ride with you, Citizen Evrémonde, will you let me hold your hand? I am not afraid, but I am little and weak, and it will give me more courage.'
> As *the patient eyes* were lifted to his face, he saw a sudden doubt in them, and then astonishment. (Bk. III, Ch. 13)

2.3 Repetition of "hand" and "finger"

Now, I will investigate the repetition of the words "hand" and "finger." First, as I have done in the examination of "hair / head" and "eye / eyebrows," I will show likewise how the words "hand" and "finger" are distributed and used throughout *A Tale of Two Cities*. The word "hand" (370 instances) is realized in the word-forms, "hand" (247), "hands" (112), and "handed" (11). I would like to confine my investigation to the word "hand" contextually referring to "the terminal part of the arm beyond the wrist,"[25] so the following 33 instances are exclud-

---

[24] The *OED2* defines "open-eyed" as "having the mental 'eyes' or perceptive powers open." (s.v. Open-eyed 2)
[25] *OED2* s.v. Hand n. 1.

Chapter II Repetition of Words for Character Description   117

ed: "handed" (11); "hand" (7), which means "the cards dealt to each player" in the games of cards; "hands" (1), which means "the pointer of a clock"; "hand" (1), which serves as a verb; some phrases, "on the other hand" (3), "at hand" (4), "in hand" (4), "second-hand" (2). As a result, I will discuss 337 instances of "hand." The word "finger" (51) contains the word-forms, "finger" (18) and the plural form "fingers" (33). The frequencies of the two words, "hand" and "finger," in serial order of chapter are represented in Figure 2-11 below.

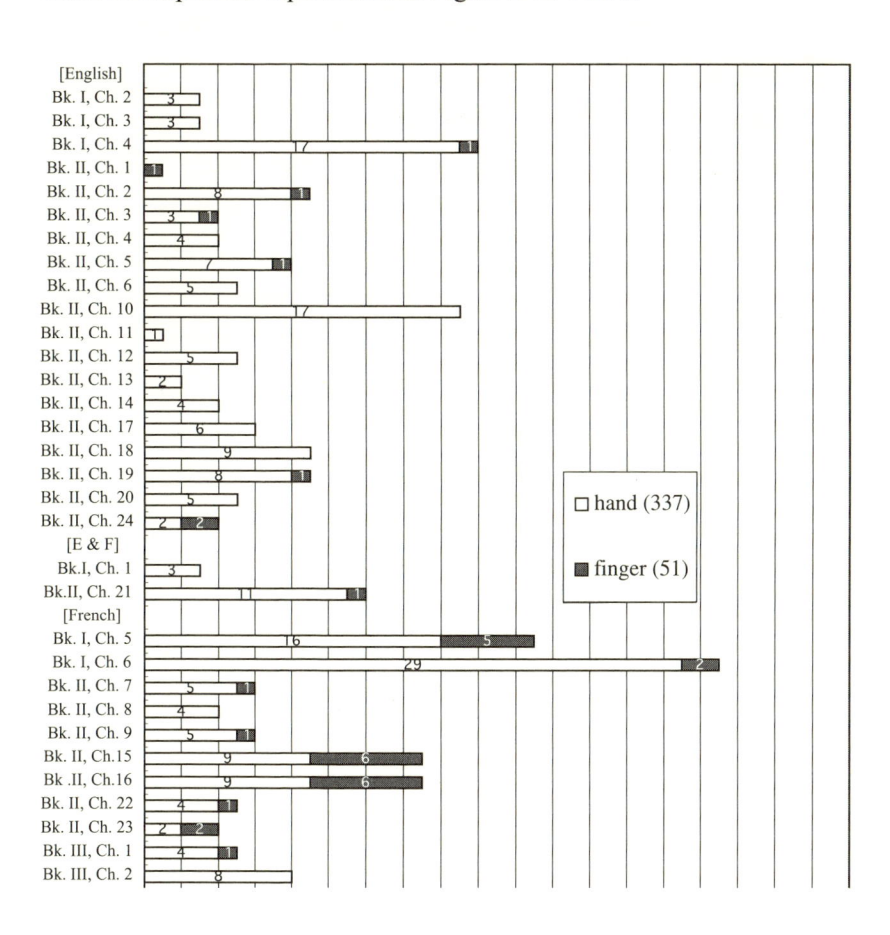

118   Repetition in Dickens's *A Tale of Two Cities*

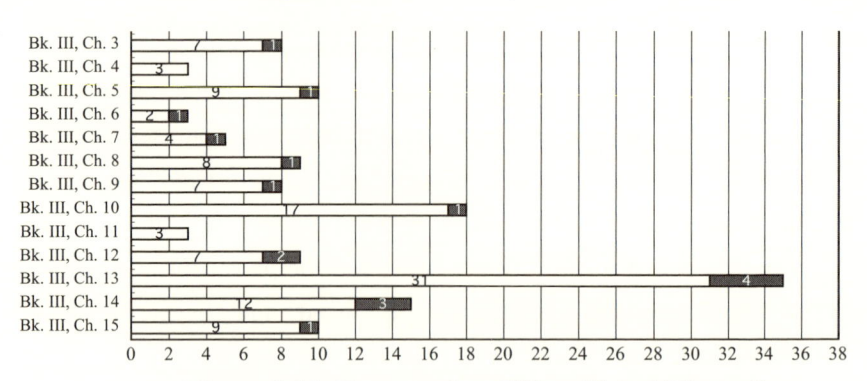

Figure 2-11 Frequencies of "hand" and "finger"

An inspection of Figure 2-11 shows the following: (i) the word "hand" occurs in almost all the chapters of the novel like "hair" / "head" and "eye"; (ii) the two words "hand" and "finger" occur more frequently in the French chapters, especially, most recurrently in Chapters 5 and 6 of Book I and Chapter 13 of Book III. The high frequencies of these two words in the three chapters are closely connected with the emergence of Dr. Manette, Lucie and Sydney Carton. For example, Chapter 6 of Book I represents the poignant reunion between Dr. Manette and Lucie. Dr. Manette is completely stripped of his identity by the suffering of his imprisonment at first, but through his intimate and physical contact with Lucie he is gradually regaining his sanity. Their contact is visually described through the repetition of their "hand" / "finger," which contributes to the second highest frequency of the words indicative of the body parts (19 instances to Dr. Manette, 10 to Lucie, and 2 to Mr. Lorry). Some of the instances of Dr. Manette's and Lucie's "hand" / "finger" are listed below:

1) ... *the unsteady fingers* of one of *his hands* strayed to his lips

Chapter II Repetition of Words for Character Description

as he looked at it...

2) ... he laid the knuckles of *the right hand* in the hollow of the left, and then the knuckles of *the left hand* in the hollow of the right, and then passed *a hand* across his bearded chin...

3) With the tears streaming down her face, she put *her two hands* to her lips, and kissed them to him; then clasped them on her breast...

4) He recoiled, but she laid *her hand* upon his arm.

5) Advancing *his hand* by little and little, he took it up and looked at it.

6) Releasing his arm, she laid *her hand* upon his shoulder.

7) He took her hair into *his hand* again, and looked closely at it.

8) *His hands* released her as he uttered this cry, and went up to his white hair, which they tore in a frenzy.

9) Hailing his softened tone and manner, his daughter fell upon her knees before him, with *her appealing hands* upon his breast.

10) He readily responded to his daughter's drawing her arm through his, and took – and kept – *her hand* in both his own.

In instances 1) and 2), the repetition of "hand" and "finger" serves to describe Dr. Manette's irrational motions. Instances 3) to 10) depict not only the movement of Lucie's "hand" to comfort her father but also that of Dr. Manette's "hand," indicative of both his confused state of mind and his temporary recovery from delirium. Dickens exploits the repetition of Dr. Manette's "hand" as a means of rendering his mental states visible. In other words, the repetitive descriptions of the outward appearances of the characters are used for psychological characterization. To take a typical example, the transferred epithet "appealing" in Lucie's "appealing hand" in instance 9) appropriately depicts her psychological state of calling for help, as will be discussed in more detail later.

Next, I demonstrate how the words "hand" and "finger" are allocated to each character.[26]

Table 2-12 Frequencies of "hand" and "finger" for each character

Characters	"hand"	"finger"	Total
Dr. Manette	64	3	67
Lucie	41	1	42
Carton	38	1	39
Madame Defarge	21	9	30
Mr. Lorry	23		23
Darnay	15	1	16
Defarge	16		16
Jacques Three	4	7	11
Miss Pross	9	1	10
Stryver	7	3	10
Marquis	6	3	9
Jerry	5	3	8
road-mender	3	2	5
seamstress	3	1	4
Barsad	2	1	3
Lucie's daughter	1		1
Others	79	15	94
Total	**337**	**51**	**388**

Table 2-12 indicates that the word "hand" is repetitively used in the descriptions of most of the characters in the novel with various frequencies like the words "hair," "head," and "eye." Higher frequencies of the word "hand" are assigned to Dr. Manette, Lucie and Sydney Carton. It is noteworthy that, compared with the frequencies of "head / hair" (see Table 2-4) and "eye / eyebrows" (see Table 2-8), more

---

[26] In some instances of "hands," they refer to two characters' "hands." Such instances are put in "Others."

Chapter II Repetition of Words for Character Description 121

instances of "hand" are applied to Carton.

The word "finger" is more frequently employed in the depictions of Madame Defarge and Jacques Three. Madame Defarge's "finger" often co-occurs with "knitted" or "knitting" as in the sentence, "Madame Defarge knitted with nimble fingers and steady eyebrows, and saw nothing" (Bk. I, Ch. 5). The word "finger" is recurrently employed to portray her habitual gesture of knitting. The similar thing is applied to Jacques Three, as will be mentioned later.

Furthermore, I exemplify what words qualify the "hand" / "finger" in the descriptions of characters. The collocations I deal with are in the construction [(determiner +) modifiers + "hand" / "finger"]. In the following table, the collocations are shown individually for each character.

Table 2-13 Collocations of "hand" and "finger" by character

Lucie	E	the hesitating little hand (I, 4) / the supplicatory fingers (I, 4) / "her cold hands" (I, 4) / delicate hands (II, 6) / her agitated hand (II, 18)
	F	her appealing hands (I, 6) / her appealing hand (III, 3)
Dr. Manette	E	emaciated hands (I, 3) / "this honoured hand" (II, 10) / his two hands (twice) (II, 10) / his own hand (II, 18)
	F	The unsteady fingers (I, 6) / the right hand (I, 6) / the left hand (I, 6) / "this gaunt hand" (III, 10) / "my own hands" (III, 10)
Carton	F	his open hand (III, 8) / his eager but so firm and steady hand (III, 12) / a cautionary finger (III, 13) / his right hand (III, 13) / "your brave hand" (III, 13)
Mr. Lorry	E	his left hand (twice) (I, 4) / both hands (I, 4)
	F	the clasping hand (III, 2) / his troubled hand (III, 8)

Madame Defarge	F	a large hand (I, 5) / her left hand (I, 5) / nimble fingers (I, 5) / her right hand (II, 16) / her extended hand (II, 16) / Madame's resolute right hand (II, 21) / "these two hands" (III, 12) / The two hands (III, 14) / griping fingers (III, 14)
Defarge	F	a large hand (I, 5) / his soiled hand (I, 5) / his strong hand (II, 21) / his own hand (II, 21) / his anxious hand (III, 3)
Jacques Three	F	his agitated hand (II, 15) / the restless hand (II, 15) / the usual hand (III, 9) / the restless fingers (III, 12) / his cruel fingers (III, 14)
seamstress	F	her cold hand (III, 13) / the work-worn, hunger-worn young fingers (III, 13) / her patient hand (III, 15) / The spare hand (III, 15)
Miss Pross	E	a brawny hand (I, 4)
	F	a strong hand (III, 14) / unsteady hand (III, 14)
Jerry	E	his rusty hands (II, 14)

The combinations of "hand" / "finger" with their modifiers, compared with those of "hair," "head," "eye," and "eyebrows," do not clearly show the meaningful collocational patterns peculiar to each character for individualization. The words "hand" and "finger" display a tendency to combine with modifiers expressive of the characters' attitudes and states of mind in context. The author provides a situational description of the characters through the repetition of "hand" / "finger" with modifiers (e.g. Lucie's "appealing hand(s)") and the intensive use of the two words in one scene.

It should also be added that the collocations of the words "hand" and "finger" sometimes include the same words and their synonyms that are seen in those of "hair," "head," "eye," and "eyebrows." For example, as pointed out in the repetition of Madame Defarge's "eye" (Section 2.2.4), the use of the adjectives "watchful," "steady," and "quick" suggests her personality traits as seen in the various functions of her "eyes." Here again, the modifiers "nimble" and "resolute," which are the near-synonyms of "quick" and "steady" respectively, produce an accumulative effect of characterization.

Furthermore, when my observations are extended to words and phrases that co-occur with the words "hand" and "finger," I cannot help noticing Dickens's deliberate use of the co-occurring words for characterization. Now, I investigate five characters' cases: Lucie, Carton, Jacques Three, a seamstress, and Jerry Cruncher. I do not examine the case of Dr. Manette because the combinations of his "hand" and "finger" with modifiers do not seem to present his predominant features of character.

2.3.1 Repetition of Lucie's "hand" and "finger"

Lucie's "hair," "head," "eye," and "eyebrows" often collocate with the modifiers illustrative of their color (e.g. "golden" and "blue"), but her "hand" and "finger" recurrently co-occur with modifiers denotative of her attitude and mentality, such as "supplicatory," "hesitating," "agitated," and "appealing." It is worth mentioning that the collocations "supplicatory fingers" and "appealing hand(s)" (twice) are only seen in the descriptions of Lucie in the novel.[27] Let me consider the three instances of such collocations:

(30)　'Pray,' said Mr. Lorry, in a soothing tone, bringing his left

---

[27] In the description of a female peasant, the collocation "appealing touch" (Bk. II, Ch. 8) is seen.

hand from the back of the chair to lay it on *the supplicatory fingers* that clasped him in so violent a tremble…

(Bk. I, Ch. 4)

(31) Hailing his[Dr. Manette's] softened tone and manner, his daughter fell upon her knees before him, with *her appealing hands* upon his breast. (Bk. I, Ch. 6)

(32) But, the suppressed manner had enough of menace in it — not visible and presented, but indistinct and withheld — to alarm Lucie into saying, as she laid *her appealing hand* on Madame Defarge's dress:
'You will be good to my poor husband. You will do him no harm. You will help me to see him if you can?'

(Bk. III, Ch. 3)

In each case, Lucie is in expectation of a sympathetic response from her interlocutors: Mr. Lorry, Dr. Manette, and Madame Defarge. Lucie has a compassionate nature and the power to inspire great love and peace of mind in other characters, but she does not play an active role by herself. The people surrounding her, such as Mr. Lorry and Sydney Carton, draw their strength from her and act on her behalf. Each instance of these collocations situationally represents Lucie's attitudes and states of mind in context, and at the same time, suggests her role in the novel.

2.3.2 Repetition of Carton's "hand" and "finger"

Carton's "hand" and "finger" occur at the third highest frequency in Table 2-13, but the combination of his "hand" and "finger" with modifiers recurrently occurs only in the three French chapters: Chapters 8, 12, and 13 of Book III. Table 2-14 demonstrates how the 39 instances of his "hand" and "finger" are distributed among chapters.

Table 2-14   Distribution of Carton's "hand" and "finger"

	English Chapters					French Chapters				
Chap.	II, 2	II, 3	II, 5	II, 13	II, 20	III, 8	III, 9	III, 12	III, 13	III, 14
Freq.	1	1	4	1	1	3	2	2	21	3

Table 2-14 illustrates that Carton's "hand" and "finger" are present most frequently in Chapter 13 of Book III (21 out of 39, 54%). In this chapter, Carton causes Darnay to slip into unconsciousness and substitutes himself for him in prison. The very frequent and intensive use of his "hand" in this chapter brings his heroic self-sacrifice to the foreground. More concretely, the process of Carton's action of drugging Darnay is depicted through the repetition of his "hand," which is reiterated as many as 11 times within three pages. The repetition is presented as follows:

1) Carton, with *his right hand* in his breast, stood close beside him.
2) Carton still had *his hand* in his breast.
3) Carton, standing over him with *his hand* in his breast, looked down.
4) He was drawing *his hand* from his breast...
5) ... *the hand* stopped, closing upon something.
6) ... *his hand* slowly and softly moved down close to the writer's face.
7) ... Carton – *his hand* again in his breast – looked steadily at him.
8) ... *Carton's hand* was again watchfully and softly stealing down...
9) ... *the hand* was at the prisoner's face...
10) *Carton's hand* moved back to his breast no more.
11) ... *Carton's hand* was close and firm at his nostrils...

In this scene, the repeated combination of "his (right) hand" with "in his breast" (1 to 3) suggests Carton's waiting for the opportunity to take out a sleeping drug. The initiating action is represented in 4 with the combination "drawing his hand" with "from his breast." From 5 to 11 (excluding 7), the action of Carton's drugging Darnay is vividly described through the repetitive construction [Carton's "hand" + predicate verb]. In this way, Dickens makes a graphic description of Carton's heroic conduct.

Additionally, the arrangement of the combinations of his "hand" and "finger" with modifiers attracts my attention. The combination "his eager but so firm and steady hand" occurs at the end of Chapter 12 of Book III just before Carton tries to take Darnay's place in the prison in Chapter 13 of Book III, as discussed above. The transferred epithets "eager," "firm," and "steady" in the combination represent Carton's positive features, which have not been mentioned by the novelist before. The combination does not directly foreshadow Carton's heroic act of self-devotion, but leads the reader to expect his unprecedented action in the following scene.

2.3.3 Repetition of Jacques Three's "hand" and "finger"

Jacques Three is a member of the secret revolutionary committee, of which Defarge is a leader, and is also on the jury of the Tribunal. He illustrates the repulsive and immoral aspects of the Revolution. The modifiers or the transferred epithets — "agitated," "restless" (twice) and "cruel" — in the collocations of his "hand" and "finger" directly reveal his character to be "averse of being quiet and settled," and "taking pleasure in another's pain or distress."[28]

Chapter II Repetition of Words for Character Description   127

What is more, scrutinizing the words and phrases that co-occur with his "hand" and "finger," I am brought to notice that such synonymous words as "hungry" and "craving" frequently recur with his body parts, and that he makes a habitual gesture with his "hand" and "finger." Let me consider the following passages:

(33)   ... Jacques Three, equally intent, on one knee behind them, with *his agitated hand* always gliding over the network of fine nerves about his mouth and nose... (Bk. II, Ch. 15)

(34)   'And once again listen, Jacques!' said the kneeling Number Three: *his fingers* ever wandering over and over those fine nerves... (Bk. II, Ch. 15)

(35)   The hungry man gnawed one of *his fingers* as he looked at the other three, and *his finger* quivered with the craving that was on him. (Bk. II, Ch. 15)

(36)   Eager and prominent among them, one man with a craving face, and *his fingers* perpetually hovering about his lips, whose appearance gave great satisfaction to the spectators. A life-thirsting, cannibal-looking, bloody-minded juryman, the Jacques Three of St. Antoine. (Bk. III, Ch. 9)

(37)   'It is a great pity,' croaked Jacques Three, dubiously shaking his head, with *his cruel fingers* at his hungry mouth...
(Bk. III, Ch. 14)

All the passages describe Jacques Three's habitual gesture of fidgeting with his "hand" and "finger" around the mouth. This repeated behavior with his "hand" and "finger" help identify him among lots of

---

[28] *OED2* s.v. Restless 2.a. and Cruel 1.

revolutionists of the same name.[29]

Moreover, the recurrent use of "craving" and "hungry" in passages (35), (36), and (37) indicates the fact that Jacques Three has an intense longing or an insatiable hunger for something, but we cannot first make out exactly what it is. In the unfolding of the plot, we come to learn that he is a "life-thirsting, cannibal-looking, bloody-minded"[30] man as seen in passage (36), and therefore that his "hand" and "finger" are "agitated," "restless," or "cruel," and are always hovering about his mouth.

2.3.4 Repetition of a seamstress's "hand" and "finger"

As examined in Section 2.2.5, the adjective "patient" and its synonym "uncomplaining" are repeatedly employed in the collocations of a seamstress's "eye." Here again, the adjective "patient" collocates with her "hand," and the accumulative use of the word contributes to individualizing the seamstress. In addition, the less familiar collocation of her "fingers" with "work-worn" and "hunger-worn"[31] attracts attention. Dickens demonstrates that the seamstress is society's innocent victim, a sacrificial heroine both before and during the Revolution through such collocations:

---

[29] In the description of Jacques Three, the collocation "gnaw his finger" is seen twice.
[30] The *OED2* records this example as the earliest of "life-thirsting."
[31] The *OED2* records this example as the earliest of "hunger-worn." Furthermore, the dictionary records the earliest use of "work-worn" as 1865, but Dickens uses this in the combination "the work-worn, hunger-worn young fingers" as early as 1859.

(38)   As *the patient eyes* were lifted to his face, he [Carton] saw a sudden doubt in them, and then astonishment. He pressed *the work-worn, hunger-worn young fingers*, and touched his lips. (Bk. III, Ch. 13)

Incidentally, both the seamstress and Lucie have "cold hand(s)." Lucie's "cold hands," which appear in Miss Pross's speech, suggest her state of unconsciousness because of the severe shock when Mr. Lorry explains that her father, whom she believes to be dead, is alive in Paris after a long imprisonment. On the other hand, the seamstress's "cold hand" suggests her dispirited and disheartened condition as seen in the phrase "the work-worn, hunger-worn young fingers."

2.3.5 Repetition of Jerry Cruncher's "hand" and "finger"

Though only one instance of "his rusty hands" is listed in Jerry's column of Table 2-13, we often come across the co-occurrence of his "hand" / "finger" with "rusty" / "rust." It is likely that the habitual combinations of these words indicate one of the themes of the novel — resurrection — as well as his characterization. Now, let me investigate some instances of the combinations below:

(39)   Mr. Cruncher had by this time taken quite a lunch of rust off *his fingers* in his following of the evidence. (Bk. II, Ch. 3)

(40)   After taking a timid peep at him lying on his back, with *his rusty hands* under his head for a pillow, his son lay down too, and fell asleep again. (Bk. II, Ch. 14)

(41)   Jerry hoarsely professed himself at Miss Pross's service.

He had worn <u>all his rust off</u> long ago, but nothing would file his spiky head down. (Bk. III, Ch. 7)

The words "rust" and "rusty" convey not merely a literal meaning, i.e. "a red, orange, or tawny coating formed upon the surface of iron or steel by oxidation,"[32] which Jerry Cruncher's "hand" and "finger" get from the corpses he exhumes, but also a figurative meaning, "moral corrosion or canker."[33] The combinations of "rust" / "rusty" with "hand" / "finger" in passages (39) and (40) represent his corrupt resurrectionist business before he falls to the horror of death and murder during the Revolution, just like his "black hair" is connected with his midnight work. After he experiences the sheer horror in Paris, however, he resolves to relinquish his task of grave-robbing, and thus wears "all his rust off" as observed in passage (41), where "rust" is not connected with his "hands" or "fingers" any longer. Viewed in this light, the discrepancy of the combinations of his "hand" / "finger" before and during the Revolution makes a cohesive web and reflects Cruncher's reformation or resurrection.

2.4 Key words in *A Tale of Two Cities*

Before I make a further examination of the relationship between repetition and character description, I will identify key words in *A Tale of Two Cities*, as compared to Dickens's other novels. For the statistical analysis of repetition, I adopt a computer-assisted approach to the selfmade Dickens Corpus of his 22 novels. In order to make Table

---

[32] *OED2* s.v. Rust 1.a.
[33] *OED2* s.v. Rust 2.a.

Chapter II Repetition of Words for Character Description   131

2-15 below, I use Mike Scott's "Key Words Tool" of "WordSmith Tools" program.[34] The key words are calculated by comparing the frequency of each word in *A Tale of Two Cities* with that of the same word in the Dickens Corpus. Any word which is found to be unusually frequent in *A Tale of Two Cities* is considered a key word. For instance, the word "madam" occurs 193 times at the frequency of 0.14 % in *A Tale of Two Cities*, while it appears 263 times at the frequency in the Dickens Corpus. The word is not expected to occur at such high frequency on the basis of the Dickens Corpus, and therefore it is given the highest numeric value of keyness, in other words, the highest log likelihood (744.0). On the other hand, the conjunction "and" is not regarded as one of key words, though it occurs at the second highest frequency in *A Tale of Two Cities* (5,000 times; 3.65 %), and in the Dickens Corpus (156,900 times; 3.56 %) (see Table 2-5). The reason for this is because the word is present with almost the same rate between *A Tale of Two Cities* and the Dickens Corpus as expected.

Table 2-15
Key words in *A Tale of Two Cities* as compared to the Dickens Corpus

No.	Key words	*A Tale of Two Cities* (Approx. 137,000 words)		Dickens Corpus (Approx. 4,380,000 words)		Keyness (Log likelihood)
		Freq.	%	Freq.	%	
1	madame	193	0.14	263	0.00	744.0
2	prisoner	169	0.12	306	0.00	581.8
3	doctor	226	0.16	1,199	0.03	407.3
4	spy	72	0.05	66	0.00	316.3
5	mender	48	0.03	4	0.00	307.5

---

[34] To calculate log likelihood I also refer to the site: http://ucrel.lancs.ac.uk/llwizard.html.

6	citizen	64	0.05	65	0.00	272.5
7	knit	65	0.05	98	0.00	241.1
8	the	8,024	5.85	214,911	4.91	239.5
9	wine	120	0.09	671	0.02	206.8
10	patriot	33	0.02	11	0.00	181.8
11	prison	91	0.07	433	0.00	178.9
12	chateau	27	0.02	3	0.00	169.4
13	courtyard	36	0.03	27	0.00	167.2
14	guillotine	27	0.02	6	0.00	157.8
15	fountain	42	0.03	69	0.00	150.6
16	gaoler	23	0.02	2	0.00	146.9
17	tribunal	23	0.02	7	0.00	128.6
18	tumbril	18	0.01	1	0.00	118.0
19	village	52	0.04	220	0.00	111.6
20	bank	65	0.05	387	0.00	105.9
21	husband	99	0.07	874	0.02	105.8
22	jackal	15	0.01	0	0.00	104.8
23	road	106	0.08	1,009	0.02	102.7
24	father	197	0.14	2,720	0.06	102.4
25	plane-tree	15	0.01	1	0.00	97.4
26	shoemaker	18	0.01	9	0.00	92.0
27	flop	15	0.01	3	0.00	88.8
28	citizeness	13	0.00	1	0.00	83.7
29	passenger	45	0.03	236	0.00	81.8
30	emigrant	23	0.02	40	0.00	80.5
31	jury	32	0.02	107	0.00	80.3
32	business	134	0.10	1,760	0.04	77.0
33	stone	74	0.05	689	0.02	73.8
34	hill	42	0.03	231	0.00	73.4
35	ladybird	12	0.00	2	0.00	72.5

In Table 2-15, 35 key words are presented in order according to the log likelihood values. Of course, the proper names of characters can rank among the top because most of them appear only in *A Tale of Two Cities*. In the Table, these character names like "Carton" and "Lucie," the place names like "Soho" and "France," and such French words as "Monseigneur" and "Monsieur" are excluded.

Observation of Table 2-15 leads me to notice that the words to refer back to characters are at the head of the list: for example, the word "madame" for Madame Defarge; "doctor," "father," and "shoemaker" for Doctor Manette; "prisoner," "emigrant," and "husband" for Darnay; "ladybird" for Lucie; "spy" for Barsad; "mender" for one of the French patriots; and "jackal" for Carton. Moreover, the words related to France and the French Revolution also show keyness, for example, "citizen," "citizeness," "patriot," "republic," "guillotine," "tribunal," "tumbrel," and so on.

Among the remaining words in Table 2-5, the key words, "knit," "wine," "fountain," "plane-tree," and "business" catch my special attention. In the following sections, I will focus my attention on the repetitive use of the words "knit" and "business" for character description. The repeated use of the other keywords, "wine," "fountain," and "plane-tree," should be examined later in Chapter III.

2.5 Repetition of "business" and "knit"

As Table 2-15 above indicates, the two words "business" and "knit" show outstandingness in their frequencies in *A Tale of Two Cities* against Dickens's other novels. In particular, the word "knit" occurs just 98 times in Dickens's 22 novels, while it appears as many as 65 times in *A Tale of Two Cities*, showing the very high log likelihood of 241.1. The word "business" also occurs more in *A Tale of Two Cities* than in Dickens other novels, showing the high log likelihood of 77.0. Both words are unusually frequent in *A Tale of Two Cities* in comparison with what we would expect on the basis of the Dickens Corpus. The two key words are recurrently used not only for an individualization of the characters but also for indication of the subject matter of the novel. My concern turns to the repeated use of the two words and of words that co-occur with them in the same sentence, or in adjacent sentences.

2.5.1 Repetition of "business"

As pointed out in Section 2.2.2, the word "business" occurs most frequently to depict Mr. Lorry: 50 of 89 instances in the dialogue and 15 of 45 in the descriptive and narrative parts. The combination of the repetitive word and its collocates, for example, [plodding/strict + a man of business] in "a plodding man of business" (II, 19) and "a strict man of business" (III, 3), serve to display Mr. Lorry's distinctive feature, or his businesslike manner. However, Mr. Lorry's way of coping with his relations with the other characters is not always businesslike. He often displays his great affection for Lucie and her father even though he frequently uses "a man of business" in his speech. His human aspect of character is reflected through words co-occurring with "business" in the descriptive part, as seen in the passage below:

>(42) (Mr. Lorry tactfully asks Doctor Manette what caused the relapse and how it can be prevented.)
>   'Now, my dear Manette," said Mr. Lorry, at length, <u>in his most considerate and most affectionate way</u>, "I am *a mere man of business*, and unfit to cope with such intricate and difficult matters. I do not possess the kind of information necessary; I do not possess the kind of intelligence; I want

guiding...' (Bk. II, Ch. 19)

In the underlined phrase, the adjectives "considerate" and "affectionate" present some semantic features which are incompatible with aspects of "a man of business" — thoughtfulness, gentleness, tenderness. The repetition of "business" directs our attention to Mr. Lorry's businesslike manner, while the use of these adjectives, which are contextually antonymous with "businesslike," offer a glimpse into his unobtrusive but significant traits. We observe a conflict of meanings between the two adjectives and his habitual use of the phrase "a man of business." This is one of Dickens's methods for character creation. That is to say, the author repeats a word peculiar to his characters, dramatizing a particular semantic feature that constitutes them, and then gradually reveals new aspects of the characters' personality through a semantic conflict between the repeated word and words co-occurring with it, as the novel progresses. In this way, Dickens often builds up manifold aspects of his characters.

The recurrent use of the word "business," which works as a key word, not only serves to characterize Mr. Lorry as discussed above, but also denotes other characters' "business," or their work, concerns, and roles. For instance, Carton's "business" implies his heroic act of self-sacrifice, Cruncher's is indicative of his work of body-snatching, and Madame Defarge's is suggestive of her cruel revenge on the aristocracy. As a typical example, let us examine Carton's "business":

(43)   Carton's negligent <u>recklessness</u> of manner came powerfully in aid of his <u>quickness</u> and <u>skill</u>, in such *a business* as he had in his secret mind, and with such a man as he had to do with.
(Bk. III, Ch. 8)

In the context of the passage, Carton threatens Barsad and forces him to co-operate in his plan to rescue Darnay from prison. The phrase "a business" contextually alludes to Carton's future action. The underlined words, "recklessness," "quickness," and "skill" represent the qualities and abilities needed for Carton to perform his risky and self-sacrificing act in the near future. My interpretation of Carton's "business" is based on the repetitive use of "business" in his speech, as discussed below:

> (44) 'And indeed, sir,' pursued Mr. Lorry, not minding him, 'I really don't know what you have to do with the matter. If you'll excuse me, as very much your elder, for saying so, I really don't know that it is *your business*.'
> '*Business*! Bless you, *I*[35] have *no business*,' said Mr. Carton.
> 'It is a pity you have not, sir.' (Bk. II, Ch. 4)

The word "business" occurs several times in Carton's speech. When he refers to his own "business," Carton repeats the expression "I have no business" twice.[36] One such instance is shown in the passage above.

Here, Carton makes fun of Mr. Lorry by pointing out his job restraints as a banker after Darnay's trial in the Old Baily. Mr. Lorry refutes Carton's argument and says, "I really don't know that it is your

---

[35] This italic is in the original.
[36] Another instance of "I have no business" is observed in the following passage:

> (After telling Carton that he has decided to marry Lucie, Stryver criticizes Carton for making himself so unattractive to women.)
> 'You have *no business* to be incorrigible,' was his friend's answer, delivered in no very soothing tone.
> 'I have *no business* to be, at all, that I know of,' said Sydney Carton.
> (Bk. II, Ch. 11)

business." In Mr. Lorry's utterance, "business" means "a matter with which one has the right to meddle."[37] On the other hand, in Carton's reply "I have no business," "business" is defined as "work to be done or matters to be attended to in his service or on his behalf" or "a particular matter demanding attention."[38] The word "business" conveys two different meanings between the two speeches in passage (44). Carton states a seemingly unrelated thing in spite of the repetition of the same word, but his reply "I have no business" hints at an existence of his future "business," that is to say, what is implied in a "business" in passage (43) in terms of foreshadowing.

Through the repetitive use of "business," Dickens directs the reader's attention to the word, and suggests the different or contrastive roles between the characters. In other words, Mr. Lorry and Carton independently carry on their own "business" to rescue Darnay. The repeated use of "business" is not directly but intimately related to the themes of fate and resurrection.

In short, Dickens repeats a particular word instead of using different words or phrases of similar meaning, exploiting polysemy of the repeated word, and directs the reader's attention to the word and its connotation. This technique shows one aspect of Dickens's use of repetition.

2.5.2 Repetition of "knit"

In this section, my concern turns to the repetition of "knit" and related

---

[37] *OED2* s.v. Business 16.c.
[38] *OED2* s.v. Business 13.d and 1.a.

words. The knitting of the female revolutionists is a well-known figure of the *tricoteuse* during the French Revolution. The word "knit" frequently happens in the descriptions of Madame Defarge, and seems not only to represent her character, but also to closely relate her to one of the dominant themes of the book — fate. In other words, Madame Defarge and the word "knit" are in mutual expectancy with each other, and in a metaphorical sense she seems to weave "the threads of the characters' fates" by "knitting."

First, let me note the frequency of the word "knit" in each chapter of the novel in Figure 2-16 on the next page. The word occurs 65 times in total throughout *A Tale of Two Cities*. The total frequency of the word "knit" (65) consists of "knitting" (46), "knitted" (17), and "knit" (2). Out of the 65 instances, 62 happen in the French chapters. As a result, the uneven distribution of the word statistically illustrates the close and important connection between the word "knit" and the characters or the incidents in the French scenes.

A close examination of the word "knit" and words that co-occur with it in context reveals the relationship between those words and the subject matter of *A Tale of Two Cities*, as seen in the following passage:

> (45) (The coach of Marquis St. Evrémonde accidentally runs down a helpless child, and Madame Defarge witnesses the accident.)
> (i) The father had long ago taken up his bundle and hidden himself away with it, when the women who had tended the bundle while it lay on the base of the fountain, sat there watching the running of the water and the rolling of the Fancy Ball — when the one woman[Madame Defarge] who had stood conspicuous, *knitting*, still *knitted on* with *the steadfastness of Fate*. (ii) The water of the fountain ran, the

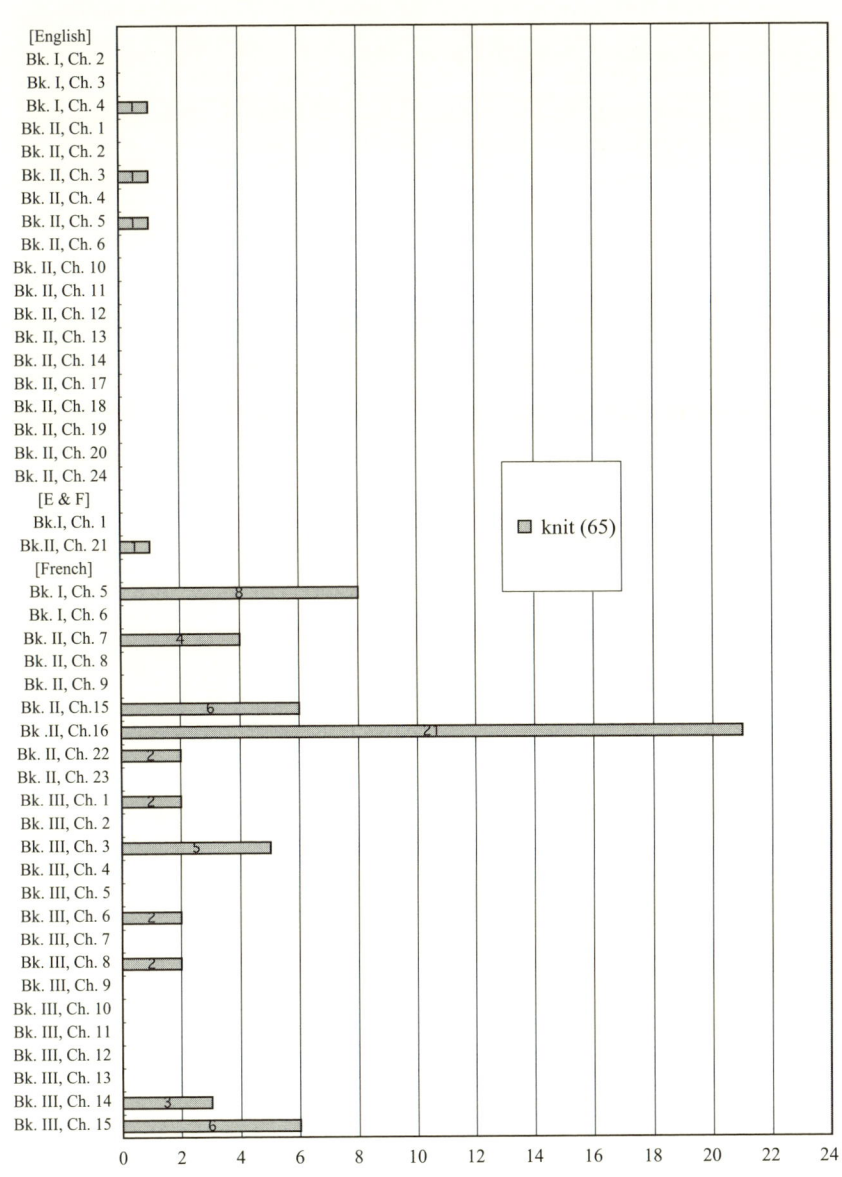

Chapter II Repetition of Words for Character Description 139

Figure 2-16 Frequency of "knit"

swift river ran, the day ran into evening, so much life in the city ran into death according to rule, time and tide waited for no man, the rats were sleeping close together in their dark holes again, the Fancy Ball was lighted up at supper, all things ran their course. (Bk. II, Ch. 7)

In sentence (i) of the passage, the words "knitting" and "knitted" co-occur with the phrase "the steadfastness of Fate" in proximity in the description of Madame Defarge. As Glancy (1991: 95) notes, "Madame Defarge represents fate, but fate in the hands of man rather than God and therefore flawed and unjust." The co-occurrence of Madame Defarge's "knitting" and "the steadfastness of Fate" suggests the fate in her hands.

Moreover, in the clauses of sentence (ii), the workings of nature and human activities are represented. The operations of nature are subject to the laws of nature, and behind the laws exists fate in the hands of God. The clauses of the sentence can be classified according to two kinds of fate, fate in the hands of God and fate in the hands of man:

(A) the clauses indicative of fate in the hands of God:
(a) The water of the fountain ran
(b) the swift river ran
(c) the day ran into evening
(d) so much life in the city ran into death according to rule
(e) time and tide waited for no man[39]

(B) the clauses indicative of fate in the hands of man:
(f) the rats were sleeping close together in their dark holes again

---

[39] Dickens exploits this homely proverb to describe the social situation in which more and more people are dead because of hunger and poverty. cf. Yamamoto (2003), 327.

(g) the Fancy Ball was lighted up at supper

(C) the clause indicative of interwoven fates:
(h) all things ran their course

Clauses (a), (b), (c), (e) in group (A) contain the things of nature as their grammatical subjects, and describe the natural phenomena on which humankind cannot act. In three clauses, excluding (e), the intransitive verb "ran" is repetitively used. Clause (d) suggests human beings' mortality along with the verb "ran." These clauses all indicate fate in the hands of God. On the other hand, in clauses (f) and (g) in group (B), where the verb "ran" is not used, the lives of the people of the two classes, the aristocrats and the common, are compared through the contrastive use of the words "dark" and "lighted." The two clauses describe the causes of the Revolution indicative of fate in the hands of man. The two kinds of fate between groups (A) and (B) are contrasted mainly by the presence or absence of "ran," and of the things of nature as grammatical subjects. Furthermore, clause (h) in group (C) denotes that the two kinds of fate are interwoven by a similar procedure of "knitting" depicted at the end of sentence (i). Would it not be better to say that "knitting" foreshadows both the inevitable outbreak of the French Revolution as a manifestation of fate in the hands of God and the bloody revenge of the revolutionists as a suggestion of fate in the hands of man?

The foreshadowing of the outbreak of the Revolution and its bloodshed can often be observed in the descriptions of "knitting" by Madame Defarge and the revolutionary women, especially in Chapter 16 of Book II, where the word "knit" occurs most frequently, as Figure

2-16 shows. The chapter is the last one that describes France before the French Revolution. The recursive employment of "knitting" in the chapter appears as a prologue to the French chapters. As a typical example, see the use of "knitting" with the repetitive use of "dark" in the passage at the very end of Chapter 16 of Book II:

> (46)   (i) <u>Darkness</u> closed around, and then came the ringing of church bells and the distant beating of the military drums in the Palace Court-Yard, as the women sat *knitting, knitting*. (ii) <u>Darkness</u> encompassed them. (iii) <u>Another darkness</u> was closing in as surely, when the church bells, then ringing pleasantly in many an airy steeple over France, should be melted into thundering cannon; when the military drums should be beating to drown <u>a wretched voice</u>, that night all-potent as the voice of Power and Plenty, Freedom and Life. (iv) <u>So much</u> was closing in about the women who sat *knitting, knitting,* that they their very selves were closing in around <u>a structure yet unbuilt</u>, where they were to sit *knitting, knitting*, <u>counting dropping heads</u>. (Bk. II, Ch. 16)

In the passage, a pair of present participles "knitting, knitting" are repeated three times, as many as six times in total. The very repetitive use of the word serves to create an atmosphere where the French Revolution is near at hand.

In addition, scrutinizing words co-occurring with "knitting" in the passage, I notice the use of words characteristic of the Revolution and its atrocity: the repeated use of "darkness" in sentences (i), (ii), and (iii) is associated with the Revolution and Madame Defarge; the phrase "a structure yet unbuilt" and "counting dropping heads" in (iv) remind us of the guillotine and beheading; and "a wretched voice" in sentence (iii) suggests the voice of a guillotine victim. In a word, the recurring word "knitting" and the related words indicate the evil omen of the Revolution.

After the Revolution breaks out, Madame Defarge's "knitting" is depicted as "her knitted registers" and "that fatal register" as seen in the passage below:

(47) He[Barsad] always remembered with fear and trembling, that that terrible woman[Madame Defarge] had *knitted* when he talked with her, and had looked ominously at him as her fingers moved. He had since seen her, in the Section of Saint Antoine, over and over again produce *her knitted registers*, and denounce people whose lives the guillotine then surely swallowed up. He knew, as every one employed as he was did, that he was never safe; that flight was impossible; that he was tied fast under the shadow of the axe; and that in spite of his utmost tergiversation and treachery in furtherance of the reigning terror, a word might bring it down upon him. Once denounced, and on such grave grounds as had just now been suggested to his mind, he foresaw that the dreadful woman of whose unrelenting character he had seen many proofs, would produce against him *that fatal register*, and would quash his last chance of life. (Bk. III, Ch. 8)

The victims of "the axe" listed in "that fatal register" are described as "people whose lives the guillotine then surely swallowed up." The close relationship between the word "knit" and fate in the hands of Madame Defarge is more explicitly represented.[40]

---

[40] The phrase "the knitted register of Madame Defarge" is found in Defarge's speech before the Revolution happens, and the phrase "the fatal register" only in the description after its outbreak:

'Jacques,' returned Defarge, drawing himself up, 'if madame my wife undertook to keep the register in her memory alone, she would not lose a word of it — not a syllable of it. *Knitted*, in her own stitches and her

It should also be added that unlike passage (46), the frequent use of the present participle "knitting" is not observed in the passage above, but the word "knitted" is repeated twice. The words "knitting" and "knitted" in passages (46) and (47) are different or contrastive in the grammatical forms. Dickens makes such a deliberate use of the derivatives of the word "knit" to produce different atmospheres before the outbreak of, and during the Revolution. The novelist repeats the word "knit" and its related words, under various modifications and transformations, allowing them to accumulate thematic significance as the story unfolds.

---

own symbols, it will always be as plain to her as the sun... It would be easier for the weakest poltroon that lives, to erase himself from existence, than to erase one letter of his name or crimes from *the knitted register of Madame Defarge.*' (Bk. II, Ch. 15)

Little need to show that this detested family name had long been anathematised by Saint Antoine, and was wrought into *the fatal register*.
(Bk. III, Ch. 10)

Chapter III
Distinctive Use of Repetition

3.0 Introduction

As Monod (1968: 462) notes, "Dickens makes a broader use of the symbols and allegories that had long been dear to him." In reality, *A Tale of Two Cities* is full of repeated imagery and symbolic patterns. We hear again and again the footsteps and the rising storm; we see the drinking of wine and the staining blood. This novel achieves linguistic and stylistic contiguity through the repeated use of symbolic words like "footstep," "echo," "wine," and "blood," which are closely related to the subject matter of the novel.[1] To put it another way, repetition of symbolic words fulfills an important function of promoting the thematic cohesion, by which the themes of this novel are brought to light.

In the process of carefully and closely scrutinizing this function, I

---

[1] Stoehr (1965: 25) quotes J. H. Miller's words to explain Dickens's use of images:

> Images in a novel get their significance not simply in their immediate relation to the narrative line, but in relation to all the images in their contexts before and after. In Dickens this spatial quality results in part from the intricate plots in which everything that happens and all the characters turn out in the end to be somehow related. The revelations at the end cause the whole pattern of the novel to fall into place almost with an audible click.

cannot but notice that the linguistic device of repetition is closely related to contrast as shown in the famous opening sentences of *A Tale of Two Cities*. The sentences, presenting a series of neat antitheses, clearly illustrate Dickens's elaborate use of the two techniques of repetition and contrast. See the passage below:

(48)   (i) It was the best of times, (ii) it was the worst of times, (iii) it was the age of wisdom, (iv) it was the age of foolishness, (v) it was the epoch of belief, (vi) it was the epoch of incredulity, (vii) it was the season of Light, (viii) it was the season of Darkness, (ix) it was the spring of hope, (x) it was the winter of despair, (xi) we had everything before us, (xii) we had nothing before us, (xiii) we were all going direct to Heaven, (xiv) we were all going direct the other way...
(xv) There were a king with a large jaw and a queen with a plain face, on the throne of England; (xvi) there were a king with a large jaw and a queen with a fair face, on the throne of France. (Bk. I, Ch. 1)

The following table shows the antitheses of the passage above:

Table 3-1 Structure of the opening sentences

(i) the best	times	(ii) the worst
(iii) wisdom	the age	(iv) foolishness
(v) belief	the epoch	(vi) incredulity
(vii) Light	the season	(viii) Darkness
(ix) hope	spring / winter	(x) despair
(xi) everything		(xii) nothing
(xiii) to Heaven		(xiv) the other way
(xv) England		(xvi) France

The words and phrases, which are antonymous to each other, are framed in antithesis "to indicate the contrasting ways in which it is possible to regard the state of England and France in 1775" (Brook 1970: 36). At the same time, from clause (i) to (x), such synonymous words as "times," "age," "epoch," "season," and "spring / winter" are reiterated as a connector to associate the contrastive elements. The synonymous words are properly used according to the contrasted elements, and indicate a general to a more specific period of time. Such a seemingly simple yet deliberate choice of words within the framework of repetition manifests an important aspect of Dickens's use of repetition. As a result, through verbal and cohesive associations, the passage embodies Dickens's purpose to convince us to see London / England in comparison and relation to Paris / France, as the title of the novel implies, one scene to another, one character to another, one word to another, with their structural and thematic unity.

Here, with the above mentioned in mind, my concern is first directed to the use of such repeated symbolic words as "wine," "red," "blood," "footstep," "echo," "foot," and "tread," in context.[2] These words appear throughout *A Tale of Two Cities*, often co-occurring with one another, and convey additional and different meanings as well as their own specific ones, in accordance with the scenes or contexts,[2] especially between the English and the French scenes.

Secondly, I scrutinize cases in which different words are repeated in one context and then in another even though the two contexts are closely connected in terms of the plot. For example, the two trials of Darnay in London and Paris are compared and described by using different repeated words. Through this contrastive use of repetition we are induced to compare the legal procedures and justices in the two courts.

---

[2] As discussed in Section 2.4, the word "wine" is regarded as one of key words in *A Tale of Two Cities* (see Table 2-15).

Thirdly, I discuss the distinctive use of repetition between the English and the French scenes. A close examination of the distribution of the repeated words reveals that such key words as "plane-tree" and "fountain" only or mostly appear in either the English or the French scenes. These kinds of repetition work together to convey the main themes of the novel to the minds of the reader.

3.1 Repetition of "wine," "red," and "blood"

In this section, I focus my attention on the repetition of symbolic words of visual effects like "wine," "red," "blood." These words often co-occur with one another, and convey additional and different meanings as well as their own specific meanings, in accordance with the scenes or contexts, especially between the English and the French scenes. First, I make a comparison of the frequencies of the three words between *A Tale of Two Cities* and the Dickens Corpus, and demonstrate their log likelihood values, or keyness.[3]

Table 3-2 Frequencies of "wine," "red," and "blood"

A Tale of Two Cities (Approx. 137,000 words)			*Dickens Corpus* (Approx. 4,380,000 words)			
Word	Freq.	%	Word	Freq.	%	Keyness*
wine	120	0.09	wine	671	0.015	206.8
red	56	0.04	red	1,032	0.02	13.7
blood	35	0.03	blood	436	0.01	22.3

*Log likelihood ratio

---

[3] In *A Tale of Two Cities*, the word "wine" (120) includes "wines" (2), and "red" (56) includes "redder" (16) and "reddest" (2).

Table 3-2 shows that the three words occur more frequently in *A Tale of Two Cities* than Dickens's other novels. The key word "wine," especially, is outstanding for its frequency in *A Tale of Two Cities* in contrast to the Dickens Corpus, showing the very high log likelihood value of 206.8. The statistic data show that these words indicate some lexical properties of the novel.

Next, I examine the distribution of these three words in *A Tale of Two Cities*. See Figure 3-3 on the next page.

Figure 3-3 represents the frequencies of the three words throughout *A Tale of Two Cities*. The word "wine" occurs 120 times, "red" 56 times, and "blood" 35 times in total. As previously done, the chapters of the novel are divided into three groups: English chapters, French chapters, and English-French chapters, depending on the location of the incidents in each chapter.

Scrutiny of Figure 3-3 reveals, among other things, the following two things:

(i) Although the three words occur throughout the novel, they occur more frequently in the French chapters rather than the English ones. Furthermore, these words often co-occur with one another in the French scenes. They also co-occur in the English scenes, but not as often.

(ii) The word "wine" is remarkably obvious in the first French chapter, in Chapter 5 of Book I [37 of 120 (30.8%)]. This emphasizes a strong connection between what may be meant by the word and France, and prefigures the coming bloody Revolution at the very beginning of the French scenes. In the

150   Repetition in Dickens's *A Tale of Two Cities*

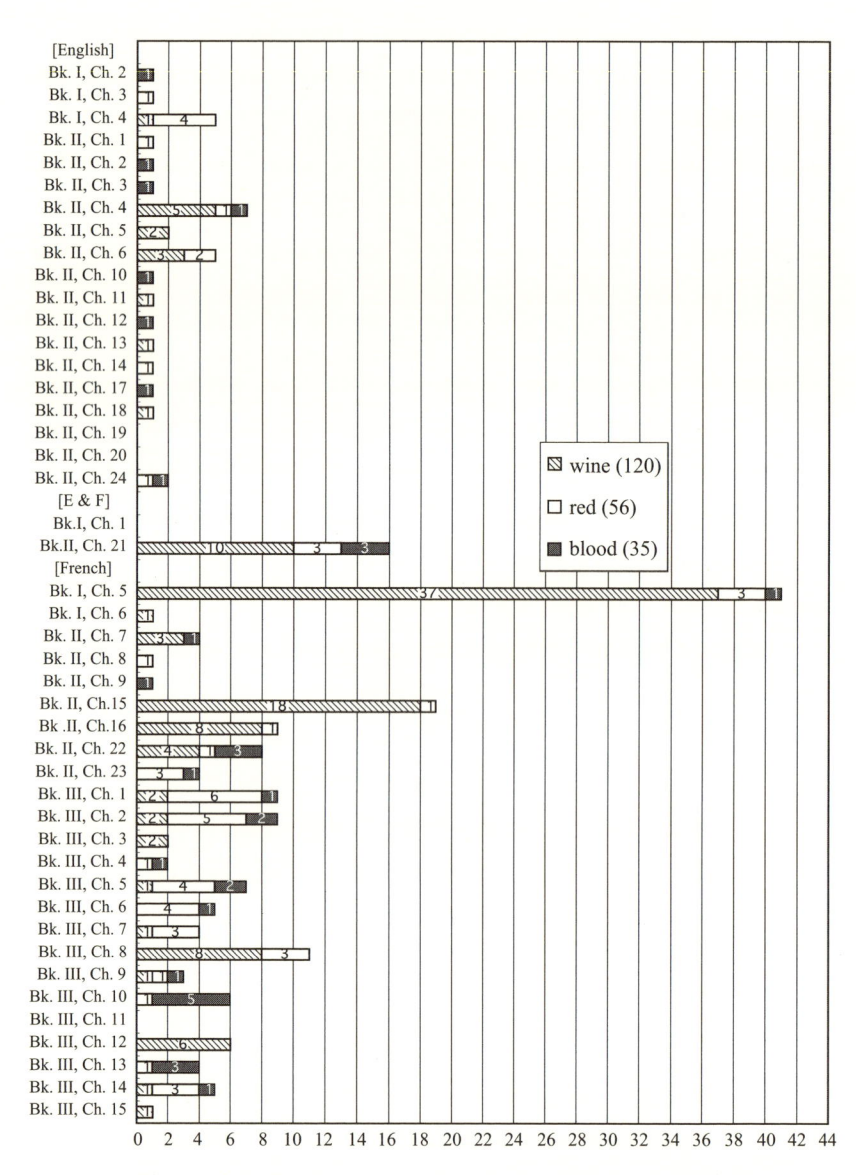

Figure 3-3 Frequencies of "wine," "red," and "blood"

English chapters, on the other hand, the word "wine" occurs only 14 times, and most instances [10 of 14, (71%)] occur in a limited context: Chapters 4, 5, and 6 of Book II.

It is often pointed out that the word "wine" and its related words "red" and "blood" frequently co-occur as an indication of the French Revolution's slaughter and bloodshed. In fact, Figure 3-3 supports this idea in quantitative terms but does not reveal how the words create the symbolical imagery of the bleeding Revolution. Needless to say, the Revolution's slaughter and bloodshed are not simply hinted at and represented through the repetition and co-occurrence of these three words, but the related words co-occurring with them in the same contexts contribute to creating the bleeding imagery. So, I will investigate how the three words and their related words work together. Moreover, it seems that Dickens attaches different meanings to the word "wine" and its related words in each context. Hence, I will next examine how the words carry variegated meanings for the French and the English scenes.

3.1.1 Use of "wine" in the French scenes

The following passage describes the breaking of a wine cask in the street, inspiring the people of the neighborhood to scoop and sop up the wine to drink it in the first French scene, Chapter 5 of Book I. The passage, long as it is, must be quoted nearly in full to preserve its peculiar effect:

(49)   (i) *A large cask of wine* had been dropped and broken, in the street. (ii) The accident had happened in getting it out of a cart; the cask had tumbled out with a run, the hoops had burst, and it lay on the stones just outside the door of *the wine-shop*, shattered like a walnut-shell.

(iii) All the people within reach had suspended their business, or their idleness, to run to the spot and drink *the wine*... (iv) Some men kneeled down, made scoops of their two hands joined, and sipped, or tried to help women, who bent over their shoulders, to sip, before *the wine* had all run out between their fingers. (v) Others, men and women, dipped in the puddles with little mugs of mutilated earthenware, or even with handkerchiefs from women's heads, which were squeezed dry into infants' mouths; others made small mud embankments, to stem *the wine* as it ran; others, directed by lookers-on up at high windows, darted here and there, to cut off *little streams of wine* that started away in new directions; others devoted themselves to the sodden and lee-dyed pieces of the cask, licking, and even champing *the moister wine-rotted fragments* with eager relish...

(vi) *The wine* was *red wine*, and had stained the ground of the narrow street in the suburb of Saint Antoine, in Paris, where it was spilled. (vii) It had stained many hands, too, and many faces, and many naked feet, and many wooden shoes. (viii) The hands of the man who sawed the wood, left red marks on the billets; and the forehead of the woman who nursed her baby, was stained with the stain of the old rag she wound about her head again. (ix) Those who had been greedy with the staves of the cask, had acquired a tigerish smear about the mouth; and one tall joker so besmirched, his head more out of a long squalid bag of a night-cap than in it, scrawled upon a wall with his finger dipped in muddy *wine-lees* — BLOOD.

(x) The time was to come, when *that wine* too would be

spilled on the street-stones, and when the stain of it would be red upon many there. (Bk. I, Ch. 5)

The repetition of the word "wine" and words related to the spilled wine in each sentence of the passage above are shown as follows.

Table 3-4 Words including "wine" and words related to the spilled wine

	Words indicating "wine"	Words related to the spilled wine
(i)	A large cask of wine	
(ii)	the wine-shop	
(iii)	the wine	
(iv)	the wine	
(v)	the wine little streams of wine the moister wine-rotted fragments	mutilated cut off sodden lee-dyed
(vi)	The wine red wine	stained spilled
(vii)		stained
(viii)		red marks stained the stain
(ix)	wine-lees	a tigerish smear besmirched BLOOD
(x)	that wine	spilled the stain red

The words representative of "wine" and its sediment recurrently occur in the passage (in sentences (v), (vi), and (vii) the pronoun "it" is used), which builds up close connections of each sentence. Observing the words related to the spilled wine, I notice the novelist's deliberate order of them: in sentence (v), the words denoting the beheading on the guillotine, "mutilated" and "cut off," first appear, and then in the following sentences, such words as "stained" and "spilled" denotative of the spilling of blood by the killer machine are repeatedly used, thereby showing a cause and effect relationship. Moreover, in sentence (vi), we are first told that the spilled wine is "red," and then the word "red" is repeated in sentence (viii). In sentence (ix), the juxtaposition of "wine-lees" and "Blood," which gains special emphasis by coming at the end of the sentence, shows a close relation between "wine" and "blood." Finally, in sentence (x), the words "wine," "spilled," "stain," "red" occur together, and the combinations "wine—red" and "wine—blood" allude to the slaughter and bloodshed of the Revolution with the help of the clause "The time was to come." Dickens not only repeats the same word, but also deliberately arranges its related or associated words around it, for emphasis of its symbolic meaning.

The word "wine" and its related words "red" and "blood" frequently occur in the various revolutionary scenes that depict the violence and horror of the Revolution, making new combinations with the words indicative of the Revolution's inhumanity. In particular, as the novel progresses, the word "wine" figuratively comes to represent the dehumanized condemned people executed on the guillotine.[4] The foreshadowing in the "wine-cask breaking" scene is realized and embodied in various scenes through the word combinations.[5] The

---

[4] One instance of the dehumanization can be observed in the following passage:

Lovely girls; bright women, brown-haired, black-haired, and grey; youths; stalwart men and old; gentle born and peasant born; *all red wine for La Guillotine*, all daily brought into light from the dark cellars of the loathsome prisons, and carried to her through the streets to slake her devouring thirst. (Bk. III, Ch. 5).

[5] The nominal form "mutilation" of the adjectival form "mutilated" in sentence

Chapter III Distinctive Use of Repetition 155

following passage is one such example. The bloodthirsty mob is sharpening their knives and weapons on the grindstone after slaying the prisoners at La Force:

> (50) (i) The grindstone had a double handle, and, turning at it madly were two men, whose faces, as their long hair flapped back when the whirlings of the grindstone brought their faces up, were more horrible and cruel than the visages of the wildest savages in their most barbarous disguise. (ii) False eyebrows and false moustaches were stuck upon them, and their hideous countenances were all *bloody* and sweaty, and all awry with howling, and all staring and glaring with beastly excitement and want of sleep. (iii) As these ruffians turned and turned, their matted locks now flung forward over their eyes, now flung backward over their necks, some women held *wine* to their mouths that they might drink; and what with *dropping blood*, and what with *dropping wine*, and what with *the stream of sparks* struck out of the stone, all their wicked atmosphere seemed *gore* and *fire*. (iv) The eye could not detect one creature in the group free from *the smear of blood*. (v) Shouldering one another to get next at the sharpening-stone, were men stripped to the waist, with *the stain* all over their limbs and bodies; men in all sorts of rags, with *the stain* upon those rags; men devilishly set off with spoils of women's lace and silk and ribbon, with *the stain dyeing* those trifles through and through. (vi) Hatchets, knives, bayonets, swords, all brought to be sharpened, were all *red* with it. (vii) Some of the hacked swords were tied to

---

(v) appears in passage (11) already quoted in 1.3. The nominal depicts Madame Defarge's hewing off the governor's head. Both words occur only once in the novel, but seem to make a close connection between the scenes in which they appear:

> ... she[Madam Defarge] had trodden on the body to steady it for *mutilation*.
> (Bk. II, Ch. 21)

the wrists of those who carried them, with strips of linen and fragments of dress: ligatures various in kind, but all deep of *the one colour*. (viii) And as the frantic wielders of these weapons snatched them from *the stream of sparks* and tore away into the streets, *the same red hue* was *red* in their frenzied eyes; — eyes which any unbrutalised beholder would have given twenty years of life, to petrify with a well-directed gun. (Bk. III, Ch. 2)

In the successive sentences of the passage, a great associative field of meaning is established by recurrence of the words significant of "wine," "red," and "blood" and the words expressive of the mob's cruelty and violence. They are shown in the following table.

Table 3-5 Words denoting "wine," "red," "blood," and the mob's cruelty

	Words denoting "wine," "red," and "blood"	Words indicating the mob's cruelty and violence
(i)		madly / horrible / cruel / the wildest savages / their most barbarous disguise
(ii)	bloody	False eyebrows / false moustaches their hideous countenances / sweaty / awry / beastly excitement
(iii)	wine / dropping blood / dropping wine / the stream of sparks / gore / fire	these ruffians / their wicked atmosphere
(iv)	the smear of blood	
(v)	the stain / the stain / the stain / dyeing	devilishly
(vi)	red	
(vii)	the one colour	
(viii)	the stream of sparks / the same red hue / red	the frantic wielders their frenzied eyes

A close scrutiny of the table shows that in sentences (i) and (ii) the words denotative of the revolutionist's cruelty and violence are first used recurrently; in the following sentences the terrible results of their actions are visually and concretely represented by the repetition of words denoting the "wine—blood" and the "red—blood" association. At the same time, in the first two sentences, the word "faces" and its synonyms "visages" and "countenances" occur, and in the subsequent sentences, such words indicative of the mob's bodily parts as "eyes," "necks," and "mouths." The repeated use of these words serves to enhance the visual impressions when we read the passage.

Needless to say, the grindstone itself contributes to the horrible description of the scene. According to Glancy (1991: 41), "part of the horror of the grindstone image is its metaphorical force: a relentless, implacable machine, it recalls the beanstalk giant who was going to grind Jack's bones to make his bread. It is always associated with Hell, the greater setting of the whole scene in both Carlyle and Dickens." The combination of the grindstone and the words designating the carnage serves to describe the inhumanity of the Revolution visually and graphically.[6]

The use of words that are related to "wine," "red," and "blood" has another function of establishing the interconnections between the two

---

[6] The word "grindstone" is also used to describe Jerry Cruncher comically, showing a sort of contrastive use:

> Growling, in addition, such phrases as "Ah! yes! You're religious, too. You wouldn't put yourself in opposition to the interests of your husband and child, would you? Not you!" and throwing off *other sarcastic sparks from the whirling grindstone of his indignation*, Mr. Cruncher betook himself to his boot-cleaning and his general preparation for business.
>
> (Bk. II, Ch. 1)

scenes by the high frequencies of use. For example, the noun "stain" occurs seven times in total throughout the novel.[7] Three of these seven instances can be seen in the "wine-cask breaking" scene, and another three instances in the "grindstone" scene.[8] In a statistical view, Dickens repeats the word "stain" in the two scenes for the purpose of indicating the foreshadowing of and the realization of the enormity of the Revolution against which the novelist imparts his satirical eyes.

It should also be added that the very high frequency of the word "wine-shop" (53 of 120 instances of "wine", 44%) attracts attention. We usually buy wine at a wine-shop, where we sometimes also enjoy drinking it. In the novel, however, Dickens conjures up a different association of "wine-shop." That is to say, the "wine-shop" of Defarge and Madame Defarge is located in Saint Antoine, where the revolutionary agitation arises and is carried into action. The wine drinking of the revolutionists at the wine-shop creates a sense of solidarity among them. Dickens evokes a strong association of "wine" with the Revolution through the repetitive use of "wine-shop."

3.1.2 Use of "wine" in the English scenes

Now my attention turns to the use of the word "wine" in the English

---

[7] The word "stained" occurs seven times: four of seven instances in the passage of the "wine-cask breaking" scene in Chapter 5 of Book II; two in Chapter 21 of Book II; and one in Chapter 10 of Book III.

[8] The last instance of "stain" is observed in the passage below:

> Château and hut, stone face and dangling figure, *the red stain* on the stone floor, and the pure water in the village well — thousands of acres of land — a whole province of France — all France itself — lay under the night sky, concentrated into a faint hair-breadth line. (Bk. II, Ch. 16)

scenes. In the revolutionary scenes in France, the word repeatedly co-occurs with words suggestive of the bleeding Revolution, while in the English scenes it co-occurs with words of different connotation. In fact, the word seems to be closely related to the development of the plot and the character's fate. That is to say, "wine" recurrently occurs in the scene where the characters of the novel first meet each other, and they are destined to share their fate. Let me examine some typical instances.

As the first example, see the passage below in which Mr. Lorry meets Lucie for the first time at a hotel in Dover:

(51) (i) When it was dark, and he sat before the coffee-room fire, awaiting his dinner as he had awaited his breakfast, his mind was busily <u>digging, digging, digging</u>, in the live *red* coals.
(ii) A bottle of good *claret* after dinner does a <u>digger</u> in the *red* coals no harm, otherwise than as it has a tendency to throw him out of work. (iii) Mr. Lorry had been idle a long time, and had just poured out his last glassful of *wine* with as complete an appearance of satisfaction as is ever to be found in an elderly gentleman of a fresh complexion who has got to the end of a bottle, when a rattling of wheels came up the narrow street, and rumbled into the inn-yard. (Bk. I, Ch. 4)

The word "wine," along with its synonym "claret," first appears in the passage above in this novel. I find no words significant of blood or death like those we have seen in the revolutionary scenes, even though the word "red" in the phrase "in the (live) red coals" is found in sentences (i) and (ii). The "wine—red" combination does not indicate the outbreak of the Revolution here in this scene, but it may be exploited to suggest the fateful encounter between Mr. Lorry and Lucie. That is to say, the repetitive use of "digging" in sentence (i), which is repeated as many as eight times in the previous chapter, attracts our attention, and becomes reminiscent of Mr. Lorry's mission: "to dig some one out of a grave" (Bk. I, Ch. 3), namely 'to bring Dr. Manette to the safety of England.' The second sentence, which describes a good effect of the drinking of wine on "a digger in the red coals (i.e. Mr. Lorry)," reminds us of the proverbial statement on wine: "some people only speak the truth after having drunk wine."[9] Third, sentence (iii) describes Mr. Lorry's drinking "his last glassful of wine." This process and the use of "wine" in this scene may indicate the disclosure of the truth about Dr. Manette. In reality, in his interview with Lucie, which follows the passage above, Mr. Lorry explains to her that they are going to rescue her father, Dr. Manette, whom she believes to be dead, in Paris.

Furthermore, let me observe the passage in which Sydney Carton and Charles Darnay first meet and dine together in a tavern after the trial in the Old Baily:

> (52) Drawing his arm through his own, he took him down Ludgate-hill to Fleet-street, and so, up a covered way, into a tavern. Here, they were shown into a little room, where Charles Darnay was soon recruiting his strength with a good plain dinner and good *wine*: while Carton sat opposite to him at the same table, with his separate bottle of *port* before him, and his fully half-insolent manner upon him. (Bk. II, Ch. 4)

Here, in the fateful encounter between Carton and Darnay, Dickens properly exploits the "wine" and its synonym "port" to individualize the two characters. That is to say, the word "wine" is assigned to Darnay, "port" to Carton. The novelist does not repeat the same word "wine," in

---

[9] de Vries (1976), s.v. Wine 5.

spite of the fact that Carton himself uses "wine" when he orders another glass in the later scene: "bring me another pint of *this same wine.*" Through the reiterated use of "wine" (4 times) in the scene of the encounter between Carton and Darnay and the deliberate use of "wine" and "port" between them, Dickens represents not only their fateful meeting but also their characteristic differences despite physical resemblances. It might be said that Dickens creates a kind of symbolic meaning of "wine" in addition to its conventional symbolic meaning.

It seems that the use of the word "wine" in the English chapters is almost always associated with the inevitable development of the plot, among others, the fateful encounter between the characters.

3.2 Repetition of "footstep," "foot," "tread," and "echo"

It is said that the symbolic word "footstep," its synonyms "foot" and "tread," and its related word "echo" are closely related to, and suggestive of, the outbreak of the French Revolution, by which the characters' fates are greatly affected. Here, I will examine how Dickens creates such symbolic imagery of the four words by means of repetition.

In the same way as before, I will show the frequencies of the four words in serial order of chapters in Figure 3-6 on the next page, and then I will closely examine the repetitive use of the four words.[10]

---

[10] The total number of "footstep" (21) in Figure 3-6 contains "footstep" (2) and its plural form "footsteps" (19); that of "echo" (30), "echo" (2), and "echoes" (28); and that of "foot" (68), "foot" (24), and "feet" (44). I exclude one instance of "echo," which works as a verb.

162   Repetition in Dickens's *A Tale of Two Cities*

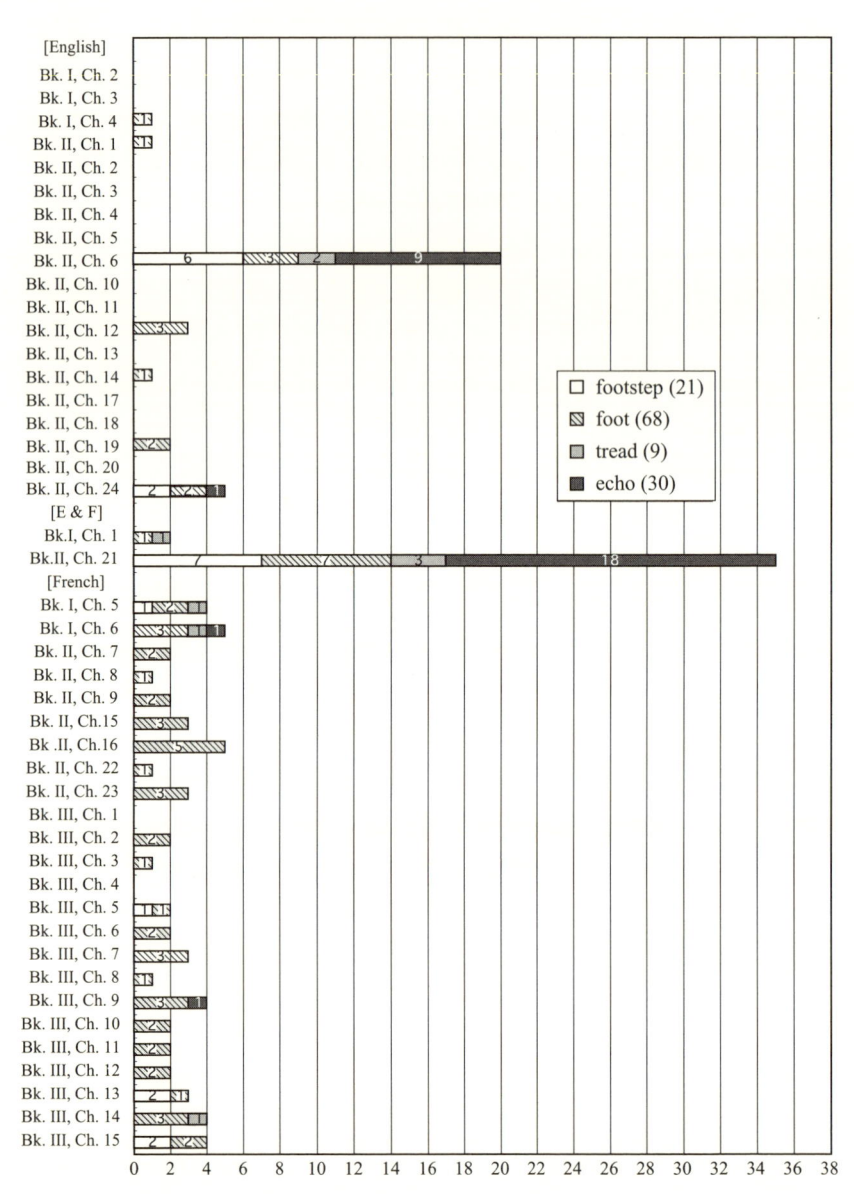

Figure 3-6 Frequencies of "footstep," "foot," "tread," and "echo"

Legend:
- ☐ footstep (21)
- ▨ foot (68)
- ▤ tread (9)
- ■ echo (30)

Figure 3-6 shows that the word "footstep" often co-occurs with its synonyms and related words; sometimes in isolation, and more often in association. The word may create its symbolic meaning of rapidly approaching footsteps of the Revolution with the help of those words. In other words, it often goes hand in hand with them, and then the symbolic meaning becomes particularly emphatic. The figure also tells us that these four words occur together most frequently in Chapter 6 of Book II among the English chapters, and in Chapter 21 of Book II, where the French Revolution breaks out. In quantitative terms, the two chapters are closely connected to each other. It seems that the repeated use of these words not only expresses tight cohesiveness within each of the two chapters but also establishes a strong connection between them. Now, I will proceed to observe the use of "footstep" and its related words in the two chapters respectively.

First, I observe the recurrent use of the four words in Chapter 6 of Book II among the English chapters. Mr. Lorry, Charles Darnay, and Sydney Carton visit Lucie's house in Soho, and they hear footsteps of people in the street, hurrying for shelter so as not to get wet in a rainstorm:

> (53)　(i) There was a great hurry in the streets, of people speeding away to get shelter before the storm broke; *the wonderful corner for echoes* resounded with *the echoes of footsteps* coming and going, *yet not a footstep was there...*
>
> 　(ii) 'It will seem nothing to you. Such whims are only impressive as we originate them, I think; they are not to be communicated. I have sometimes sat alone here of an evening, listening, until I have made *the echoes* out to be *the echoes of all the footsteps that are coming by-and-by into our lives.*' ...

> (iii) *The footsteps* were incessant, and the hurry of them became more and more rapid. The corner *echoed* and *re-echoed* with *the tread of feet*; <u>some</u>, as it seemed, under the windows; <u>some</u>, as it seemed, in the room; <u>some</u> coming, <u>some</u> going, <u>some</u> breaking off, <u>some</u> stopping altogether; all in the distant streets, and <u>not one within sight</u>. (Bk. II, Ch. 6)

This passage is expressive of the scene where the word "footstep" first appears again and again in the English chapters, and therefore attracts attention. In paragraph (i), the place where Dr. Manette and Lucie live is depicted as "the wonderful corner for echoes," and the repeated use of the word "footstep" can be found in the phrases "the echoes of footsteps" and "a footstep."

Paragraph (ii) expresses Lucie's imagination of "the echoes" of the people's footsteps as "the echoes of all the footsteps that are coming by-and-by into our lives." The connection of the "footsteps" of the people in the street with the "footsteps" in Lucie's mind is just hinted at.

Furthermore, paragraph (iii) more concretely represents the tumult of the people in the street through the recurrent use of the word "footsteps," the related words "tread" and "feet," the verbs "echoed" and "re-echoed," and the words "some" and "all" with ellipsis of "footsteps." The repetition of these words is kept in the foreground because they repeatedly occur in close proximity. Through the repetition, the echoes of the people's footsteps are engraved in our mind.

On the other hand, the state of Lucie's house is described in the clause "yet not a footstep was there" in paragraph (i) and the phrase "not one within sight" in paragraph (iii). These contrast the calm and stillness of her house with the noise and disturbance of the people in the street.[11]

---

[11] The quietness of Lucie's house is also reinforced by the recurrent use of the word "quiet" in the passage, which occurs in the same context:

Chapter III Distinctive Use of Repetition 165

The repetitive and contrastive use of "footsteps" and the related words in this scene carries an implication that the echoes of the footsteps would be entering their lives in the near future. However, we cannot immediately grasp what meaning lies behind the repetition and the contrast, and therefore we are kept in suspense.

Next, I investigate the use of the word "footstep" and its related words in Chapter 21 of Book II, which contains the words "footstep," "echo," "tread" and "feet" most frequently. Figure 3-6 shows that the word "footstep" never occurs from Chapter 7 to Chapter 20 of Book II. The recursive use of the word after an interval of 14 chapters may connect Chapter 6 of Book II with Chapter 21 of Book II, or the English scene with the French one. I observe the use of these words in the latter chapter in the following passages:

(54) A wonderful corner for *echoes*, it has been remarked, that corner where the Doctor lived. Ever busily winding the golden thread which bound her husband, and her father, and herself, and her old directress and companion, in a life of quiet bliss, Lucie sat in the still house in the tranquilly resounding corner, listening to *the echoing footsteps* of years.
(Bk. II, Ch. 21)

(55) *Headlong, mad*, and *dangerous footsteps* to force their way into anybody's life, *footsteps* not easily made clean again if once stained red, *the footsteps* raging in Saint Antoine afar off, as the little circle sat in the dark London window. (Bk. II, Ch. 21)

The *quiet* lodgings of Doctor Manette were in a *quiet* street-corner not far from Soho-square. On the afternoon of a certain fine Sunday when the waves of four months had rolled over the trial for treason, ... After several relapses into business-absorption, Mr. Lorry had become the Doctor's friend, and the *quiet* street-corner was the sunny part of his life.
(Bk. II, Ch. 6)

Chapter 21 of Book II, which begins in England but ends in France, represents Lucie's house in Soho and then the outbreak of the French Revolution. In passage (54), the repetition of "echoes" and "the echoing footsteps" co-occur with the words "quiet," "still," and "tranquilly," which indicate the calm and peaceful situation in her house.

On the contrary, passage (55) depicts the footsteps of the revolutionists with the repetition of "footsteps" modified by the adjectives "headlong," "mad," and "dangerous" and with the omission of the predicate verbs.[12] These adjectives are not found in the descriptions of the footsteps in the English chapters. The repetition of "footstep" cultivates a close connection between the scenes, or Chapter 6 of Book II with Chapter 21 of Book II, and at the same time shows the change of "footstep" in quality or its modifications and transformations. To put it another way, the footsteps often heard by Lucie in Soho are realized in those in Saint Antoine with alteration, more accurately, with "headlong," "mad," and "dangerous" qualities. The repetition provides a semantic network in which Dickens charges "footstep" with the symbolic meaning of the foreshadowing and outbreak of the Revolution.

Furthermore, the word "footstep" never occurs from Chapter 22 of Book II to Chapter 4 of Book III, as Figure 3-6 indicates. The repetitive use of the word after an interval of seven chapters is seen in the next passage:

> (56) (Lucie stands beneath the prison wall in the hope that Darnay may be able to see her there.)
>   *A footstep* in the snow. Madame Defarge. 'I salute you, citizeness,' from the Doctor. 'I salute you, citizen.' This in

---

[12] Yamamoto (2003: 362) points out Carlyle's influence over this passage.

passing. Nothing more. Madame Defarge gone, like a shadow over the white road. (Bk. III, Ch. 5)

"A footstep" of Madame Defarge after such a long interval is brought to the foreground. The close association between the word "footstep" and Madame Defarge is evoked. After the passage, we are to see Madame Defarge's wicked and diabolical design to carry out her revenge on Charles Darnay, Dr. Manette, and Lucie. The use of the word in this scene symbolically suggests the ominous figure of Madame Defarge.[13]

The gradually accumulated associated meanings of "footstep" and the related words, with some modifications and transformations in their recurrent occurrences, build up a strong connection between the chapters as well as within them, producing a kind of rhythm according to the frequencies of the words in this novel as shown in Figure 3-6.

3.3 Repetition of words indicative of "light" and "dark"

The contrast of "light" and "dark" is one of the leitmotifs that run throughout the whole work. In this section, I examine how repeated words, which are themselves contrastive in meaning, are distributed throughout the novel: the arrangement of words indicative of "light" and "dark." The repetition of the contrastive words with different configurations conveys additional meanings as well as their own specific ones in accordance with the scenes. First of all, I will investigate the configuration of words suggestive of "light" and "dark." Figure 3-7 on

---

[13] Needless to say, the use of the elliptical sentences omitting the predicate verbs in the passage makes some of their elements salient: "Madame Defarge," and her "footstep."

the next page shows the frequencies of these words throughout the text.[14] In the table, the chapters of the novel are divided into three groups: English chapters, French chapters, and English-French chapters.

Scrutiny of Figure 3-7, among other things, reveals the following the three things:

(i) Words indicative of "light" and "dark" appear again and again in most of the chapters throughout the novel, yet almost always together in the same chapters with different occurrences of frequency.

(ii) Either of the words occurs at a greater frequency in some chapters than others. Especially, words expressive of "light" have several chapters in which they appear with extremely higher frequencies. For example, in Book I, Chapter 6, where Lucie is reunited with her father in a defective mental state, the words are repeated most frequently in the novel in contrast with the low frequency of the words indicative of "dark."

---

[14] The words (196 in total) exhibitive of light in Figure 3-7 comprise "light" (78), "lights" (11), "daylight" (3), "moonlight" (6), "starlight" (2), "sunlight" (2), "twilight" (4), "fire-light" (1), "lighted" (15), "dimly-lighted" (1), "newly-lighted" (1), "lighter" (3), "lighting" (3), "lightning" (8), "bright" (26), "brightened" (1), "brighter" (8), "brightly" (3), "brightness" (3), "brilliant" (1), "brilliantly" (2), "radiance" (2), "radiant" (3), "ray" (5), "rays" (2), and "kindled" (2). The words (198 in total) indicative of dark are composed of "darkness" (28), "dark" (89), "darkened" (5), "darkening" (5), "darker" (1), "darkest" (1), "darkly" (5), "shadow" (31), "shadows" (21), "shade" (5), "shades" (1), "shaded" (3), "shadowy" (2), and "shady" (1). Several instances of "light" meaning "of little weight" or "of small importance," and the examples of "lightly" meaning "with little weight" or "easily" are excluded.

Chapter III   Distinctive Use of Repetition

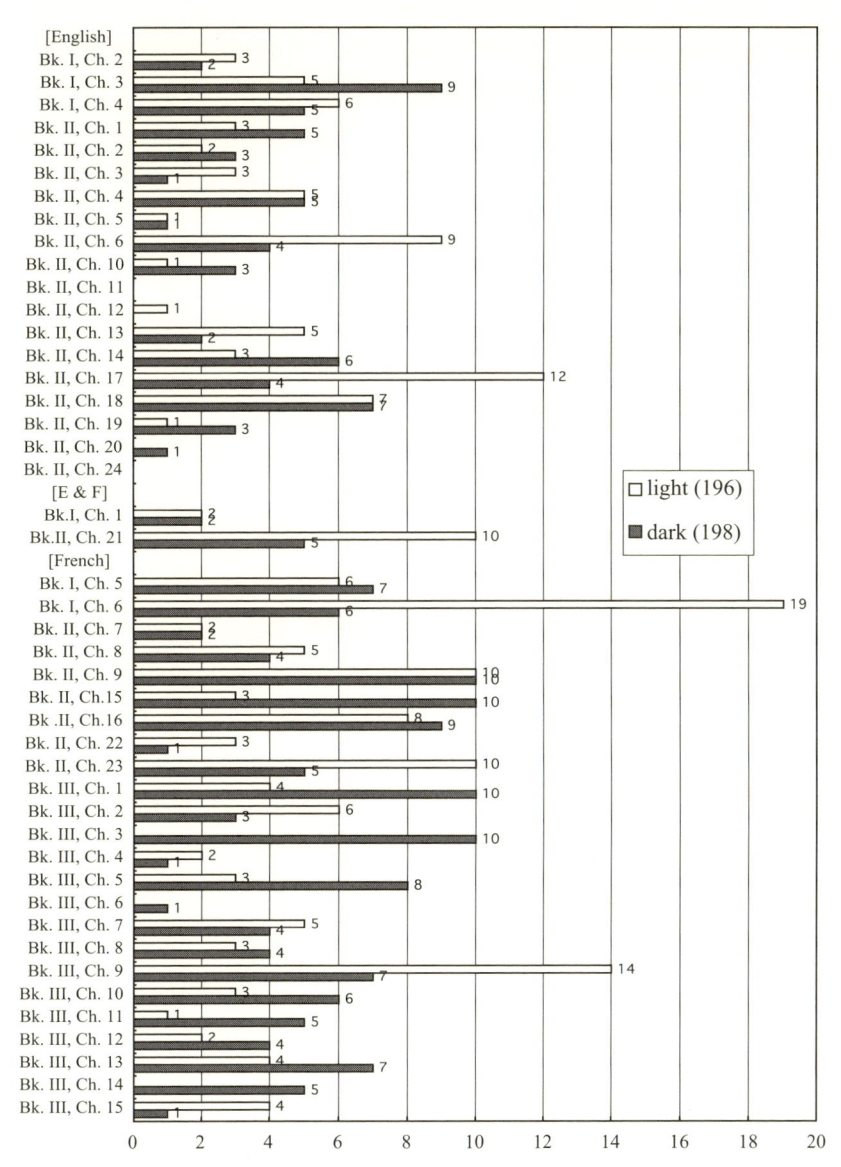

Figure 3-7 Frequencies of words indicative of "light" and "dark"

(iii) I also find the differences in frequencies of the words suggestive of "light" and "dark" in successive chapters. For instance, Chapter 8 and 9 of Book III depict a relevant and serial event, but the frequencies of those words are significantly different or contrastive. Concretely, in the former chapter, three examples of words denoting "light" and four examples denoting "dark" occur, while in the latter chapter 14 instances of words indicative of "light" and 7 instances indicative of "dark" are present.

In this way, repetition of words indicative of "light" and "dark" seems to be inevitably connected with individualization of the characters, their roles, foreshadowing of the plot, and the subject matter of *A Tale of Two Cities*.

Now, I will examine cases in which the distribution of words denoting "light" and "dark" contributes to characterization. For example, words indicative of "dark" occur frequently in Chapter 3 of Book III, while in the following chapter, where Madame Defarge does not appear, the same repetitive use of these words is not found. Yet, in Chapter 5 of Book III, in response to the reemergence of Madame Defarge, the words occur at a high rate of recurrence (8 times). The shift of frequencies of words denoting "dark" in the chapters leads to the realization that Madame Defarge and these words are in mutual expectancy with each other.

In contrast, words indicative of "light" often occur in the descriptions of Lucie at higher frequencies than words denoting "dark" as seen in the descriptions of Lucie's hair: "golden hair" (I, 4), "her radiant hair" (I, 6), "the bright golden hair" (II, 18) (see Section 2.1.1). More concretely, in

Chapter 5 of Book I, where Lucie meets with Dr. Manette after 18 years' absence, I cannot find a striking discrepancy of frequencies between the words denoting "light" and "dark" (six instances of words denoting "light" and seven denoting "dark"). However, in Chapter 6 of Book I, where she actually tries to rescue her father, the highest frequency of words indicating "light" are observed as Figure 3-7 shows (19 instances of words denoting "light" and six denoting "dark"). Such a contrastive use of the words between two consecutive chapters lays special emphasis on the mutual expectancy between Lucie as the support of her mentally deranged father and the words indicative of "light" in the earlier part of the novel.

Furthermore, I turn my attention to cases in which repetition of words indicative of "light" and "dark" contributes to the foreshadowing of the novel. The passage below is seen in the chapter where words denoting "dark" occur at the highest frequency among the English chapters:

> (57) (Mr. Lorry has the dream about digging up a dead man and questioning him on his will to live after having been buried for 18 years.)
> Yet even when his eyes were opened on the mist and rain, on the moving patch of light from the lamps, and the hedge at the roadside retreating by jerks, *the night shadows* outside the coach would fall into the train of *the night shadows* within. The real Banking-house by Temple Bar, the real business of the past day, the real strong-rooms, the real express sent after him, and the real message returned, would all be there. Out of the midst of them, the ghostly face would rise, and he would accost it again. (Bk. I, Ch. 3)

The italicized phrase "the night shadows," which is also the title of Chapter 3 of Book I, and its related phrase "the shadows of the night" recur again and again in this chapter; more concretely, the former phrase three times and the latter four times. The repetitive and cumulative use of the phrases serves to create a dark and mysterious atmosphere in the very early part of the novel together with other words indicative of "dark." In other words, the above-mentioned phrases intensify the theme of secrecy with the help of the recurring use of the word "real" and foreshadow the reality of the story being disclosed behind them. The reality is to be revealed as the novel progresses, just as the "shadow" of Dr. Manette is exposed with the reading of his denunciation in Chapter 10 of Book III, which is titled "The Substance of the Shadow."

Foreshadowing is sometimes signified through the shift from "dark" to "light." Such a shift is recognized in the descriptions of Sydney Carton. That is to say, in Book II of this novel, words suggestive of "dark" are frequently found in delineating Carton. On the contrary, in Book III, words significant of "light" repeatedly occur to depict the hero. Compare the two passages below:

> (58)　If Sydney Carton ever *shone* anywhere, he certainly never *shone* in the house of Doctor Manette. He had been there often, during a whole year, and had always been the same moody and morose lounger there. When he cared to talk, he talked well; but, the cloud of caring for nothing, which *overshadowed* him with such *a fatal darkness*, was very rarely pierced by *the light* within him. (Bk. II, Ch. 13)

> (59)　But, *the glorious sun,* rising, seemed to strike those words, that burden of *the night*, straight and warm to his heart in *its long bright rays*. And looking along them, with *reverently shaded eyes, a bridge of light* appeared to span the air between him and *the sun*, while the river *sparkled* under it.
> (Bk. III, Ch. 9)

Passage (58) describes Carton's confession. Carton professes his undying love to Lucie, knowing that he is not worthy of her. Words expressive of light, "shone" and "the light," go with the negatives "never" and "rarely." The phrase "the light within him" as indicative of his inner reality is just hinted at, and "a fatal darkness" which overshadows him is emphasized by contrast as if to mirror his role here.

On the other hand, passage (59) is found in Chapter 9 of Book III, which has the second highest frequency of words expressive of "light." In the scene, words and phrases denoting "light" such as "glorious sun," "its long bright rays," and "a bridge of light" recur, thus visually highlighting the change of role Carton plays. He prowls the streets of Paris alone with the settled decision to sacrifice himself for Lucie and her husband. However, Carton's decision is not clearly announced or narrated, and we are led to expect his future heroic self-devotion through the drastic shift of words significant of light from Chapter 8 to Chapter 9 of Book III (3 to 14 instances).

Additionally, in passage (58), words denoting "light" are inevitably linked to negatives, while in passage (59) I find the example of Dickens's collocating of "shaded eyes" with "reverently," suggesting a new aspect to Carton's character.

3.4 Distinctive use of repetition among characters or scenes

In this section, I will turn my attention to a case of distinctive or contrastive use of repetition in which different words are repeated in one context and in another even though the two contexts are closely associated from the viewpoint of plot.

To take a typical instance, Chapter 10 and Chapter 11 of Book II describe Darnay's and Stryver's declaration of love for Lucie respectively. We find the repetitive use of the word "confidence" in Darnay's and Dr. Manette's speeches in the former chapter (5 times), whereas we find no instance of Stryver's in the latter.

In addition, in Chapter 13 of Book II, where Carton resolves to reveal his feelings to Lucie, the word "confidence" is repeated in Carton's and Lucie's speeches (3 times in total).

Such contrastive use of the reiterated word among characters and chapters deserves special attention, and makes the reader aware of Darnay's and Carton's earnest attitudes and Stryver's flippant one toward love.

The following table represents how many times the word "confidence" is used in the dialogue of each character throughout the novel.

Table 3-8 Frequency of "confidence" in the dialogue

Mr. Lorry	7	Carton	2
Darnay	4	Madame Defarge	1
Dr. Manette	4	Marquis	1
Lucie	3	**Total**	22

Seen from the table above, the word "confidence" is repetitively used in the speeches of Mr. Lorry, Darnay, Dr. Manette, Lucie, and Carton (91% of the total), and shows the mutual trust or love between them.

As a similar case, observe the two court trial scenes in London and Paris:

> (60) Mr. Lorry sat at a table, among the gentlemen in *wigs*: not far from a *wigged* gentleman, the prisoner's counsel, who

had a great bundle of papers before him: and nearly opposite another *wigged* gentleman with his hands in his pockets, whose whole attention, when Mr. Cruncher looked at him then or afterwards, seemed to be concentrated on the ceiling of the court. (Bk. II, Ch. 2)

(61)   When the Attorney-General ceased, a *buzz* arose in the court as if a cloud of great *blue-flies* were swarming about the prisoner, in anticipation of what he was soon to become.
(Bk. II, Ch. 2)

(62)   His judges sat upon the Bench in *feathered hats*; but *the rough red cap* and *tricoloured cockade* was the head-dress otherwise prevailing. Looking at the Jury and *the turbulent audience*, he might have thought that the usual order of things was reversed, and that the felons were trying the honest men. (Bk. III, Ch. 6)

(63)   'Take off his head!' *cried the audience*. 'An enemy to the Republic!'
   The President rang his bell to silence those *cries*, and asked the prisoner whether it was not true that he had lived many years in England? (Bk. III, Ch. 6)

In the trials in London and Paris, Darnay is accused of treason, and such words as "attorney," "jury," "judge," "accused," "prisoner" occur repeatedly. At the same time, different kinds of recurring words are seen in the descriptions of the lawyers and the court audience. In the Old Bailey in London, the words "wig(s)" (4 times) and "wigged" (6 times) are reiterated to represent the lawyers; on the other hand, in Paris, "feathered hats," "red cap," and "tricoloured cockade" as a covering for the head occur as seen in passage (62).

Likewise, in the English court, the audience is given an image of "blue-flies" over a dead body and they recurrently "buzz": "blue-flies"

(4 times), "great flies" (twice), and "buzz" (5 times). In the French court, however, the court spectators are given the variant expressions of "the populace" (6 times), its context-bound synonyms, "the crowd" (6 times), "the audience" (5 times), "spectators" (once), and "concourse" (once), and they are heard to "cry" (5 times) and "shout" (twice). Some repeated words in the one scene are not resounded in the other even though the two scenes are closely related with each other in context, and the different words are repeated. The different or contrastive use of the repeated words in the two courts are represented as follows.

Table 3-9 Descriptions of the English and the French courts

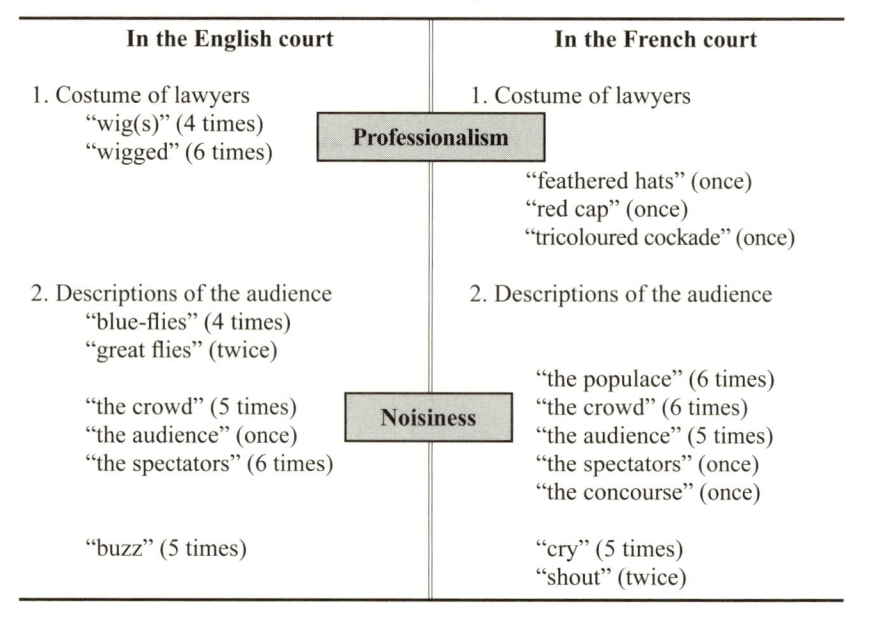

In the English court	In the French court

1. Costume of lawyers
    "wig(s)" (4 times)
    "wigged" (6 times)   **Professionalism**
	1. Costume of lawyers
	
	"feathered hats" (once)
	"red cap" (once)
	"tricoloured cockade" (once)

2. Descriptions of the audience
    "blue-flies" (4 times)
    "great flies" (twice)
	2. Descriptions of the audience

"the crowd" (5 times) **Noisiness** "the audience" (once) "the spectators" (6 times)	"the populace" (6 times) "the crowd" (6 times) "the audience" (5 times) "the spectators" (once) "the concourse" (once)
"buzz" (5 times)	"cry" (5 times) "shout" (twice)

Of course, Dickens's satirical eyes are cast on both trials to vilify the legal systems, but the difference of repeated words leads to a realization of the dissimilarity of legal procedure and quality of the audience in the two courts. The descriptions of the French lawyers without the typical "wigs" as part of a professional costume disclose a lack of professionalism. The author's intentional use of "cry" and "shout" as expressive of the court audience's "noisiness" highlights the revolutionists' bloodlust nature in the French court. To put it another way, the fact that different words are reiterated in contextually similar scenes demonstrates a semblance of justice in the English court and, by stark contrast, the total lack of justice in the Revolutionary Tribunal.

3.5 Repetition of "plane-tree" and "fountain"

We can see another distinctive or contrastive use of repeated words when close examination of the distribution of other repeated words reveals that particular words only or mostly appear in either the English or the French scenes. Needless to say, such Anglicized French expressions as "Good day," "I salute you, citizenness," and "the sun going to bed" (cf. Sanders 1988: 9-10, 45-47 & Monod 1968: 459-60) occur only in the French scenes. In the same way, words specific to the French Revolution like "Tribunal" and "guillotine" are repeated only in the French scenes. In particular, among others, I notice the frequent use of the key word, "plane-tree," which shows the high log likelihood value of 97.4, in the English scenes (see Table 2-15). The word, which is symbolic of "friendliness" or "charity,"[15] occurs 15 times in total in the novel, and 14 of them are found in the English chapters. The only instance in the French chapter, Bk. III, Ch. 13, is used in a retrospective

---

[15] de Vries (1976), s.v. Plane (tree).

description of the English scene.[16] Moreover, the word repeatedly co-occurs with the adjective "pleasant," which is found 15 times only in the English chapters, notably 10 times in Chapter 6 of Book II.

On the other hand, another key word "fountain" (all 42 times), whose log likelihood value is 150.6, and its related word "fate" (10 of 12 times) occur mainly in the French scenes. The word "fountain" repeatedly occurs in the earlier French chapters, and is observed particularly in the scenes depicting the characters' death and the misery of the French commoners. The words "fountain" and "fate" appear at some intervals as a running leitmotif in the French scenes. Figure 3-10 represents the distribution of these four words.[17]

The different or contrastive use of repeated words in the English and the French scenes in *A Tale of Two Cities* enables the reader to realize the author's deliberate exploitation of words in terms of the subject

---

[16] The "plane-tree" occurs predominantly in *A Tale of Two Cities* in Dickens's novels; only one instance is found externally in *The Uncommercial Traveller*. The instance is found in the following passage:

> The illegible tombstones are all lop-sided, the grave-mounds lost their shape in the rains of a hundred years ago, the Lombardy Poplar or *Plane-Tree* that was once a drysalter's daughter and several common-councilmen, has withered like those worthies, and its departed leaves are dust beneath it. (*UT* 23)

Moreover, when I checked the use of the word "plane-tree" in *Nineteenth-Century Fiction* (2000, Chadwyck-Healey), I find 14 instances excluding the 15 examples in *A Tale of Two Cities*: one instance in *Belinda* (1801) by M. Edgeworth, 2 instances in *Romola* (1863) by G. Eliot, 1 instance in *A Pair of Blue Eyes* (1873) by T. Hardy, and 10 instances in *The Mysteries of Udolpho* (1794) by A. W. Radcliffe.

[17] In the Dickens Corpus, the word "fountain" includes "fountains" (8); "pleasant" includes "pleasanter" (23) and "pleasantest" (40); and "fate" includes "fates" (10). In *A Tale of Two Cities*, the word "fountain" (42) includes "fountains" (2).

Chapter III Distinctive Use of Repetition   179

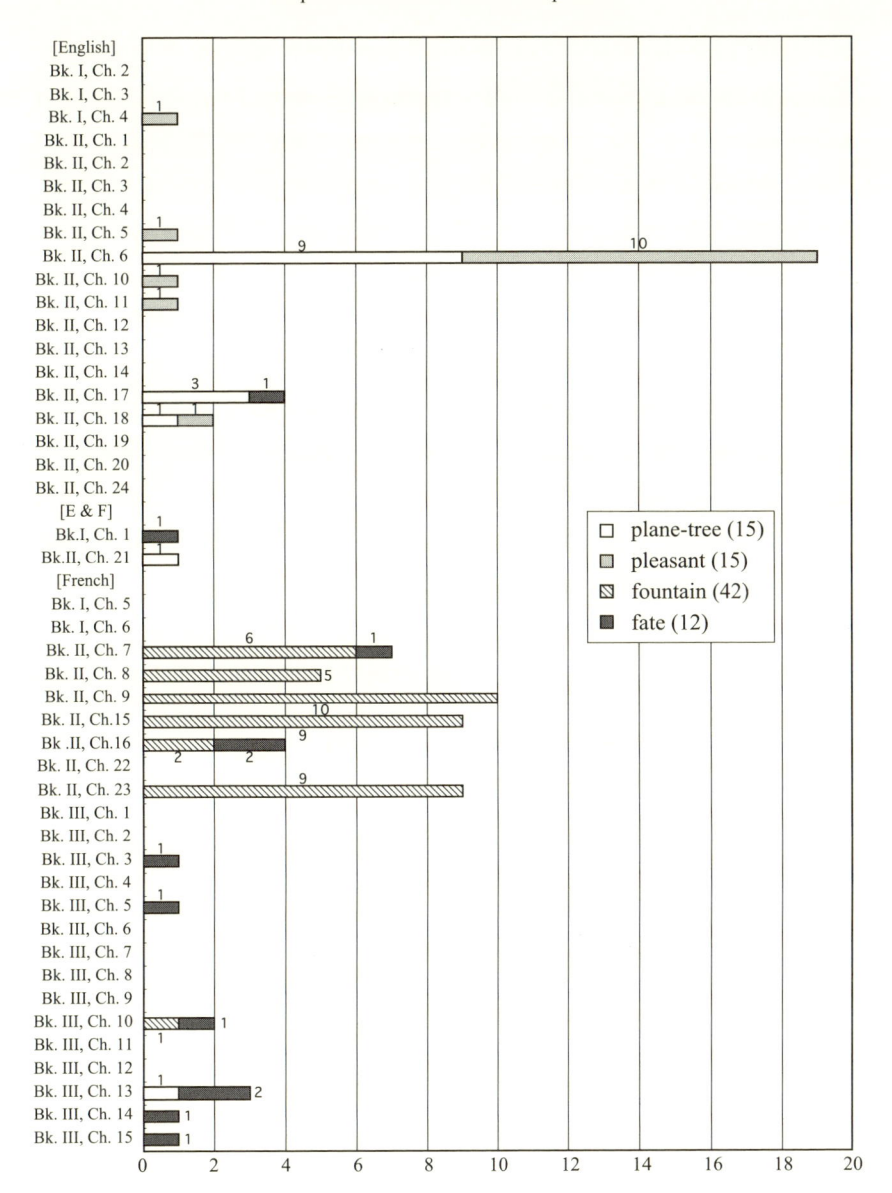

[English]
Bk. I, Ch. 2
Bk. I, Ch. 3   1
Bk. I, Ch. 4
Bk. II, Ch. 1
Bk. II, Ch. 2
Bk. II, Ch. 3
Bk. II, Ch. 4
Bk. II, Ch. 5   1
Bk. II, Ch. 6   9   10
Bk. II, Ch. 10
Bk. II, Ch. 11
Bk. II, Ch. 12
Bk. II, Ch. 13
Bk. II, Ch. 14
Bk. II, Ch. 17   3   1
Bk. II, Ch. 18
Bk. II, Ch. 19
Bk. II, Ch. 20
Bk. II, Ch. 24
[E & F]
Bk.I, Ch. 1   1
Bk.II, Ch. 21
[French]
Bk. I, Ch. 5
Bk. I, Ch. 6   6   1
Bk. II, Ch. 7
Bk. II, Ch. 8   5
Bk. II, Ch. 9   10
Bk. II, Ch.15   9
Bk .II, Ch.16   2   2
Bk. II, Ch. 22   9
Bk. II, Ch. 23
Bk. III, Ch. 1
Bk. III, Ch. 2
Bk. III, Ch. 3   1
Bk. III, Ch. 4
Bk. III, Ch. 5   1
Bk. III, Ch. 6
Bk. III, Ch. 7
Bk. III, Ch. 8
Bk. III, Ch. 9
Bk. III, Ch. 10   1
Bk. III, Ch. 11   1
Bk. III, Ch. 12   1
Bk. III, Ch. 13   2
Bk. III, Ch. 14   1
Bk. III, Ch. 15   1

Legend:
☐ plane-tree (15)
▨ pleasant (15)
▧ fountain (42)
■ fate (12)

Figure 3-10
Frequecies of "plane-tree," "pleasant," "fate," and "fountain"

matter. The repetition of "plane-tree" together with that of "pleasant" serves to create a favorable family atmosphere in the English scenes. In sharp contrast to this, in the French scenes, the words "fountain" and "fate" directly convey some of the dominant themes of the book: death, future life, fate, and resurrection.[18] It seems that Dickens suggests the inevitable outbreak of the French Revolution and the characters' sealed destinies through the verbal associations of such repetitive words arranged mainly in the French scenes.

It is worth examining the repetitive use of "plane-tree" and "fountain" more closely and concretely. The words convey not only their own meanings but additional ones as well, for instance, foreshadowing. First, I make an investigation of the repeated use of "plane-tree" and "pleasant" in the following passage:

> (64)　On this occasion, Miss Pross, responding to Ladybird's <u>pleasant</u> face and <u>pleasant</u> efforts to please her, unbent exceedingly; so the dinner was very <u>pleasant</u>, too.
> 　　It was an oppressive day, and, after dinner, Lucie proposed that <u>the wine</u> should be carried out under *the plane-tree*, and they <u>should</u> sit there in the air. As everything turned upon her, and revolved about her, they went out under *the plane-tree*, and she carried <u>the wine</u> down for the special benefit of Mr. Lorry. She had installed herself, some time before, as Mr. Lorry's cup-bearer; and while they sat under *the plane-tree*, talking, she kept his glass replenished. Mysterious backs and ends of houses peeped at them as they talked, and *the plane-tree* whispered to them in its own way above their heads. (Bk. II, Ch. 6)

---

[18] cf. de Vries (1976), s.v. Fountain 1.

In the context of the passage above, Dr. Manette, Lucie, Mr. Lorry, and Miss Pross are in the courtyard after dinner. The repeated use of "plane-tree" in close proximity serves to create a comfortable and cozy atmosphere of domestic peace. At the same time, however, I find the repetition of the word "wine." As already discussed in Section 3.1.2, "wine" in the English scenes is associated with a serious development in the plot. Through the co-occurrence of "plane-tree" with "wine" we can sense an impending misfortune to ruin Lucie's happy family life, even though the "plane-tree" itself carries a good connotation. In fact, in the scene which follows the passage above, all the characters who gather under the "plane-tree" hear the footsteps of the people in the street caught in the sudden storm, as has been observed in Section 3.2. Additionally, the personification of the "plane-tree" and "houses" in the last sentence also serves as an ominous harbinger.

As another example of the repeated use of the "plane-tree," let me examine the following two passages. Passage (65) is observed at the very beginning, and passage (66) at the very end of Chapter 17 of Book II:

> (65) Never did the <u>sun</u> go down with a <u>brighter</u> glory on the quiet corner in Soho, than one memorable evening when the Doctor and his daughter sat under *the plane-tree* together. Never did the <u>moon</u> rise with a milder <u>radiance</u> over great London, than on that night when it found them still seated under *the tree*, and <u>shone</u> upon their faces through its leaves.
>
> Lucie was to be married to-morrow. She had reserved this last evening for her father, and they sat alone under *the plane-tree*.
>
> 'You are happy, my dear father?'
> 'Quite, my child.' (Bk. II, Ch. 17)

(66) (Lucie sits by her father's bedside for a while.)
  She[Lucie] timidly laid her hand on his[Dr. Manette's] dear breast, and put up a prayer that she might ever be as true to him as her love aspired to be, and as his sorrows deserved. Then, she withdrew her hand, and kissed his lips once more, and went away. So, <u>the sunrise</u> came, and <u>the shadows</u> of the leaves of *the plane-tree* moved upon his face, as softly as her lips had moved in praying for him. (Bk. II, Ch. 17)

The first passage appears in the context where the night before Lucie's wedding, she and her father sit outside under the "plane-tree," and she reassures her father that her love for Darnay will not alter her love for him. The repetitive use of the "plane-tree" (and also the words "the tree") along with the words indicative of light, "sun," "brighter," "moon," "radiance," "shone" is closely related with the domestic happiness and hope that Lucie and her father feel.

Furthermore, in passage (66), the word denoting light, "sunrise," also happens. At the same time, however, the "plane-tree" co-occurs with the word "shadow," which seems to carry ominous implication for Dr. Manette's future. In reality, in the following chapter, Chapter 18 of Book II, Dr. Manette has temporarily reverted to shoemaking because of the shock of Charles Darnay's revelation, on the morning of his wedding to Lucie, of his identity as a member of the St Evrémonde family.

It can be said that the repeated use of the "plane-tree" itself symbolically suggests the Manettes' domestic peace, co-occurring with the words significant of light. Yet, the change of words co-occurring with the "plane-tree," that is to say, the new combination of "plane-tree" and "shadow," implies the characters' future fate in terms of foreshadowing.

Next, as the last instance of this section, I explore what additional meanings the repetitive use of "fountain" carries. The passage is present in the scene where the Marquis St. Evrémonde is killed:

(67)   (i) He[St. Evrémonde] moved from end to end of his voluptuous bedroom, looking again at the scraps of the day's journey that came unbidden into his mind; the slow toil up the hill at sunset, the setting sun, the descent, the mill, the prison on the crag, the little village in the hollow, the peasants at *the fountain*, and the mender of roads with his blue cap pointing out the chain under the carriage. (ii) *That fountain* suggested *the Paris fountain*, the little bundle lying on the step, the women bending over it, and the tall man with his arms up, crying, "Dead!"...

(iii) *The fountain in the village* flowed unseen and unheard, and *the fountain at the château* dropped unseen and unheard — both melting away, like the minutes that were falling from the spring of Time — through three dark hours. (iv) Then, the grey water of both began to be ghostly in the light, and the eyes of the stone faces of the château were opened.

(v) Lighter and lighter, until at last the sun touched the tops of the still trees, and poured its radiance over the hill. (vi) In the glow, the water of *the château fountain* seemed to turn to blood, and the stone faces crimsoned. (Bk. II, Ch. 9)

The word "fountain" appears in three places: on a Paris street, in the village, and at the country estate of the Marquis. At the Paris "fountain," an innocent child is accidentally run over by the Marquis's carriage. At the village "fountain," the poor peasants gather together for a living; the child's father, Gaspard, is seen riding under the carriage. The château "fountain" is a decoration at the Marquis's mansion. The three fountains refer to different things, but in the passage above, the repetitive use of "fountain" denotes their close association. The association is illustrated as follows.

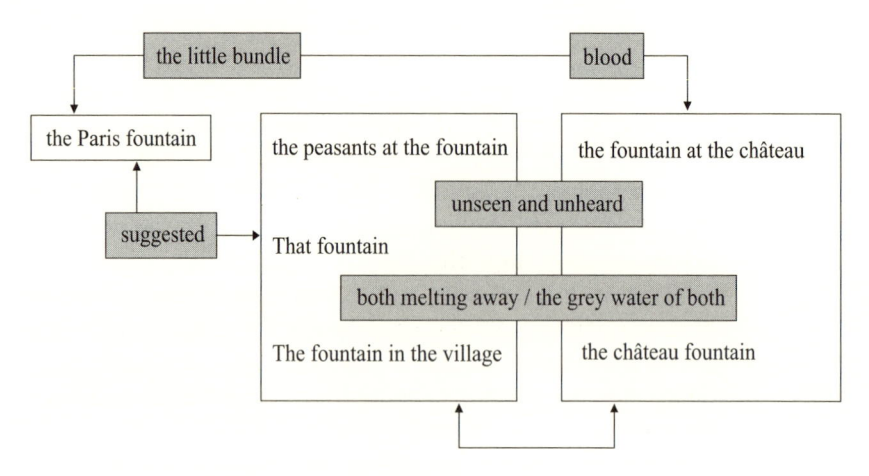

Figure 3-11　Verbal chart of "fountain"

The linkage between the fountain in the village and the Paris fountain is clearly shown in the clause "That fountain suggested the Paris fountain" in sentence (ii). The village fountain is connected with the château fountain through the repetition of "unseen and unheard" in (iii) and "both" with the ellipsis of "fountain" in (iii) and (iv). Moreover, the château fountain is connected with the Paris fountain through the assistance of the village fountain and the "blood" association of the two fountains, that is to say, the association of "the little bundle" in (ii), which refers to the child killed by the carriage, with the word "blood" in (vi). Through the association, by the construction of a verbal circle, we are made to realize the murder of the Marquis.

　Dickens often repeats a word with different referents and meanings in different scenes, and attempts to establish a close link between the scenes. The technique contributes to indicating a cause and effect relation and foreshadowing.

Final Remarks

I have approached the language and style of *A Tale of Two Cities* with special reference to three types of repetition: repetition of participant items, repetition of words for character description, and the distinctive use of repetition. Here, let me summarize the results gained from the preceding three chapters.

First, Chapter I, recapitulated as follows, looked at the repetition of the characters' participant items:

1. Dickens devotes much care to the choice and allocation of suitable participant items, such as proper names, personal pronouns, and other alternative expressions for characterization.

2. The repetitive use of the participant items not only contributes to individualizing the characters, including the depiction of their states of mind, but is also closely related to the progress of the plot and the subject matter of the novel. For example, the number of proper names applied to Sydney Carton tactfully alters between Books II and III in accordance with the roles he plays. The change of frequencies of his proper names allows us to realize one

of the dominant themes of the work — resurrection, as well as it serves to make salient his existence and his unselfish act of self-sacrifice, and at the same time.

3. Personal pronouns are normally unmarked referent items, but Dickens deliberately repeats and exploits such seemingly insignificant items to differentiate the characters, to obscure the identity of the referents intentionally, and to indicate the characters' states of mind.

4. Dickens's repetitive use of the participant items is made in different contexts as well as in an immediate context. Each instance of the participant items in different scenes in the novel corresponds with other scenes, forming a cohesive network of relationships, and produces various effects in the accumulated contexts.

Second, Chapter II, abstracted as follows, looked at the repetition of words used to describe the characters:

1. The statistical data (Table 2-1) shows that Dickens has a strong predilection for particular words such as "head," "eye," and "hand" in describing his characters.

2. Examining the combinations or collocations of these words with words co-occurring with them, I have established that the novelist varies the co-occurring words for the purpose of individualizing the characters. Some combinations of words expressive of body parts with their modifiers are apparently regarded as familiar or

conventional, while some are less familiar or unconventional. Both combinations serve to give vivid and realistic pictures of the characters and their psychological states in the contexts. The feelings of the characters especially, though not directly described, are deliberately suggested by these combinations.

3. Dickens also provides a situational description of the characters through the repetition of words expressing the body parts. To restate a typical instance, Lucie's "lifted eyebrows," unlike her "blue eyes," serves to appropriately describe the situation in which she is kept.

4. The key words "business" and "knit," which are unusually frequent in *A Tale of Two Cities* in comparison to the Dickens Corpus, are recurrently used not only for individualization of the characters but also for presenting the subject matter of the novel. Through repetition, Dickens transforms the significance of the word "knitting," expressive of a simple and innocent activity, into something ominous and fatal. The recurrent use of the word "business" denotes each character's own work, concern, and role.

5. The connected interwoven collocations of the repeated words and the words co-occurring with them contribute to producing a network of relationships, which exposes Dickens's deliberate intention of unifying the structure of the novel.

Finally, Chapter III, epitomized as follows, looked at Dickens's distinctive use of repetition:

1. Dickens makes a broad and insistent use of such symbolic or thematic key words as "footstep," "wine," "red," "fountain," and "plane-tree." The repetition of these words conveys their own specific meanings as well as additional and different ones, in accordance with the scenes or contexts; this is especially seen in the juxtaposition of the English and the French scenes. For example, the recurrent use of "wine" in the French scenes indicates the bloodshed of the French Revolution, while the use of the word in the English scenes is associated with the fateful encounter between the characters.

2. The effects of the symbolic words are augmented in terms of their iterated co-occurrence with their related words. For instance, the word "footstep" sometimes occurs in isolation, but more frequently co-occurs with "foot," "tread," and "echo." Consequently, the use of the word "footstep" establishes its symbolic meaning of the rapid approach of the Revolution through the assistance of the co-occurring words. Furthermore, the novelist repeats the symbolic words and their related words through various modifications and transformations, commanding them to accumulate the thematic significance as the story unfolds.

3. Dickens obtrusively repeats symbolic words closely related to the themes; moreover, I have found cases where he does not reiterate the co-occurring words in the same context but consistently uses their synonymous words. For instance, in the description of

Lucie's house in Soho, the recurrent use of the words "footsteps," "tread," "feet," and "echo" represents the tumult of the people in the street; on the other hand, the synonymous words "quiet," "still," and "tranquilly" contrastively indicate the calm and peaceful atmosphere in her house. The symbolic words are foregrounded by brute repetition, whereas the synonymous ones are unobtrusively hidden in the background. Dickens brilliantly manages to heighten the stylistic effects of the repetition by the use of synonymous words or phrases within a context.

4. Instead of using different words or phrases of similar meaning, Dickens exploits polysemy by repeating the same words, and directs the reader's attention to the word and its connotation in the context. This technique reveals one aspect of Dickens's use of repetition.

5. The different or contrastive use of repetition between the English and the French scenes in *A Tale of Two Cities* enables us to realize the author's deliberate exploitation of the technique. The words "plane-tree" and "pleasant" repeated in the English scenes serve to create a favorable family atmosphere. In stark contrast, in the French scenes, the words "fountain" and "fate" directly convey some of the main themes of the novel: death, future life, fate, and resurrection.

The foregoing arguments and the above-mentioned summary justify stating that Dickens deliberately exploits the technique of repetition with great artistry in order to individualize characters, to make creative use of conventional symbolic meanings, to prefigure or foreshadow future events, and to convey the main themes of the novel, say, fate and resurrection, to the minds of the reader. The novelist's use of repetition for the stylistic effects of emphasis and irony can also be found in his other novels. However, in *A Tale of Two Cities*, the repetitions of words and phrases are well organized and structurally used, and thus have the obvious function of creating a strong sense of unity in the structure of the novel. In a metaphorical sense, as various kinds of threads are woven together into texture, various kinds of repetition are skillfully interwoven into the story, and provide a strong sense of continuity and association within the novel. Such structural use of repetition is one of the linguistic peculiarities of the novel.

Interesting enough, the very events of the plot of this novel repeat themselves to gain even greater significance. That is to say, Dr. Manette and Lucie escape from France twice; Dr. Manette falls into mental illness several times; aristocrats' cruel acts before the Revolution are followed by the equally cruel revolutionists; two trials are conducted; and, among others, Sydney's death and rebirth. The repetition of those events contributes to making tight the construction of this novel as a historical tribute. In other words, verbal repetition, closely related to such repetitively successive events, makes this novel an excellent work of art as well as a historic one. What impresses me above all is the last passage of *A Tale of Two Cities*, where instances of repetition occur intensively:

> '*I see* Barsad, and Cly, Defarge, The Vengeance, the Juryman, the Judge, long ranks of the new oppressors who have risen on the destruction of the old, perishing by this retributive instrument, before it shall cease out of its present use. *I see* a beautiful city

and a brilliant people rising from this abyss, and, in their struggles to be truly free, in their triumphs and defeats, through long years to come, *I see* the evil of this time and of the previous time of which this is the natural birth, gradually making expiation for itself and wearing out.

'*I see* the lives for which I lay down my life, peaceful, useful, prosperous and happy, in that England which I shall see no more. *I see* Her with a child upon her bosom, who bears my name. *I see* her father, aged and bent, but otherwise restored, and faithful to all men in his healing office, and at peace. *I see* the good old man, so long their friend, in ten years' time enriching them with all he has, and passing tranquilly to his reward.

'*I see* that I hold a sanctuary in their hearts, and in the hearts of their descendants, generations hence. *I see* her, an old woman, weeping for me on the anniversary of this day. *I see* her and her husband, their course done, lying side by side in their last earthly bed, and I know that each was not more honoured and held sacred in the other's soul, than I was in the souls of both.

'*I see* that child who lay upon her bosom and who bore my name, a man winning his way up in that path of life which once was mine. *I see* him winning it so well, that my name is made illustrious there by the light of his. *I see* the blots I threw upon it, faded away. *I see* him, fore-most of just judges and honoured men, bringing a boy of my name, with a forehead that I know and golden hair, to this place — then fair to look upon, with not a trace of this day's disfigurement — and I hear him tell the child my story, with a tender and a faltering voice.

'It is a far, far better thing that I do, than I have ever done; it is a far, far better rest that I go to than I have ever known.'

(Bk. III, Ch. 15)

Here, Sydney Carton looks back upon the past and foretells the future in which the same events repeat themselves. This is Dickens's idea of eternity — hope for "a far, far better rest" which follows the repeated follies of mankind.

The research from the viewpoint of repetition in the present treatise is chiefly confined to *A Tale of Two Cities*, but serves to reveal the writer's stylistic and linguistic artistry that inheres, with some qualitative alternations and transformations, throughout his other works. Therefore, my continuing task will be to undertake further exhaustive and systematic observations on the lexical structure and style of the author's entire work from the similar viewpoint. Such an approach will undoubtedly throw greater light on the system and structure of Dickens's language which reached full maturity in English prose.

Select Bibliography

Andrews, M. (1994) *Dickens and the Grown-up Child*. Iowa: University of Iowa Press.

Bentley, N., M. Slater, and N. Burgis, (eds.) (1988) *The Dickens Index*. Oxford: Oxford University Press.

Booth, W. C. (1961) *The Rhetoric of Fiction*. Chicago: The University of Chicago Press.

Bradford, R. (1997) *Stylistics*. London: Routledge.

Brook, G. L. (1970) *The Language of Dickens*. London: Andre Deutsch.

Carter, R. (ed.) (1982) *Language and Literature: An Introductory Reader in Stylistics*. London: George Allen & Unwin.

—— (1998) *Vocabulary: Applied Linguistic Perspectives* 2nd ed. London: Routledge.

Chapman, R. (1994) *Forms of Speech in Victorian Fiction*. London: Longman.

Collins, P. (ed.) (1971) *Dickens: The Critical Heritage*. London: Routledge and Kegan Paul.

Connor, S. (1985) *Charles Dickens*. Oxford: Basil Blackwell.

Crystal, D. and Davy, D. (1969) *Investigating English Style*. London: Longman.

Curme, G. O. (1931) *Syntax*. Boston: D. C. Heath and Company.

Curry, M. J. C. (1994) "Anaphoric and Cataphoric Reference in Dickens's *Our Mutual Friend* and James's *The Golden Bowl*" in S. G. Bernstein (ed.), *The Text and Beyond: Essays in Literary Linguistics*.

Tuscaloosa: The University of Alabama Press.

de Vries, Ad. (1976) *Dictionary of Symbols and Imagery*. London: North-Holland Publishing Company.

Dijk, T. A. van. (ed.) (1985) *Discourse and Literature*. Philadelphia: John Benjamins Publishing Company.

Firth, J. R. (1957) *Papers in Linguistics* 1934-1951. London: Oxford University Press.

Forster, E. M. (1927) *Aspects of the Novel*. London: Hodder & Stoughton.

Fowler, H. W. (1965) *A Dictionary of Modern English Usage* 2nd ed., revised by Sir Ernest Gowers. Oxford: Oxford University Press.

Fowler, R. (1977) *Linguistics and the Novel*. London: Methuen.

—— (1996) *Linguistic Criticism* 2nd ed. Oxford: Oxford University Press.

Glancy, R. (1991) *A Tale of Two Cities: Dickens's Revolutionary Novel*. Boston: Twayne Publishers.

Golding, R. (1985) *Idiolects in Dickens*. London: Macmillan.

Gordon, I. A. (1966) *The Movement of English Prose*. London: Longman.

Greaves, J. (1972) *Who's Who in Dickens*. London: Elm Tree Books.

Greenbaum, S. (1970) *Verb-Intensifier Collocations in English: An Experimental Approach*. Mouton: The Hague.

—— (1988) *Good English and the Grammarian*. London: Longman.

Greimas, A. J. (1966) *Sémantique Structurale*. Paris: Larousse.

Gross, J. and Pearson, G. (1962) *Dickens and the Twentieth Century*. Toronto: Toronto University of Toronto Press.

Gutwinski, W. (1976) *Cohesion in Literary Texts: A Study of Some Grammatical and Lexical Features of English Discourse*. Hague: Mouton.

Halliday, M. A. K. (1971) "Linguistic Function and Literary Style: An

Inquiry into the Language of William Golding's *The Inheritors*" in Seymour Chatman (ed.), *Literary Style: A Symposium*. London: Oxford University Press.

—— (1985) *An Introduction to Functional Grammar* 2nd ed. London: Edward Arnold.

—— and Hasan, R. (1976) *Cohesion in English*. London: Longman.

Hasan, R. (1989) *Linguistics, Language, and Verbal Art*. Oxford: Oxford University Press.

Hawes, D. (1998) *Who's Who in Dickens*. London: Routledge.

Hayward, A. (1924) *The Dickens Encyclopedia*. London: Routledge & Kegan Paul.

Hori. M. (1981) "Some Aspects of the Participant Line in Charles Dickens's *Oliver Twist*," *Kurokami Review*, 4: 50-63.

—— (1993) "Some Collocations of the Word 'Eye' in Dickens: A Preliminary Sketch" in *Aspects of Modern English*. Tokyo: Eichosha, 509-27.

—— (1999) "Collocational Patterns of Intensive Adverbs in Dickens: A Tentative Approach," *English Corpus Studies*, 6: 51-65.

—— (2004) *Investigating Dickens' Style: A Collocational Analysis*. New York: Palgrave Macmillan.

Imahayashi, O. (2006) *Charles Dickens and Literary Dialect*. Hiroshima: Keisuisha.

Imai, M. (2004) "Repetition in Middle English Metrical Romances," in Risto Hiltunen and Shinichiro Watanabe (eds.), *Approaches to Style and Discourse in English*. Osaka: Osaka University Press.

Ingham, P. (1992) *Dickens, Women and Language*. Hemel Hempstead: Harvester Wheatsheaf.

Ito, H. (1980) *The Language of The Spectator: A Lexical and Stylistic*

Approach. Tokyo: Shinozaki Shorin.

—— (1989) *Some Aspects of Eighteenth-Century English*. Tokyo: Eichosha.

Jespersen, O. (1909-49) *A Modern English Grammar on Historical Principles* 7 vols. London: George Allen & Unwin.

Kenny, A. (1982) *The Computation of Style: An Introduction to Statistics for Students of Literature and Humanities*. Oxford: Pergamon Press.

Koguchi, K. (1993) "Some Stylistic Observations on Charles Dickens's *Hard Times*: With Special Reference to Conflict between Fact and Fancy," *Kumamoto Studies in English Language and Literature*, 36: 101-115.

—— (2001) *The Language of Charles Dickens's* A Tale of Two Cities: *From a Cohesive Point of View*. Hiroshima: Research Institute for Language and Culture, Yasuda Women's University.

—— (2003) "Repetition and Contrast in *A Tale of Two Cities*" in *Studies in Modern English: The Twentieth Anniversary Publication of the Modern English Association*. Tokyo: Eichosha.

Kumamoto, S. (1999) *The Rhyme-structure of* The Romaunt of the Rose-A: *In Comparison with its French Original* Le Roman de la Rose. Tokyo: Kaibunsha.

Lambert, M. (1981) *Dickens and the Suspended Quotation*. New Haven: Yale University Press.

Leavis, F. R. and Leavis, Q. D. (1970) *Dickens the Novelist*. Harmondsworth: Penguin Books.

Leech, G. N. (1966) "Linguistics and the Figures of Rhetoric" in R. Fowler (ed.), *Essays on Style and Language: Linguistic and Critical Approaches to Literary Style*. New York: The Humanities Press.

—— (1969) *A Linguistic Guide to English Poetry*. London: Longman.

—— (1970) "'This Bread I Break' — Language and Interpretation" in D. C. Freeman (ed.), *Linguistics and Literary Style*. New York: Holt, Rinehart and Winston.

—— (1981) *Semantics* 2nd ed. Harmondsworth: Penguin Books.

—— and Short, M. H. (1981) *Style in Fiction: A Linguistic Introduction to English Fictional Prose*. London: Longman.

Levit, F. (1990) *A Dickens Glossary*. New York: Garland Publishing.

Lodge, D. (1966) *Language of Fiction: Essays in Criticism and Verbal Analysis of the English Novel*. London: Routledge & Kegan Paul.

—— (1977) *The Modes of Modern Writing: Metaphor, Metonymy, and the Typology of Modern Literature*. Chicago: The University of Chicago Press.

Mahlberg, M. (2007) "A Corpus Stylistic Perspective on Dickens' *Great Expectations*" in M. Lambrou and P. Stockwell (eds.), *Contemporary Stylistics*. London: Continuum.

Mansion, J. E. (1972) *Harrap's New Standard French and English Dictionary* 2 vols. revised and edited by R. P. Ledésert and M. Ledésert. London: George G. Harrap.

McMaster, J. (1987) *Dickens the Designer*. New Jersey: Barnes & Noble Books.

Miller, J. H. (1959) *Charles Dickens: The World of His Novels*. Massachusetts: Harvard University Press.

Monod, S. (1968) *Dickens the Novelist*. Norman: University of Oklahoma Press.

—— (1970) "Some Stylistic Devices in *A Tale of Two Cities*" in R. B. Partlow, Jr. (ed.), *Dickens the Craftsman: Strategies of Presentation*. Illinois: Southern Illinois University Press.

Mukařovský, J. (1970) "Standard Language and Poetic Language" in D.

C. Freeman (ed.), *Linguistics and Literary Style*. New York: Holt, Rinehart and Winston.

Page, N. (1988) *Speech in the English Novel* 2nd ed. London: Macmillan.

Peer, W. V. (1986) *Stylistics and Psychology: Investigations of Foregrounding*. London: Croom Helm.

Phillipps, K. C. (1984) *Language and Class in Victorian England*. Oxford: Basil Blackwell.

Quirk, R. (1974) *The Linguist and the English Language*. London: Edward Arnold

—— et al. (1985) *A Comprehensive Grammar of the English Language*. London: Longman.

Sanders, A. (1988) *The Companion to* A Tale of Two Cities. London: George Allen & Unwin.

Short, Mick. (1996) *Exploring the Language of Poems, Plays and Prose*. London: Longman.

Simpson, J. and E. S. C. Weiner, (eds.) (2004) *The Oxford English Dictionary* 2nd ed. CD-ROM, Version 3.1. Oxford: Oxford University Press.

Simpson, P. (1997) *Language through Literature*. London: Routledge.

Sinclair, J. (1991) *Corpus, Concordance, Collocation*. Oxford: Oxford University Press.

Shepherd, V. (1994) *Literature about Language*. London: Routledge.

Sørensen, K. (1985) *Charles Dickens: Linguistic Innovator*. Aarhus: Arkona.

Spitzer, L. (1962) *Linguistics and Literary History: Essays in Stylistics*. New York: Russell & Russell.

Stoehr, T. (1965) *Dickens: The Dreamer's Stance*. New York: Cornell

University Press.

Sucksmith, H. P. (1970) *The Narrative Art of Charles Dickens*. London: Oxford University Press.

Tabata, T. (2002) "Investigating Stylistic Variation in Dickens through Correspondence Analysis of Word-class Distribution" in T. Saito, J. Nakamura, and S. Yamazaki (eds.), *English Corpus Linguistics in Japan*. Amsterdam: Rodopi.

—— (2004) "Differentiation of Idiolects in Fictional Discourse: A Stylo-statistical Aproach to Dickens's Artistry" in Risto Hiltunen and Shinichiro Watanabe (eds.), *Approaches to Style and Discourse in English*. Osaka: Osaka University Press.

Turner, G. W. (1973) *Stylistics*. Harmondsworh: Penguin Books.

Ullmann, S. (1967) *The Principles of Semantics*. New York: Barnes & Noble.

Wales, K. (2001) *A Dictionary of Stylistics* 2nd. ed. London: Longman.

Watt, I. (1964) *The Rise of the Novel*. California: University of California Press.

Yamamoto, T. (2003) *Growth and System of the Language of Dickens: An Introduction to A Dickens Lexicon* 3rd ed. Hiroshima: Keisuisha.

Index of Names and Subjects

A

alternative / alterntive expression 19, 31-32, 71-74, 76-79, 185
anaphoric 44, 66
Anglicized French expression 177
antithesis → contrast
Austen, Jane 84-85

B

Barnaby Rudge 16
Barsad → Pross, Solomon
Battle of Life 16
Biblical 79
blame by praise → irony
Bleak House 4, 12, 17
    Dedlock, Lady 18
    Dedlock, Sir Leicester 17
    Richard 13
    Vholes 12-13
Brook, G. L. 3, 4, 14, 17, 94, 147

C

Carton, Sydney 5, 17, 21, 29-40, 43, 44, 45-53, 63, 66-71, 72, 76-79, 88, 89, 90, 104, 106, 108, 115, 118, 120, 121, 124-126, 132, 133, 135, 136, 137, 160, 161, 172, 173, 174, 185, 191
cataphoric(ally) 44, 69, 75
characterization 6, 8, 78, 81, 99, 106, 119, 123, 129, 170, 185
Chimes, The 16
Christmas Carol, A 16, 18
    Scrooge 18
cohesion 50, 145
    between paragraphs 50
    co-referential 33, 48
    thematic 145
    within a paragraph 50
cohesive
    chain 50, 99
    element 33, 48
    indicator 97
    net(work) 21, 186
    structure 74
    tie 48, 50, 68, 93
    web 130
cohesiveness, tight 163
Collins, Wilkie 29
collocation 4, 8-10, 81, 82, 88-102, 105, 107, 108, 110, 111, 113, 115, 121, 122, 123, 124, 126, 128, 186, 187
    familiar 91, 110, 128, 186
    unique 92, 114
collocational pattern 85, 88, 122, 123, 124, 126, 128, 186, 187
color adjective 88, 90, 91, 94, 95, 99

CONC 16
configuration 167
connotation 10, 11, 12, 13, 137, 159, 181, 189
content word 82-84
context 5, 6, 8, 12, 19, 21, 32, 44, 68, 122, 138, 147, 174, 176, 186, 188, 189
   accumulated 14, 186
   different 12, 13, 14-15, 107, 186
   extralinguistic 68
   immediate 12, 13, 20, 27, 107, 186
contrast / contrastive 5, 18, 20, 32, 37, 38, 39, 40, 43, 45, 47, 59, 93, 94, 100, 111, 137, 141, 144, 146, 147, 157, 165, 167, 170, 171, 173, 174, 176, 177, 178, 180, 189
Cricket on the Hearth, The 16
Cruncher, Jerry 38-39, 87, 89, 90, 91, 99-101, 106, 120, 122, 123, 129-130, 135
cumulative 15, 97, 172,

D

Darnay, Charles 17, 29, 40, 43, 45-53, 57, 59, 62-63, 69-70, 87, 89, 97-98, 106, 110, 112, 120, 125-126, 133, 136-137, 147, 160-161, 174-175, 182
David Copperfield 6, 10, 11, 18, 108
   Agnes 10
   Crupp, Mrs. 11-12
   David 6, 10, 11
   Dick, Mr. 11, 107

   Dora 10, 108
   Micawberism 18
   Omer 6
   Trotwood, Miss. 11
Defarge, Madame 17, 19, 21-29, 43, 44, 72-76, 78, 88, 89, 90, 91, 99-102, 106, 107, 109-110, 114-115, 120, 122, 123, 133, 134, 138-144, 158, 166-167, 170, 174
Defarge, Monsieur 26, 88, 89, 99, 101, 104, 106, 107, 120, 122, 126, 158, 190
dehumanization 54, 154
de Vries, Ad 78, 91, 96, 105, 108, 160, 177, 180
Dickens Corpus, the 16, 82-85, 92, 107, 131-134, 148-149, 187
Dombey and Son 16

E

echo (resounding) 12, 109, 114
Edwin Drood 16
elegant variation 17, 19
elliptical sentence 167
Evrémonde, (Marquis) St. 27, 54, 58, 59, 60, 182, 183
experimental use of language 4

F

family name 43, 143
flat character 44
foreshadowing 4, 99, 137, 141, 154, 158, 166, 170, 171, 172,

180, 182, 184
Forster, E. M. 44
Fowler, R. 74
Free Direct Speech (FDS) 47, 51
Free Indirect Speech (FIS) 12, 30, 41, 77
Frozen Deep, The 29
   Wardour, Richard 29
function word 82

G

Glancy, R. 4, 5, 18, 29, 43, 140, 157
graphic description 126
Great Expectations 7-8, 17-18, 109
   Estella 8-9
   Drummle 8-9
   Joe 8-9, 109
   Pip 9
   Wemmick, John 13-15
Greaves, J. 8
Gross, J. and Pearson, G. 5

H

habitual co-occurrence 81, 82
Halliday, M. A. K. and Hasan, R. 50, 81
Hard Times 7, 16, 17, 20
   Sissy 7-8, 20
   Gradgrind, Thomas 7, 20
Hasan, R. 4
Haunted Man, The 16
Havelok the Dane 109
Hawes, D. 18
Hori, M. 4, 69, 82, 109

I

Imai, M. 109
imagery 145, 151, 161
individualization 4, 17, 19, 20, 44, 88, 91, 100, 107, 110, 122, 134, 170, 187, 189
   use of language for 4
initial capital (in a pronoun) 70
inter-textual repetition 109
irony / ironical 6, 12, 13, 18, 20, 74, 190

J

Jacques Three 88, 89, 90, 120, 122, 126-128

K

keyness 131, 133, 148
key word 130-133, 134, 147, 148, 187, 188
Koguchi, K. 20

L

Leech, G. N. and Short, M. H. 6, 18, 19
Leech, G. N. 4, 11, 74
lemmatization 82
linguistic artistry 3, 15, 192
Little Dorrit 16
log likelihood (value) 131, 132, 133, 148, 149, 177, 178
Lorry, Mr. 56, 57, 58, 64, 71, 87,

89, 104, 106, 107, 110-111, 118,
120, 121, 123-124, 129, 134-137,
159-160, 174, 181

M

Manette, Dr. 17, 52, 54-66, 71, 87,
  89, 90, 91, 93-99, 100, 101, 105,
  107-108, 111-114, 118, 119, 120,
  121, 160, 164, 167, 171, 172,
  174, 181-182, 190
Manette, Lucie 17, 18, 21, 27, 28,
  40-44, 45, 52, 53, 62, 66-71, 74,
  79, 87, 89, 90, 91-93, 95, 97,
  100, 101, 105, 107, 108-110,
  111, 115, 118, 119, 120, 121,
  122, 123-124, 129, 132, 133,
  134, 159, 160, 163-167, 168,
  171, 174, 180-182, 187, 188, 190
Mansion, J. E. 27
Martin Chuzzlewit 16, 18
  Gamp 18
McMaster, J. 107
meaning
  additional 21, 167, 183
  affective 74
  associative 39, 74
  conceptual 11
  connotative → connotation
  conventional symbolic 161, 189
  figurative 115, 130
  literal 130
  symbolic → symbol(ic)
Miller, J. H. 145
modifier 81, 88, 90, 91, 92, 100,
  105, 106, 107, 108, 110, 111,

115, 121, 122, 123, 124, 126,
  186
Monod, S. 3, 5, 145, 177

N

Nicholas Nickleby 16
Nineteenth-Century Fiction 110,
  178

O

Old Bailey 175
onomatopoeia / onomatopetic word
  6, 7
Old Curiosity Shop, The 16
Oliver Twist 16, 69
  Monks 69
Our Mutual Friend 16, 18, 92
  Podsnap, Miss 92
  Podsnappery 18

P

participant line 26
personification 181
Pickwick Papers, The 16
  Pickwick 107
polysemy 137, 189
professionalism 79, 177
pronoun
  extensive use of 57, 59
  neuter 66
  structural use of 57-58
Project Gutenberg 15
pronominalization 68

Pross, Miss 38, 87, 89, 90, 104, 106, 120, 122, 129, 181
Pross, Solomon / Barsad, John 20, 32, 33-36, 37-40, 88, 89, 90, 99, 104, 120, 133, 136

Q

Quirk, R. 4, 110
Quirk, R. et al. 68

R

reference
  anaphoric → anaphoric
  cataphoric 44, 69, 75
  situational 44, 69
  textual 44
Reprinted Pieces 16
road-mender, a 26, 104, 120
round character 44

S

Sanders, A. 102, 177
satire / satirical 8, 18, 158, 177
Scott, M. 131
seme / semantic feature 74, 107, 109, 135, 149
seamstress, a 106, 115-116, 120, 122, 128-129
semantic conflict 135
semantic network 166
situational description 110, 122, 187
Sketches by Boz 16

Sørensen, K. 4, 15, 68
Stoehr, T. 145
structure / structural 3, 12, 29, 50, 58, 65, 74, 96, 146, 187, 190, 192
  structural unity 20, 147
  structural use of language 4
Stryver, Mr. 5, 106, 120, 174
style / stylistic 3, 4, 6, 12, 15, 18, 20, 44, 68, 91, 94, 113, 145, 185, 189, 190, 192
stylistic contiguity 145
symbol(ic) 4, 28, 96, 145, 147, 148, 151, 154, 161, 163, 166, 177, 188, 190
synonym / synonymous 76, 88, 100, 114, 122, 123, 128, 147, 157, 159, 160, 161, 163, 188, 189
context-bound 176

T

theme / thematic 3, 4, 6, 12, 79, 129, 137, 138, 144, 145, 147, 148, 172, 180, 186, 188, 189
transferred epithet 90, 94, 95, 96, 119, 126
Tribunal 52, 57, 59, 126, 132, 133, 177
typification, use of language for 4, 110

U

Uucommercial Traveller 16, 178

V

Vengeance, the 27, 110, 115
verbal iconicity 6

W

WordSmith Tools 131

Y

Yamamoto, T. 3, 140, 166
Young Jerry 88, 104

Index of Words

B

blue flies 175, 176
business
    man of business, a 111, 134, 135
    business eye → eye
breast 49, 50, 125, 126
buzz 175, 176

C

claret 159
confidence 174
cordially 11, 12

D

dig / digging 159, 160, 171
dry / drier / drily 13-14

E

eye 82, 84, 85
    blue 105, 107, 108, 109, 110, 187
    bright 106, 107, 112
    business 106, 107, 110, 111
    contemptuous 106
    dark 106, 107, 114, 115
    exceedingly bright 105, 112, 113, 114
    frenzied 156,
    haggard 105, 112, 113
    kindled 105, 113
    opened 106, 116
    patient 106, 115, 116, 129
    reverently shaded 106, 108, 172, 173
    sharp 106
    troubled 106
    uncomplaining 106, 115, 128
    watchfull 106, 114, 123
eyebrows
    lifted 105, 109, 110, 187
    dark 106, 112, 114
    darkly defined 106, 101
    steady 106, 107, 121

F

fate 17, 51, 53, 116, 137, 138, 140, 141, 143, 159, 161, 178, 180, 182, 189
    steadfastness of 140
far, far better rest, a 191
fatal darkness 173
fatal register 143
finger
    cautionary 121
    cruel 122, 126, 127, 128
    nimble 121, 122, 123
    resolute 122, 123

restless 122, 126, 128
supplicatory 121, 123, 124
work-worn, hunger-worn 122, 128, 129
footstep
  echoes of 163, 164, 166
  Headlong, mad, and dangerous 165, 166

G

Good day 177
grindstone 155, 157, 158
guillotine 27, 45, 115, 133, 142, 143, 154, 177

H

hair
  black 89, 99, 130
  dark 89, 90, 101, 102, 114, 115
  golden 67, 89, 91, 92, 93, 95, 100, 101, 108, 109, 170, 191
  radiant 89, 92, 93, 95, 170
  spiky 89, 100, 101
  white 89, 94-99, 100, 112, 119
hand
  agitated 122, 126, 127, 128
  appealing 119, 121, 123, 124
  brave 121
  cold 121, 122, 129
  eager but so firm and steady 121, 126
  restless 122, 126, 128
  rusty 122, 129, 130
  troubled 121

head
  (cold, confused) white 89, 90, 93, 94-99, 101, 112
  ruined 89, 94, 95
  steady 89, 94, 97, 99
  spiky 89, 100, 101

I

I salute you 177

J

jackal 7, 76, 77, 78, 79, 132, 133

K

knitted register 143

L

love and beauty 10
love and truth 10

M

madame 22, 23-29, 72, 131, 133

N

night shadow 171

P

pleasant 178-180
port 160

post-office 15
pride 8, 9, 10

Q

quiet 165, 166, 189

R

RAT—tat-tat 6, 7
real 24, 28, 102, 171, 172
respectable / respectability 12-13

S

shadow 28, 172, 182
spy 32-40

steady 72, 73, 75, 76
stitch 6
sun going to bed, the 177

T

tranquilly 165, 166, 189

U

unseen and unheard 183, 184

W

white locks 93
wig / wigged 76, 78, 175, 176, 177,
wine-shop 158